SAWYER & BOYD Duo

JP SAYLE

JP SAYLE

Book Cover © 2020 Design by Tina Løwén

Editing by Lucas Cornelius
Line Edits and Proofreading by HL Day (The App:
Littles)
Proofreading Abbie Nicole (The Little Side of Me)
Book Re-Formatting by Tina Løwén

References to real people, events, organisations,
locations, or establishments are only intended to give
a sense of authenticity and have been used fictitiously.

The author acknowledges the copyrighted or
trademarked status and trademark on Apple, Ikea,
Pepsi, Diesel.

Films, music, and lyrics mentioned are the
property of the copyright holders.

Warning

Some of the content of this book is sexually graphic, with the use of explicit language and adult situations involving two males. It is only intended for mature audiences.

JP SAYLE

Duet Boyd and Sawyer

An overheard conversation, an app, and secret hidden desires, can these be the basis of a relationship?

This is the duet of Boyd and Sawyer from book two, The App Series and book two, Flamingo bar Series, brought together for your guilty reading pleasure.

JP Sayle

Can trialling The App as a favour give Sawyer what he's been missing from all of his past relationships: A Daddy that understands what a Little needs?

Sawyer came from hippy parents, who were more interested in the planet than him. Hands off parenting has left Sawyer conflicted about a fundamental part of himself. A part that he has hidden from those closest to him.

Then The App changes everything.

Following an offer from Boyd, a newbie Daddy, Sawyer finds himself contemplating training the man to be his Daddy. But with the universe out to make Boyd's life difficult, can the two men work through the relationship hurdles and finish the race together?

The App: Littles, is a gay romance with Daddy kink, an age gap and age play. This is the second book in The App series and can be read as a standalone.

Warning:
This book ends on a cliffhanger. Boyd and Sawyer will **_not_** get their HEA until the concluding book in The Flamingo Bar Series, later this year.

Thank you to Tina, Mandy, Julie, Keren and Guy, you make me smile with your comments and feedback.

Prologue

BOYD

I was sure I hadn't hid my scepticism as Nathan held out the tub of homemade goodies to me. "Do you think offering me your boyfriend's cookies will sweeten me up?" My voice was heavy with sarcasm as I nearly snatched Nathan's hand off while taking the tub from him. Lenny, Nathan's boyfriend, was a genius in the kitchen, and Nathan had taken to bringing treats when he wanted to bribe me. The lid lasted all of a second in my hands before I practically inhaled two cookies, making Nathan laugh.

"Me, really? You think I'd be so devious as to ask Lenny to bake every day?" Nathan fluttered his eyelashes at me, going for innocent and failing miserably.

"Yep, I do. You think I'm a sucker for them," I quipped back, despite my mouth being half-full of chewed cookie.

"You are." He pointed to the tub. "Because my man can bake." Nathan was bragging, but it was the truth. Everything I'd tried that Lenny had made had been delicious.

"Okay... what do you want to change now?" I asked with resignation, laying the tub on the half-finished bar top I'd been sanding before Nathan had interrupted me.

The Flamingo Bar was the second large project I'd worked on for Nathan. The first was The Playroom, his BDSM club housed on the lower floor of the warehouse we were in. My teeth ground together as I reminded myself that Nathan had done a lot for my building contractor business by offering me my first large contract. That job had secured me several other big contracts, and therefore ensured my success.

Nathan held his hands up. "It's only a small thing—"

My gaze narrowed on him, all my good intentions flying right out the window. I jabbed him in the chest, inwardly cringing as my finger left a dirty smear on his pale grey top. "What, like when you wanted the whole section I'd built for the DJ booth moved from one side of the room to the other?" I accused angrily.

"I said I was sorry for that—"

"Yeah, the same as you were sorry about the other nine changes you had me make. I stared him down. I couldn't remember Nathan being this much of a pain in my arse the last time we'd worked together.

"It's just that sometimes you envision things that look better when they're slightly altered," I huffed, my hands going to my hips as I struggled to refrain from interrupting him again, Nathan offering me a shamefaced smile in response.

"I was thinking... that we could add a platform at the side of the dance floor. For open nights, so that those that are here for puppy or kitty play could display their pets."

Was he talking about role play? My heart skipped several beats and my palms became sweaty. Things between me and Glenn, my long-term boyfriend, had become a little stale in the bedroom department. Stale, my backside! Don't you mean non-existent? When was the last time we'd been intimate?

I stilled, my mind frantically trying to find the answer. My heart sank as I came up empty. That was why I'd been doing a little research in order to spice things up between us. There was something intriguing about some of the scenes I'd found on the internet involving different role play dynamics. There had been a few film clips with a Daddy and his boy that had left me with feelings I'd struggled to understand. Is that why you haven't mentioned it to Glenn?

I just needed to find my balls and man up. Like that is going to happen! I barely resisted rolling my eyes at myself.

Ever since Glenn had asked me to support him so that he could quit his job and set up his own business, something had changed between us. Initially I'd thought he was stressed, but as far as I could tell it was doing well. How do you know? He never talks to you anymore.

I wasn't sure what my face conveyed as Nathan shifted his gaze to mine, but frown lines appeared on his forehead. "I can't remember you mentioning that this bar was going to be for… that," I commented, working on masking my jumbled thoughts.

"That?"

"You know… role play… and such like." Heat crept up my neck as I stumbled over my words. I lowered my gaze and stared at the floor.

"Is this a problem for you?" Nathan asked, concern lacing his question.

"No… it's just… I thought this place was going to be a bar and restaurant," I added lamely, not sure how to explain why he'd thrown me for a loop.

"It is, but it will also be a place for people that are into others aspects of BDSM, particularly role play, where they can come and play in a safe space without judgement. I'll ask again, is this going to be a problem for you?" Nathan's large body seemed tense as he waited for my answer.

I shook my head slowly, lifting my eyes to meet Nathan's. "Nah, I... well..." My cheeks continued to heat as I shifted uncomfortably. "I'd be interested in a membership," I stated before I could think better of it. Why did I say that?

Nathan's gaze narrowed on me. "I'd happily give you a membership, if that's what you really want?"

"Yeah, thanks." What was I playing at? Unable to figure out what had just come over me, I walked across the room towards the dance floor. I took a few seconds to regroup and thanked my lucky stars that Nathan hadn't made a big deal out of my request.

Several hours later, sweaty and tired from the day, I opened the door to my home and shouted out to Glenn, "Hey babe, I'm home." I slung my coat over the bannister and looked down at my dirty clothes and then to the staircase leading upstairs. At the lack of response, a defeated sigh escaped, and I decided to delay facing Glenn and go and shower.

Ten minutes later, I stepped out of the shower into an empty bathroom. How long had it been since Glenn had come to talk to me about his day while I freshened up? My brow furrowed as I calculated the months. Shit.

When had things between us started to change?

The hurt I'd been tucking away at the loss of the closeness we'd once had overwhelmed me for a moment and my legs buckled. Without anything else to distract me, the discomfort I'd held at bay while I was at work returned. Quickly drying myself off, I went into the bedroom and dressed in some casual lounge pants, along with a T-shirt, before returning downstairs.

In the hallway, I took a deep breath and braced myself for what I might find when I walked into the kitchen. I'd been holding onto the hope that today might be different, the same as I had done almost every day for the last few months, but it only took the span of a few steps for that hope to wither and die. My gaze swept around the messy room, finding it empty.

With Glenn working from home, we'd agreed that he'd do the cooking during the week and I'd do it at the weekends. It seemed that, somehow, this had changed, and I was now cooking every day. I eyed the empty cooker top and sighed.

Why was I noticing all this stuff today?

As I mulled it over, my gut started to churn. I couldn't recall the last time Glenn had been affectionate towards me. Not that I'd asked for much lately when he was always too tired to do more than complain. Why did I feel like it was always me bending over backwards for him all the time? You love taking care of him. He's busy with his new business, that's all.

Aren't you busy too? Can't he take five minutes to come and give you a hug, or a kiss?

The thoughts seemed to slam into each other and the simmering anger that I often buried with excuses for Glenn's behaviour burned through me. My teeth ground together as I walked through to Glenn's home office. An office I had spent many thousands on kitting out for him so that he could fulfil his dreams.

Was I asking for too much from him?

His head never lifted from the computer and he didn't even acknowledge my presence.

"Hey." I leant forward to kiss his cheek, but he pulled away before I could touch him, causing my chest to ache.

"Your beard needs trimming. It will scratch my skin," he complained, without once looking in my direction.

"I'm sorry. I have a barber's appointment at the weekend." The apology tumbled from my lips, the need to appease him second nature when I heard the sharp edge to his voice. "What are we eating for dinner tonight?"

He shrugged his slim shoulders and still didn't glance in my direction. "Whatever you can rustle up. I'm going out with some new clients. There's a trendy new bar they mentioned in Soho that they're taking me to."

This was something else that was becoming a habit: Glenn going out and not bothering to invite me. "It won't take me long to get changed. I'll come with you." I wasn't in the mood but we hadn't spent any proper time together for weeks.

"It's not your thing." His head finally lifted and he aimed a scathing look up and down my body. "I mean, you don't really do trendy, do you?" His upper lip curled and he sounded so condescending.

I forced myself to keep a hold of my temper as my fingers clenched at my sides. Come on, think. There must be something you can do to make him look at you like he used to?

I ignored his sarcastic comment and went with the first thing that came into my head instead. "You know the place I'm working on? Well, it's going to be a bar with a difference. It'll be a place where couples can go and do role play. I asked Nathan for a membership. I thought we could try something different. You know, spice things up a little." The smile I'd plastered on my face fell as I realised my mistake.

Glenn's face turned a shade of purple that would have easily rivalled the girl's face from Willy Wonka and the Chocolate Factory. "What are you insinuating? Tell me. Are you saying I'm the cause of our bedroom issues?" He stood up, almost foaming at the mouth as he stepped closer, his face turning ugly as he sneered. "You're a pervert. Role play? What do you think I am? Some sort of plaything that likes to be shown off in front of others? I don't fucking think so! This is about those websites you've been looking at, isn't it? Don't think I don't know what you've been doing at night."

Spittle hit my face as he continued to rant at me. I opened my mouth, a wave of dizziness hitting me from the nastiness of his tone. I clamped my lips together, realising it was pointless as I listened to the barrage of abuse he was throwing at me.

Why was he acting like this?

My mind circled back to all the times he'd spoken to me in this way over the last few months. Why hadn't I noticed what a horrible shit he was being? You loved him.

It took a second to register that I was thinking in the past tense. I heaved a sigh, uncertain about what I should do. My pulse was pounding so hard that my ears had started to buzz. Four years we'd been together, and yet as I stood there listening to him, I realised I didn't even recognise the man who stood before me. Where had Glenn, the gentle loving soul gone?

"Are you even listening to me? I've had enough. The tenants in my flat vacated it last week. I'm moving out. I think you need some time to think about what's gotten into you lately. Role play, sex toys and web searches for Christ knows what! You're nearly forty. You should be past this silliness."

Not sure what my age had to do with it, I stood silently, trying to release my jaw after clenching it so hard. How was wanting to try new things, silliness?

"Don't you have anything to say?" Glenn sneered.

"I wasn't sure you were finished belittling me. I think you're right, moving out is the best idea. We need some space and maybe a little perspective on what we both want from this relationship." I swallowed another sigh as he swung around and stomped to the doorway.

He glanced back over his shoulder before throwing out a threat, "If I leave, I won't be coming back."

I didn't point out that he was the one who'd suggested that he leave. This was a game he liked to play: making me beg him to stay. Only today, I wasn't up to playing his game, not with all the hurtful things he'd said still fresh in my memory.

Why had I been putting up with this shit? He's been using you for months, living off you, spending your money. He doesn't love you. I barely stopped myself from blanching at the reality of what the voice in my head was telling me. Was it the truth?

I stared at the man I'd thought I'd be spending the rest of my life with and my heart broke a little for the dream of what could have been. A hope I'd been clinging on to for far too long.

I stood tall, keeping my thoughts hidden behind a neutral mask as he paused in the doorway, waiting for me to beg. "If you need a hand to drop your stuff off at the flat, I can get one of my guys to help you? It might need to be Monday though as they're busy at the weekends." Glenn's mouth hung open, his eyes widening. I carried on speaking. "You're right. I think it's best if you move out. This… isn't working for you, evidently, so it's probably the right time to stop before someone gets hurt." Even as I said it, I felt the tears clog the back of my throat. I stared at his face for a moment, seeing nothing but fury. No regret, no love, no remorse. I made myself walk away from him.

My head pounded and my eyes blurred even more at the sound of a door slamming shut somewhere in the house. But I kept walking until I'd reached the downstairs bathroom, only then with the door locked did I let go. Sobs tore from my throat as I shoved my fist into my mouth to muffle the sound. Oh God, what had I done?

It's going to be okay. It's going to be okay.

The words were of very little comfort to me, but I clung to them.

Chapter 1

Boyd

As I walked towards the far end of the newly fitted bar, there was too much conversation for workmen getting on with their jobs. I followed the sound, getting ready to let rip. I'd already had words with the men once that morning about the deadlines we had to meet, and stopping mid-morning to have a chat wasn't going to achieve diddlysquat.

I rounded the corner and then paused, quickly moving back out of sight of the pair talking. My mouth dried up as I registered the guy talking to Nathan. I'd noticed him before when he'd popped in to see Nathan, though I'd never been introduced to him.

Nathan's voice carried over the din of the workmen. "How has The App been working out for you, Sawyer? It's been weeks since I've heard from you and I was starting to get a little worried. I've chatted to Jake a few times and he's happy with the new online community The App is creating."

Sawyer! Who was he to Nathan?

Too intrigued to do the decent thing and step away, I remained where I was. The misery I'd felt for weeks, ever since Glenn had left, lifting, if only briefly, as I tried to figure out what they were talking about. *Admit it, it's the guy that intrigues you.*

Refusing to acknowledge the butterflies belly dancing inside me, questions popped into my head. What was The App? What online community were they talking about? Was it something connected to the new bar?

Ever since that fateful day Nathan had explained what The Flamingo Bar was going to be a month earlier, my brain had been in turmoil. My mind had gone in all different directions and was now lost at Spaghetti Junction. I still wasn't sure what had possessed me to ask for a membership, or to decide to mention it to... my now ex-boyfriend.

Let it go, you and Glenn split up over a month ago.

I rubbed my chest. The dullness inside me seemed like a constant reminder of my own stupidity. I'd tried to ring Glenn twice to sort out the delivery of the rest of his things, but all I got for my trouble was an earful of abuse.

To distract myself during the lonely evenings at home, I'd continued to surf the net, and to say that I was getting a little bit obsessed would be the understatement of the year. I was discovering a side to myself that I wasn't sure how to handle.

When Nathan had offered me the contract for the bar renovations, I'd assumed the place was going to be *just* a bar, not an extension of The Playroom.

Personally, I'd never been interested in tying anyone up, or in anything else the club had to offer. I'd even turned down his generous offer of membership to The Playroom.

This new place, though, with all the different possibilities it held... was something else entirely.

I was jerked from my thoughts by the sound of a soft dulcet-toned voice. I rubbed my face and leant against the wall that hid me from both men and focused on what they were talking about, rather than the shit storm that was my personal life.

"—slammed at work over the holiday period. And with the oldies visiting, things have been a bit all over the place for me. That's if you don't take into account all the issues I'm still having with my house. In fact... let's not talk about that. The App, yeah, what can I say? I've had a few dates this last year, and a couple in the last month or so. I was so excited about this app, you know I was. All the potential Daddies out there for someone like me. Yet, every single date I've been on they've lacked something." There was a loud mournful sigh before the man carried on complaining. "Men either wanna just shag, or they take one look at me and it's a "no thank you, you're too old." Oh, and let's not forget the men who can't be bothered to read what I've written about being a Little and then make some awful assumptions!"

The whine in his voice had increased. There was something so miserable about how upset he sounded that it gave me the absurd urge to go over and give him a hug to make him feel better. It tugged at a part of me that I didn't want to acknowledge as I pushed my back against the wall to keep myself from moving. With my palms twitching, I rubbed my hands down my legs working on quelling the daft urge to go and do what I wanted to... hug him.

Daft, that's your middle name lately.

This was all Nathan's fault for talking about the bar and what it offered. *Yeah, you keep believing that. Your relationship had hit the rocks way before that.*

Oh, stop rubbing it in.

Nathan's voice cut off my thoughts. "Listen man, it might just be that you need to try something different, or to stop searching so hard and let it just happen. You're gorgeous. A beautiful person inside and out—"

"Aw shut up, and you better keep your voice down. You don't want your boyfriend getting wind that you're giving other men compliments."

A ball lodged in my throat at the wistfulness in the guy's voice.

"It's the truth and you know it. Sometimes you have to stop to see the wood for the trees. Heck, I should know." Nathan chuckled.

"Alllrighttttt... I hear you Daddy bear," came the sassy response that didn't entirely hide his sadness.

My stomach dipped and rolled at hearing the word Daddy again.

"Hey, less of that you cheeky boy. Now let's go and see if my man has left me any treats, and then you can talk me through what you don't like about The App."

The voices moved away from me and I took the opportunity to glance around the corner, reminding myself how tiny the guy was, or at least appeared to be next to Nathan. His face was turned away as they walked towards the door that led to Nathan's apartment, the lights catching his multicoloured hair. The rainbow of colours shimmered and left my hands tingling with the urge to feel if his hair was as silky soft as it appeared.

Sawyer's body was slim and dressed in old ripped jeans and an army jacket that looked like it had been salvaged from a charity shop. Although his clothes didn't speak of affluence, there was something about his presence that said he wasn't a homeless vagrant. I was forced stop looking as they disappeared through the door leading to Nathan's apartment.

"Boyd… Boyd… hey, you with me man?"

The shout from the foreman, Brett, who I'd hired to manage the men, pulled my attention from the now-closed door. I strolled back to the central part of the bar. "What's up, Brett?"

"These fucking lights"—he jabbed at the offending box on the counter—"the wholesaler has sent us are the wrong ones. They aren't even close to what we ordered. This is the third fucking mixed up order those bastards have sent us. At this rate we'll have to add another bloody day to the work schedule if they keep getting it wrong."

He continued to grumble as I lifted up the light fitting. How the fuck had the company got it so wrong? Brett was right; there was no way you could pass these off as the ones we'd ordered. Someone was having a fucking laugh at our expense.

It had happened in the past. The building trade was dog eat dog and some people didn't like how many bids I'd won. Shaking off the worry that someone was messing with me, I stopped Brett from continuing his histrionics. "Go to Illuminatics, they're a new firm I've heard great things about. Put in an urgent order and we'll take the hit for any extra costs. Send these back to the other company and ring them to say that we want a full refund, and that we're closing our account with them."

At Brett's nod, I walked back to the booth I'd been working on, needing something to take my frustrations out on. I lifted the wood planer and started to sand it over the large slab of wood clamped to my workbench. As a teenager, I'd discovered a talent for woodwork that my dad had encouraged. He'd always liked to use his hands himself and had two sheds full of tools he still used. My mother had often said he loved his tools more than her.

She'd been very wrong. When she'd been diagnosed with pancreatic cancer, he'd been devastated, even more so when she'd died six months later, the disease having stolen the life from her. The stab of grief when I thought of her was no longer as painful as it once had been, but it still caused me to stop what I was doing and rub my chest.

Seven years was a lifetime, yet not nearly long enough to get over her death. My dad was still working on being able to function without her, my younger sister, Amelia, his motivation. Given that I was twenty-five, she'd been a surprise that neither of my parents had been expecting. My mother had thought she was going through the menopause, but instead had found herself pregnant at forty-six years old.

Amelia was fourteen now, and a complete hellion. She was going to be an absolute nightmare in the coming years. My father liked to blame me because she'd spent so much time with me when Mum had got sick and Dad had needed to nurse her. She'd run wild at the building sites, getting into all sorts of trouble, but I'd secretly loved taking care of her. Her lust for life was a joy to behold. It had helped me to cope with my own grief. Although, now that she was a teenager, it was a lot harder to curb her wildness and the phone calls from my dad were enough to make my hair turn grey with her antics.

With a grin spreading across my face at the thoughts of my sister, I resumed planing the wood.

My smile dimmed as my thoughts turned back to Sawyer. There was a fluttering in my stomach as I recalled the urge to ease his sadness. Before I knew what I was doing, I'd laid the plane down and pulled out my phone.

What harm could there be in checking The App out?

Opening up the app store, I typed in *'The App'* and my breath caught in my throat as I read the warning of what The App contained. I glanced around to check that no one was watching me as I hit the icon to download it. The fee popped up and I coughed at the hundred quid it wanted. Shutting my eyes, I hit pay. Please let it be worth it!

What the fuck are you doing?
Who knows!
Maybe I was having a midlife crisis?
Then get over it, and fast.

Chapter 2

SAWYER

As I ambled up the path to my log cabin, the waning light captured my gaze as it reflected off the half-finished timber structure that was to be my home. I blew out a breath, my fringe lifting before falling back in my eyes. Balancing my bicycle against my leg, I pushed my hair out of my face before taking hold of the bike again and going over to the shed to lock it away.

It had been weeks since the last contractor had downed tools and marched off the job, saying I was far too demanding and unrealistic. It didn't matter how many times I'd explained what I'd wanted, the guy and his team had done their own thing. And okay, I might have had a few temper tantrums, but who could blame me? This was to be my forever home and I wanted it to be perfect.

After all, they weren't the ones stuck in a cramped shed with a makeshift shower, a tiny little cooker and an uncomfortable single bed. Yes, I'd lived like that most of my life, but that was irrelevant when my childhood dreams were within my grasp.

You think so? All I can see is a half-finished house. The childish voice in my head was seriously trying to tick me off.

It will be, you'll see. I'll get my happy home.

How, when you haven't found another building contractor who was interested in building an eco-friendly house that fit your ideas?

With my eyes burning from the tears that wanted to be shed, I locked my bike away.

As I turned around, my gaze was drawn to the woodland. The sound of the breeze rustling through the trees added to the symphony of bird song. It was soothing, so instead of going into my shed as I'd planned, I went and sat down on the grassy bank next to my partially finished home.

With my elbows on my knees, I rested my chin on my hands and stared at the land I'd bought two years ago when I'd hit twenty-one and come into my inheritance. It was a good size with plenty of tall trees to shield me from prying eyes.

The scent of early spring was in the air and the daffodil bulbs I'd planted in the small patch of land I'd dug up in front of the house were starting to show signs of life. February was usually my favourite month of the year, but I couldn't find any happiness in the new budding life today. I'd thought that I'd be going on a date, but no. Here I was, back home, with only myself for company, yet again.

I swallowed my sigh and pressed my lips together as I counted how many days it had been since I'd had a message from the last guy I'd been on a date with. Evidently, he wasn't interested in a second date. Not that the first date had been particularly great. In fact, all the dates I'd been on since I'd signed up to The App had been, in a word, shit.

I'd had such high hopes, given all the messages I'd received in the beginning. But then I'd gone from one disastrous date to the next. I snorted at the memory of guy number seven, remembering his face when I'd gone and got changed and came back wearing one of my little outfits. His expression had been priceless as he'd taken in my dummy and my snuggle blanket tucked under my arm. His pale cheeks and utter shock as he'd stuttered and all but ran out the door had left me deflated and unsure whether I should carry on using The App.

I let my chin sink lower into my hands, my mouth turning down as I went through the list of men who'd said they'd be interested in dating someone like me—a Little.

The thing was, some of them only wanted to have sex, some wanted to explore their own kinks, and then there were the men who did want a boy, but only one who looked younger than me. It seemed being twenty-three was too old for some men.

I heaved a defeated sigh, my shoulders sagging as I thought about how many men had misconceived ideas about what I was like. Okay, some of the men I'd dated *had* asked what being a Little meant to me, but somehow, they'd never ignited a spark of interest in me. That was why I'd paid Nathan a visit a couple of weeks back to see if I should carry on using The App.

I'd already been explicit in the information I'd shared online, but either the men hadn't bothered to read it, or they just didn't understand what I was really looking for. Nathan had basically told me to stop trying so hard and just see what happened. Now, as another date had bombed, and I'd heard nothing since, I was thinking that I'd be better off deleting the bloody thing from my phone.

It wasn't like I'd had to pay for it as I'd initially been trialling it for Nathan. As I watched the sun sink lower in the sky, I frowned.

Delete it, or keep it?

If you delete it, you might miss the opportunity of a lifetime.

Is that not like saying I could win the lottery?

You don't do the lottery.

I huffed at how silly the conversation was getting inside my head. When my stomach growled, reminding me that it was long past lunchtime and I'd not eaten anything, I got up to go and make myself something to eat.

After unlocking the tiny space I called home, I tucked the keys back into my baggy jeans and walked the twenty steps across the floor to the little fridge that sat on a wooden stool. The large wooden shed had two rooms. The main room, the larger of the two, housed my bed, a dilapidated sofa rescued from the tip, a rickety old table that held the fridge, a cooker and two mismatched chairs. The tabletop cooker had been reclaimed from a skip. After asking the owner if they'd mind me upcycling it, I'd climbed in and pulled it out. It worked perfectly. Well, it did after I'd tinkered with it and cleaned it up.

There was no television because my parents visited and didn't approve. I'd never had one. My family were a bunch of hippies that believed children shouldn't be brainwashed by TV programmes and should go out and experience nature instead. I'd never admitted that I secretly liked to watch cartoons on my phone when I was alone.

The bathroom was a shoebox with a makeshift shower, which used a hose and a water heater I'd rigged up to warm the rainwater. The toilet was a chemical loo that visitors were somewhat reluctant to use. My lips puffed out and I blew out a breath as I took stock of the place I called home. Was this part of the reason I was single?

If my upbringing had been the same as other children, would I have been *more normal*? I chuckled to myself. I'd given up trying to figure that one out once I'd realised that doing so wouldn't alter my past.

What difference does it make, you're you?

The internal childish voice sounded irritated as I stared into the fridge.

There was a part of me that revelled in the freedom of being different, in my need to be taken care of by a Daddy. Then there was the part of me that didn't get why I couldn't just tuck all the stupidness away in a box and pretend it wasn't there, and accept something a little more traditional.

My gaze was drawn to my bed and what I knew was hidden underneath it. I'd had the box ever since I'd first figured out I was different. The expectations of people, who all thought they knew what was right for me, had been suffocating. Therefore, I'd felt compelled to keep my Little side hidden in order not to disappoint them.

I'd first worked out I was different when I'd visited the home of one of the girls I was friends with at school. We'd gone to her bedroom to study, and there on her bed had been two rather tatty dogs, Blue-blue and Pink-pink. She'd been utterly unapologetic about the fact that she slept with two stuffed dogs, and that she wouldn't go on any trips without them, totally uncaring about what others thought about it. Those stuffies had been well-loved and it had touched something deep inside me. I'd not been able to stop thinking about what it might be like to embrace my inner child and why my parents had never given me anything like that as a child. After some consideration, I'd asked my parents.

"Mum, can I ask you something?" I hopped from one foot to the next as she walked around the cabin searching for something, not really paying me much attention.

"What Sawyer? I'm a little busy. I'm looking for the book I was reading on deforestation. There's a group of us looking at travelling to the worst hit areas next week, to see the damage for ourselves."

I was so used to her and my father leaving to go on one trip or another that I didn't bat an eyelid at the fact that they weren't going to be at home for my upcoming sixteenth birthday. Spying the book she'd been reading the previous night peeking out from under a pile of clothes she'd probably put down and forgotten about, I retrieved it and handed it to her. "Here you go. Now can I ask a question?"

"If you must," she stated, sounding exasperated and still not looking at me.

I exhaled and then asked quickly, "Why did you never buy me a cuddly toy or give me a dummy when I was little?" My cheeks heated as her gaze moved from the book to me.

Her intense dark eyes peered at me thoughtfully. "Why would you need such things? A child needs to be self-sufficient and taught that from the very beginning. Useless possessions are of no importance and just make children clingy." There was something in her tone that warned me not to argue. Feeling hurt by her brusque behaviour, I nodded and quickly turned to leave, doing my best to keep the tears clogging my throat under control.

"Sawyer, why do you ask?"

My heart raced at the question. Stood at the door, I answered without turning around. "I just wondered is all." It was lame, but it was the best I could come up with at that moment.

Vibrations from the phone in my trouser pocket brought me back to the present. My blurry eyes took a moment to focus on the screen as I tugged it out of my pocket. I sniffed twice and rubbed at my eyes with my free hand—*stupid emotions.*

I blinked and then sighed when I saw that the icon for The App held a message. It was probably another loser looking for a shag.

I dithered. Should I just delete it and not bother to read it? *This could be the man of your dreams.*

I rolled my eyes at the thought, but the hope that raced around inside me wouldn't let go so I hit the icon to open up the message box.

BB: *I've never done this before and I'm not even sure why I'm doing it now, but here goes. Would you be interested in getting to know me and maybe going on a date?*

What hadn't he done before? Used an app? Been on a date with a Little? Been on a date period? What wasn't he sure about?

The more questions I came up with, the more deflated I felt. I went and sat on the saggy sofa, food forgotten and stared at the screen for long period of time. What should I do? The weird thing was, my stomach was fluttering and it hadn't felt like that in forever. The screen darkened as I chewed on my lip, so I hit the button to reread the message.

Still undecided, I went into BB's profile. There was no face pic, though there was a beautiful arty picture of a muscular forearm. *That was different.* On mine, I'd used a side profile picture of my face in shadow so you could kind of see what I looked like.

I read through the information on the profile and my heart sank. The guy was a novice with no experience of being a Daddy, or of having been with a Little before.

At least he's honest. Was that enough though? With that thought running through my head, I started to type a response.

LittleS: *I'm not sure we'd be a good match. I need someone who understands what a Little needs. Sorry.*

I hit send and was about to shut the app when the icon lit up. I held my breath, my mouth starting to dry up. My eyes widened as the message popped up. My blood heated as my heart rate went into overdrive.

BB: *Then wouldn't I be perfect because you could train me to be what you want?*

Well shit! A Daddy to train. Was this man for real?

Chapter 3

BOYD

Two weeks later, I still wasn't over what appeared to be a midlife crisis, and I'd spent my day off coming up with a plausible excuse to ask Nathan about Sawyer. Now I just needed to sound believable.

I knocked on Nathan's open office door and waited for his shout of "come in" before I poked my head around the door. "You got a minute, Nathan?"

He placed the papers he was holding down and nodded so I stepped into his office, swallowing down the ball of panic in my throat. "It's just that I noticed you talking to a young man a couple of weeks ago. He had colourful hair and I wondered if he was the delivery guy for the lights that came that day?"

Heat filled my face and I stopped talking, willing myself to act a little more relaxed. My back felt stiffer than a board as Nathan eyed me with curiosity.

"Nah… if I've got the right day then you saw me talking to a friend, Sawyer. He's a waiter at Carl's restaurant and I'm pretty sure he doesn't moonlight as a delivery guy. Why? What's up?" There was an edge to Nathan's voice as he spoke.

Thankfully, that was the hard part over and done with so I breathed more easily and told the truth, instead of some made-up bullshit. "The company we've been using for some of the fittings sent another wrong delivery. I'm starting to think someone's got it in for me," I joked. I kept my face neutral as Nathan sat forward, his massive arms flexing as he rested his elbows on the desk.

"Is this going to fuck with the deadline?" he demanded, a scowl forming.

"We've used another company who were good enough to express deliver what we needed. The men stayed all night to get them fitted so there won't be a delay," I explained as sweat gathered under my arms. "That guy, Sawyer… he… had interesting hair."

A furious heat rose up my neck as Nathan started laughing.

You were about as subtle as a sledgehammer!

"Yes, that's one way of putting it. Sawyer is a… hippy at heart." Nathan's lips pursed and he paused for a second, looking thoughtful. "In fact, I don't know why I didn't think to mention your company to him."

"Why would he be interested in my company?" I asked in alarm. Had Nathan figured out that I'd downloaded The App?

He gazed at me, a frown appearing as he answered. "Your building company. Sawyer is building his own home on some land he bought a couple of years ago. He's used several companies already and none of them seemed to stick around for very long." Nathan shrugged his powerful shoulders, eyeing me as if I'd lost the plot. "Maybe you'd be interested? It's right up your street—"

My mouth seemed to engage before my brain as I blurted out, "What have you heard?" I wished I'd kept quiet when Nathan's eyes narrowed on me.

"Am I missing something here, because it sure as hell feels like it? Sawyer is building an ECO-friendly home, something I've heard you mention is a bit of passion of yours." He barely held in his laughter as I rolled my eyes heavenward.

Why had I thought this was a good idea?

"Yes, it is," I answered, returning to the chair to sit before I fell down. Once I was seated, Nathan leaned back in his chair, his hands clasped over his flat stomach and speculation sparking in the depth of his gaze. I took a breath and went with honesty.

***

Sitting at home later that day, I stared at the open app icon after spending hours searching for Sawyer. My heart had skipped merrily as I'd clicked on LittleS's profile and instantly recognised Sawyer's face, even though it was in profile.

Are you really going to do this?

It didn't matter how many times I told myself not to, I knew differently. Even though I'd never met him in person, there was something about Sawyer, that called to a part of me I'd never acknowledged before.

The time I'd spent going through all the contacts in The App to find Sawyer had been hellish. Who the heck could have known there were so many kinks out there? Or that they were way more interesting than I'd ever considered. Up until now, I'd have described myself as a meat and two veg kind of guy—plain and simple. *That's why you spoke to Glenn about trying something different and asked Nathan for a membership?*

Oh, shut up.

As I'd searched through the different profiles, I hadn't been able to escape how much my heart had raced with excitement, or how captivated I'd been by certain things I'd read.

I eyed the phone clutched in my sweaty palm and then I started to type. Exhaling the breath that had become caught in my lungs, I hit send before I could change my mind. I reread what I'd written and swallowed the pitiful sigh at how dorky it sounded.

BB: *I've never done this before and I'm not even sure why I'm doing it now, but here goes. Would you be interested in getting to know me and maybe going on a date?*

For a couple of minutes, I stared at the screen, willing Sawyer to answer. I couldn't help but curse at how desperate I was probably coming across as. *No, there's no probably about it, you're definitely desperate.*

My hand jerked as my phone buzzed.

LittleS: *I'm not sure we'd be a good match. I need someone who understands what a Little needs. Sorry.*

I replied without thinking about it.

BB: *Then wouldn't I be perfect because you could train me to be what you want?*

What the fuck had compelled me to write that?

Reeling from my own audacity, I sat there frozen.

Why couldn't I just let it go? *You know full well, why… Daddy.*

Oh, shut up.

I refused to have a debate with myself as I stared at the screen, waiting with bated breath to see how Sawyer would respond.

Unnerved by my own needs, I laid the phone down as the seconds ticked by and there was still no response. My stomach rumbling, I got up in the hope that I could distract myself with dinner.

When my phone buzzed to alert me to a message from The App, I spun around too fast, losing my balance and crashing into the wall with a resounding *thud*. The alert reminded me of the time I'd spent ensuring that the sound to alert me to a message was different from any other I had. I ran back to pick up my phone, ignoring the pain in my shoulder.

You're a foolish old man, I scolded myself, but it made no difference as my heart beat against my ribs in a rapid staccato rhythm that left me breathless. Willing myself to stop acting like a bloody fool, I paused before picking up the phone with shaky fingers.

Pull yourself together, you idiot.

Shaking my head, I read the message and then reread it, a smile spreading across my face.

LittleS: *Are you serious? This isn't some sort of joke?*

Chapter 4

Sawyer

My fingernails dug into my palm as I resisted the urge to open the door of my locker and grab my phone. Seb had a hard and fast rule—no phones when you were working in the restaurant.

I understood why, but that still didn't stop me from wanting to carry mine. BB... Builder Boyd, had been messaging me frequently ever since he'd asked me to train him. I'd avoided the subject of teaching him as we'd chatted about ourselves. Boyd, I'd found out, had a great sense of humour and liked to send me funny jokes and memes throughout the day to entertain me.

I'd not brought up the subject of whether he was actually a builder, a little wary after all the issues I'd had with the ones I'd employed to build my dream home.

What if he was one of the builders I'd worked with and he was taking the piss out of me?

I blanched, the thought stopping me dead in my tracks. Why hadn't I thought of that before?

Had I worked with someone called Boyd? An attempt to recall all the contractors I'd previously employed left me feeling a little anxious, so I stopped thinking about it. *Boyd's a decent guy. He doesn't set off any alarm bells.*

Then why haven't you agreed to a date with him?

That was a good question and one I wasn't sure I could answer. I was undecided whether it was a good idea to date a novice, regardless of his offer that I could train him. Although, after a week of messaging I was starting to weaken. I found myself getting excited waiting for his random messages throughout the day. It was getting harder and harder not to give in to the temptation.

Changing into my work pants, I eyed the skinny black trousers. Could I hide my phone in my pocket? *Hide* might be a bit of a stretch, given the way they fitted my slender legs. With a sigh of resignation, I wandered away from the lure of my phone.

In the restaurant, I was distracted as Adam's head popped out from behind the kitchen door. "Ohh Sawyer, just the man. Are you free for a sec?" Adam asked, his voice filled with excitement. His face was glowing with a healthy tan from his recent holiday. He'd been on his honeymoon with Carl, the head chef and half owner of the restaurant chain I worked for.

He disappeared back into the kitchen as I walked towards the door. The noise level increased as I stepped into the kitchen. My gaze swept the busy room and a smile lit up my face. Carl had Adam wrapped in his arms and he was attempting to kiss him. Although, Adam was putting up a little bit of a fight, I could tell it was just for show.

"You two need to get a room before things get too heated," I joked. Adam and Carl's actions had a tendency to cause quite a stir with the staff. There were a few occasions where they'd been caught in the locker room getting up to all sorts of kinky stuff. The fact Carl was a Dom Daddy and liked to punish Adam for his sassy mouth gave the staff a lot to talk about. Not that Carl or Adam seemed to care.

No one needed to know about the surge of jealousy I felt at seeing how happy Adam looked in his Daddy's arms. I forced a chuckle past my tight throat as Seb walked out of his office and gave a loud, defeated sigh.

"What have I told you about making out in the kitchen? I mean it, Carl. I'll change Adam's shifts so you never get to see him again at work." The threat sounded real enough that Carl released Adam and gave Seb a wide arse grin.

"Now, there's no need for that. I'll behave," Carl answered, not sounding in the least bit guilty.

Adam smirked and strolled towards me while Seb scratched his head. One of his dark brows rose. "Really, you'll behave? How long have we known each other?" Seb didn't let Carl answer. "Long enough to know that you'll never behave, regardless of what I say, that's how long."

"Aww, give over. You know I can behave myself," Carl mumbled, even as his gaze moved to Adam with a look of longing.

My chest tightened as I moved my gaze to meet Adam's.

His smile dimmed, creases appearing around his mouth. "You okay, Sawyer?" he asked in a hushed tone.

"Yeah, I'm cool. What did you want?" I kept my voice upbeat in the hope Adam wouldn't push. I wasn't sure that telling him I was jealous of his relationship with Carl would go down that well.

"If you wanna talk to me anytime, you can," he continued, keeping his voice down as he rubbed my arm.

I nodded and sucked in a breath before releasing it. "Thanks, I'm fine. Did you need me for something in particular?"

Adam held my gaze for another moment, concern still evident in his pinched brow. "I need someone to go over to Nathan's to deliver the final layout for the new restaurant. I can't go because I'm interviewing, and neither Theo nor Lachlan are quite sure where the place is. As you've been before, I was hoping you wouldn't mind. We should be able to muddle along fine until you get back." He gave me a sappy smile and fluttered his eyelashes at me. "I'll get Carl to bake you a cake."

"Something with cherries?" I asked, my stomach overtaking my concern at how difficult travelling across London at midday was going to be.

"Absolutely. Anything you want." He leant closer and whispered in my ear. "I have an in with the chef."

I chuckled as he pulled back "That you do. Okay, get me the stuff. I'll go and get changed... *again*." I stressed the last part.

Adam blushed, looking a little sheepish. "Yeah, I'm sorry about that. I was going to catch you before you got changed but I got distracted."

I shook my head and went back to the locker room, knowing full well what had distracted him.

Five minutes later and dressed in my own clothes, I smiled at the message I'd found on my phone.

BB: *I wake up with a good attitude every day. Then idiots happen ;)*

Not wanting to get caught messaging, I shoved my phone into my coat pocket with plans to respond after I'd left. Any thoughts of stopping to message Boyd fled, though as I encountered shitty traffic and roadworks. Then ten minutes in, the sky turned an ominous grey before starting to rain. The traffic and wind made it impossible to avoid the rain. The journey through London was torturous. My jeans stuck to my legs, making it harder to pedal and my chest heaved as I tucked my head down to avoid the stinging rain from hitting me directly in the face.

An hour later, I finally arrived at the warehouse where the new restaurant was going to be, looking like a drowned rat. The rain had soaked through all the layers of my clothes. My hair was plastered to my skull and my teeth were chattering from the icy water running down my neck into my coat.

My mood not at its best, I headed into the underground garage. Once inside and out of the wind and rain, my body started to shake. With my bike leaning against the wall by the lift, I tugged out the plastic wallet I'd tucked inside my jacket with trembling fingers. Thankfully, the plastic had kept the worst of the rain off the paper.

I made a squelching sound as I walked to the lift. I cursed and eyed my feet, a puddle starting to appear on the floor as I waited for the lift to arrive. My teeth continued to chatter as shivers raced down my spine. When the lift door opened, a cloud of warm air hit me. I all but jumped into it, my hand hesitating over the buttons. Where would Nathan be? Had Adam mentioned I was coming?

The warehouse had three other levels; I hit the button to take me to The Playroom. When the lift stopped and I got out, I avoided the puddle I'd created.

The plush carpet in the foyer was enough to make me pause.

No one is going to thank you for traipsing around in soggy shoes and dripping water all over the place.

"Why did I have to be the one that knew where the building was? Hey, why me?" I grumbled to myself, stripping off my coat, shoes and socks. I rolled up the dripping hems of my jeans for good measure as well.

That will have to do.

Doing my best to stop the sulk from taking hold, I walked into the club. I glanced around the room and spotted Isaac behind the bar. Pasting a smile on my face with difficulty, I strolled up to the bar acting like nothing was wrong.

"Hey Isaac, is Nathan about?" I asked through chattering teeth.

Isaac's head lifted and I couldn't fail to notice his eyes widening and a spark of amusement dancing in their depths as he took in my appearance. I'd had a membership to the club ever since I'd turned eighteen and I'd got to know Isaac pretty well over the years. He was a big bear of a man, who'd looked incredibly intimidating when I'd first met him. I'd soon discovered though that he was a big softie at heart. He was attractive, but he'd never ignited my interest. I was sure that the feeling was mutual as he'd never tried to initiate anything between us.

"Did you forget your coat and shoes, little man?"

"Ha ha ha! You're real funny, you know? You could maybe give me a towel or something to help me dry —"

"Isaac, you got a minute?" asked a deep, husky voice, interrupting me.

My gaze locked on the guy who was hovering in the stairwell that led up to the second floor. Melted caramel eyes held me captive as they lingered on me. Heat spread through my chilled body as his gaze swept over me with a level of possession that caused me to shudder.

Is he really looking at me like that?

Stop being ridiculous, you're seeing things that aren't there.

Even as the thought lingered, the guy was striding towards me. He exuded power and confidence; his dark hair was slightly messy but his beard was neatly trimmed. His workman clothes didn't do anything to conceal his solidly built body that looked like it was used to manual labour.

"You're soaking. You'll catch a chill if you don't get out of those clothes."

Dumbfounded by the note of affection and concern the guy was displaying to a complete stranger, I didn't know how to respond, his striking eyes continuing to draw me in.

"I'll get Sawyer a towel, don't worry about it, Boyd..."

Boyd?

I heard nothing else Isaac said as my brain latched onto the guy's name. Boyd. Was Boyd, BB? There was no way this could be *my* Boyd? Could it?

I licked my lips and tried to get my shaking limbs under control. "I... are... I..." I wasn't sure whether it was my teeth chattering, or that my mind was trying to figure out how to ask if he used a kink app that made it impossible to speak coherently.

When Isaac shoved a towel at me a few seconds later, I sighed and took it, doing my level best to pretend that everything was okay when Isaac gave me a questioning look.

I swiped at my wet hair. "Thanks."

After only a few seconds of trying to soak up the water, I could see it was futile. I was going to have to get out of my wet things.

Maybe Boyd would like to help?

Chapter 5

ℬOYD

It was as if I'd somehow conjured Sawyer up. I'd been thinking about him as I'd entered the club, and there he was. Only the state he was in had affected my brain and I'd rushed over there, acting more like an anxious boyfriend than a stranger.

Now I didn't know what to do.

Should I come clean? It was evident from the confusion on his face when Isaac had used my name, as well as the stuttering that had followed, that he'd probably figured out who I was. But with Isaac stood watching us closely, I'd kept quiet about our connection.

"Isaac, can he use the changing rooms to get out of his wet things? You have robes in there, don't you?" I swallowed a sigh at the level of concern in my own voice that I was unable to mask. There was no way Isaac wasn't going to get suspicious, never mind Sawyer, who was eyeing me like I was a bug under a microscope.

There was a pause before Isaac answered. "Yep there is, but we have the robes laundered by a company. We don't have a drier or any spare clothes." He shrugged his massive shoulders as he moved his gaze from me to Sawyer, who was shaking hard enough for his teeth to rattle.

Something that I didn't want to examine too closely, demanded that I help Sawyer, regardless of what Isaac might think. "I'll figure something out. Come on, let's get you out of those wet things and warm you up."

Isaac coughed and his eyes filled with what looked like amusement, but he gave me a nod before wandering off. Sawyer, on the other hand, blushed. His mouth opened and shut before he closed his eyes. His chest rose quickly, several times, before he opened his eyes and chose to look at me again.

"Seriously, we need to get you dry before you catch your death." Not giving him a chance to say anything, I took the wet towel from him and laid it on the closest table. Cupping his elbow, I guided him across the room. He came without protest, his gaze occasionally drifting in my direction as we walked into the changing room. Once we were inside, I let go of his arm, albeit reluctantly.

When Sawyer just stood there doing nothing more than shivering uncontrollably, I gave in to the urge to take care of him. "Let me help you get these wet things off?"

I took his silence as agreement and gently lifted one of his arms, and then the other tugging them out of the sleeves of his top. I slipped my hands under the bulky, wet jumper and widened the neck to ease it over his head. A breathy gasp was his only response as his face came back into view.

His eyes darkened and his nostrils flared as he met my gaze. There was a vulnerability about him as he stood there trembling, allowing me to help him. Emotions flowed through me, leaving my own hands quivering as we faced each other. The moment of connection resonated within me, his trust doing strange things to me.

"You're… BB?" he mumbled through blue lips.

Seeing no point in denying it, I nodded. His expression was hard to read with all the fleeting emotions that crossed it. "Are you… disappointed?" When his brow pinched, I wanted to curse my own neediness.

"Why would I be disappointed?" he questioned with a look of confusion.

Unsure how to answer, I dropped the jumper I was still holding and assisted with removing his T-shirt.

His icy hand came up and took hold of mine, stopping me. "Please, why would I be disappointed?" His eyes implored me to be honest.

Taking a deep breath before exhaling, I clasped his hand in mine. "You've been reluctant to meet up with me. And now you've had the choice taken from you." He gave me the most beautiful smile and I had to will my heart to listen to reason when all it wanted to do was leap out of my chest and land at his feet.

You're just out of one relationship, are you really ready for another one so soon?

With that thought running through my head, my lips clamped together to stop any chance of a silly confession popping out of my mouth.

"I'm not disappointed. I'm a little shocked to find you here. But in a good way, I suppose." His uncertainty as he finished speaking didn't instil confidence in me.

"Oh, right," I answered lamely. Releasing his hand, I took hold of the edge of his T-shirt for something to do. "Lift up, angel boy."

He did as I asked, although I hadn't missed the look of yearning that crossed his face. It took a second to register that it was probably connected to the term of endearment I'd used. It was how I'd thought of him ever since I'd seen his profile picture on the app. The soft light behind him in the picture had given him an ethereal appearance that made me think of angels.

Now, as he stood before me, his body language betraying how much he wanted to be taken care of, I wanted him to be my angel boy. I couldn't come up with a reasonable rationale for why I felt like this, so all I could do was just go along with it. Understanding dawned on me that nothing had been the same ever since I'd started to search for more in my relationship with Glenn. *Look how that ended for you.*

I ignored the snippy voice.

This is different. I know it is.

Something inside of me was pushing for me to let go of the past and just go with the flow. For the life of me, I couldn't deny this thing between Sawyer and myself.

To avoid dwelling on it, I removed his top. His pale torso was slim and hairless and his nipples were a dark pink and pebbled, making my mouth dry at the thought of touching them. I clutched at the wet T-shirt as I stepped back from temptation. My gaze moved to the clinging material of his jeans and I exhaled in a rush. Oh fuck!

A flash of heat rode up my neck and I blamed it on the warmth in the locker room. *Get a grip, you've seen naked men before.*

That is so not the same.

With that thought ringing in my ears, I dropped his top and hesitantly stepped closer. "Do you want me to help take off your jeans… and pants?"

The sound of a low moan was followed by a full body shudder. Sawyer's eyelashes lowered to hide his eyes from me as he nodded.

My fingers felt clumsy as they worked to open the button, the back of my hand touching his damp, silky skin. Gritting my teeth at the sensation, I gave a sigh of relief as the button popped open. I got down on my knees and tugged the zip down. As the wet fabric clung to him and drew my gaze to his crotch; the air became stuck in my lungs. Was this arousing him?

The cock pressing against the front of Sawyer's jeans said yes, but when I glanced up at his face, I wasn't so sure. Seeing a great deal of uncertainty clouding his face, I quickly pulled his jeans down his slim legs.

Keeping my gaze from straying to his arousal, I asked, "Lift your leg, Angel."

His response was to place his hands on my shoulders to steady himself and then he lifted one foot at a time, waiting for me to release his legs from his jeans. The sight of him stood in just his underpants gave me a fluttering sensation in the pit of my stomach as I stood up. "I'm sure you can take your pants off while I get you a robe."

When he huffed out a sigh, I met his gaze. "Is there something you want, Angel?"

He fidgeted for a moment. "You said... you'd undress me," he finished in a breathy whisper, his cheeks turning crimson.

His eyes locked with mine, begging... but for what?

"Do you want me to take your pants off?" I asked, wanting to be sure what he was asking for. I worked to keep my voice neutral, even as my pulse rammed itself into my throat, trying to choke me.

"Yes."

That one word nearly brought me to my knees.

What the fuck was I doing? *Removing Sawyer's pants, evidently.* The snarky answer was nearly enough to make my knees buckle as I realised I was going to do what he'd asked. My hands clenched at my sides as I lowered myself at his feet again. I kept my gaze averted from his crotch, praying that I could do this. His hands returned to my shoulders and I gingerly tugged the damp material down his pale limbs. The silence seemed to stretch between us as I held my breath, waiting for him to lift his legs for me. As he did, the movement drew my gaze to the arousal that was only inches from my face. His actions had caused his cock to raise towards me as if in offering and the scent of arousal filled my nose as I breathed in.

With shaking hands, I quickly removed his underwear. I averted my gaze from the beautiful bare cock bobbing in front of me. Then I found my gaze had shifted back to his lower body.

Realising what I was doing, I jumped up, forcing him to release my shoulders. When he wobbled, I grabbed hold of him. "Sorry," I growled, my fingers digging into his soft flesh for a moment before I released him.

Needing a moment to get myself under control, I went to get one of the robes I could see hanging on the far wall next to a row of lockers. When I returned, I ensured my gaze remained on his face. Convinced there was amusement there, I rolled my eyes heavenward. The fucker was testing me. Slipping the robe around his shoulders, I ensured that I didn't touch his skin and kept my body well away from his.

With the robe secured, I arched my brows. "You know that pushing can get you into trouble, Angel?"

His eyelashes fluttered as he pulled an innocent expression that would make any angel proud. "I don't know what you're talking about." His voice dropped to a soft whisper as his chin lowered.

I pointed at him. "I'm on to you." Even as I said it, my heart thundered, his expression affecting me deeply.

Sawyer's giggle was drowned out by the sound of an angry voice. "What the heck is going on in here?"

I glanced towards the open door, finding Nathan stood with a none too happy expression on his face as he glanced between the two of us.

"Sawyer got wet cycling here and I... was... just seeing he was okay." A resurgence of heat spread up my neck as I stuttered my way through the explanation.

Nathan's expression didn't lighten as he pinned me with a stare that could have melted metal. "Is that right? You were just seeing if Sawyer was okay? Does that involve *helping him dress*?"

The accusation cut through me, leaving me unsure how to proceed. I glanced at Sawyer, looking for some direction. Would he mind me revealing our... our what? What was I supposed to call what we'd been doing? Never having used any kind of dating app, I was at a loss to come up with an answer.

"It's alright Daddy bear, you can back off. Boyd and I are working some stuff out. Stuff, I might add that is none of your business."

The snippy tone provoked a growl from Nathan, his lips clamping together as he gave me a moody stare. But I couldn't have cared less how he was feeling as bile burned the back of my throat. I

67

hated Sawyer calling Nathan, daddy. Although, I knew deep down that he was only being flippant with Nathan, I had the urge to demand that he never do it again. What was that all about? *As if you don't know.*

Unable to face the truth, I concentrated on Nathan standing in the doorway. He met my stare and folded his arms over his chest, indicating that he was going nowhere. I met his gaze with a 'give me a moment' look. Tension filled the room as Nathan continued to stare at me seemingly unprepared to leave us even for a minute. Sensing the stare off was futile, I took a deep breath and looked back at Sawyer.

"Do you think Lenny would mind lending Sawyer some dry clothes?" Sawyer gave a sigh of relief at the change of subject as Nathan nodded.

"I'll sort Sawyer out. I'm sure you've got a lot to be doing." Nathan's tone brooked no argument.

My stomach dropped at the realisation that I was going to have to leave Sawyer when I really didn't want to. "Yeah, right. Okay. I'll message you later, Sawyer." I stared at him as I spoke, trying to convey that leaving him was the last thing I wanted to do.

At the slight head bob he gave me, I bent and whispered in his ear. "I'll be seeing you later."

His mouth hung open as he registered my meaning, his reaction making me feel much happier. I strolled over to Nathan. "Make sure you take care of Angel." The edge to my voice was enough to make Nathan's forehead furrow.

"I see."

I didn't respond because I still hadn't figured it all out myself. But I knew one thing: I wanted to work it out now that Sawyer had opened the door for me. A thought niggled at the back of my mind that now the door was open I wasn't sure I'd ever be able to close it again.

Back in the bar, I kept myself busy with work, trying not to think about a naked Sawyer in the same room with Nathan. What had brought Sawyer here in the middle of the day?

Distracting myself didn't work when all I could envision was Sawyer's slim, naked body. My fingers clenched around the sandpaper I was using to smooth down the tabletop. "Jesus, stop being a fucking dope."

"Who you talking to?" Brett asked, making me jump as I realised he was standing next to me.

"Don't creep up on folks like that!" I growled, trying to get my heart rate to settle back down.

"Keep your hair on! I just came over to see if you wanted to look at the plans that Nathan had delivered for the layout of the restaurant." Realising that Brett had answered my question, I glanced around the room to find Nathan talking to Jake, the architect. The tightness in my chest released now that I knew that Nathan was nowhere near Sawyer.

"Boss, are you okay? You're acting a bit weird," Brett asked, interrupting my train of thought.

"Yeah, sorry. I have a lot on my mind."

"Oh, is this about Glenn? I'm sorry about the break-up, but as I said before he's not worthy of you. The bastard was a user and if he can't see that you wanted to try and make things better between the two of you... then it's his fucking loss." Brett gave my shoulder a squeeze as he offered me his words of wisdom.

We'd gone for a beer one night after work, not long after Glenn had left and I'd got a little drunk before confessing to the argument I'd had that had resulted in me being single.

Fortunately, Brett was an open-minded guy and didn't like putting labels on anyone, so it had been easy to talk to him about how I was discovering a new side to myself. His opinion had been "go try it and see if it fits, and if it doesn't then move on." How could I argue with that logic?

Except, I was already worried about the feelings that I had for Sawyer and we'd not even had a date yet, so where did that leave me?

Pushing away the worry, I fibbed. "I know mate, but sometimes life is a little trickier." I gave him a smile that I hoped didn't look as fake as it felt. "Let's see what changes those plans are going to give us."

Brett groaned and I laughed as we both walked over to Nathan and Jake, knowing that this was the distraction I needed to keep my head in the game and away from a certain someone.

Chapter 6

SAWYER

As I locked my front door and leant against it, my phone vibrated in my pocket. I knew straight away who it was as I fumbled to pull it out. Boyd had been playing on my mind all afternoon as I'd worried that getting him to undress me might have put him off. My Little had needed some attention and I'd not been able to keep my mouth shut when he'd asked what I'd wanted.

My heart rate soared as I read the message.

BB: *Are you free tonight?*

Fuck yes, I was free. I cringed at the speed of the answer my head had given.

He wasn't put off by my behaviour this morning. Oh, my God!

My bum wiggled against the door before I stopped and glanced down at my wet and dirty clothes before sniffing for good measure. My nose wrinkled as I checked the time.

LittleS: *Yes. What do you have in mind?*

The seconds before a reply came through felt like forever as my gaze remained glued to my phone.

BB: *Where do you live? Do you want to go out, or would you like to come to mine for something to eat? I promise not to poison you.*

I chuckled at his promise not to poison me. He'd obviously recalled one of our app conversations about me working at La Trattoria Di Amore and my own lack of ability in the kitchen. My mother hadn't raised a fool. Why would I prepare crap food when I could have a Michelin star chef cook for me several times a week?

LittleS: *Your place would be good. I'm knackered and not up to going out.*

BB: *Do you want me to come and collect you? It will be nice to have some privacy to talk face to face.*

The air became trapped in my lungs as I typed my response.

LittleS: *No, I can ride my bike if you give me your address :)*

BB: *No, I'm not happy for you to do that, it's dark out there. I'll come and get you.*

My hand tightened around the phone at the message.

LittleS: *Cars pollute the environment. I'll ride my bike!*

I sighed at the tone of my message as I read my reply back.

BB: *Now, I want you to listen to me. It's dark out there and it's not safe for you to be cycling in the dark. I have an electric car so please don't argue with me.*

I rolled my eyes, even as a smile spread across my face at him acting all protective.

LittleS: *Alrigghtttt, I'll wait for you to come and get me...*

I chuckled as I sent another message with my address before going to shower.

Washed and changed into fresh clothes, I stood and stared out of the window, my teeth gnawing at my lower lip. Was I really going to do this? Was I going to try and train a Daddy? Had I lost my marbles? It certainly seemed like it. Maybe I was taking Nathan's advice a step too far?

Any negative thoughts died as the headlights lit up my drive. As the car pulled to a stop, I walked out the door and locked it behind me.

I searched for something to say as Boyd got out of the car. "Thank you for coming to get me, but I could have cycled," I muttered belligerently

Uncertainty crept in as Boyd paused in the light from the security light, his dark head tilted and his expression turning thoughtful. Was he trying to figure out how to navigate my behaviour? I got the distinct impression that he was as he

75

approached me. His gaze swept me from head to toe and then back again. His eyelashes shielded his thoughts from me as he stopped just in front of me.

"I wanted to come, to make sure that you were safe. Aren't I allowed to worry about you?" he asked gently, his hand lifting and his thumb rubbing my cheek.

I nodded, wondering whether I was wearing a dreamy expression from the simple action. I suspected I was. "But you don't know me, not really." I wanted to bite my tongue when his hand fell from my face as a result of my words.

"That may be so. But I want to get to know you. The messages are great but I want more."

Something in his voice prevented any protest I might have made as he ushered me into the car. A grin spread across my face at seeing his car was indeed electric. I'd invested in one too, but I preferred to cycle because it kept me fit. Days like today where I got soaked, sucked, but usually I was better prepared with a waterproof suit in my rucksack.

Sitting quietly next to Boyd as he drove, I noted the familiar street signs, and it dawned on me how close he actually lived to me. Minutes later, Boyd pulled up a long drive and parked in front of a gorgeous house.

The security lights lit up the building to reveal a two-storey structure built from glass and wood. It was made out of reclaimed timber. Colossal glass windows overlooked what appeared to be a garden, but I couldn't quite make it out in the darkness.

There was a small wind turbine at the side of the house and the roof was full of solar panels. If I was a betting man, I'd have bet that there were other aspects of the house that were ECO-friendly too. Some of the conversations we'd had via the app resurfaced as I recalled how I'd enthused about using nature's reserves, like the sun, to power my own home. If *it ever gets finished.*

Feeling a bad mood wanting to take hold, I focused on Boyd's home instead of the lack of my own. "Wow! This is a lot like what I want for my own home." Drawn to the building, I got out of the car eager to discover what surprises it held.

Once inside, I followed Boyd as he gave me a tour around the lower floor. Images of me lying on Boyd's large comfy sofa in front of the massive wood stove flooded my head. *Hey, come on. You have your own place. You don't need someone else's.*

As the thought registered, my hands clenched at my sides as I lagged behind Boyd. I tried to focus and mentally tuck away all the things he'd mentioned as he chatted about what he'd done to the place.

The noises I made after each new revelation would have been embarrassing if it weren't for how happy Boyd looked.

At the mention of a company that used old newspaper as wall insulation, I stopped to stare at the walls in the living room. *I'll need to find out more about that.*

"Are you okay?" Boyd asked, making me jump.

I coughed, feeling a little flustered. "Yeah, sorry. I was thinking about what you said about the company that does the insulation." I shrugged and shoved my hands into my pockets as I peered at Boyd from beneath my eyelashes.

Boyd indicated for me to follow him out of the lounge. My gaze moved of its own accord to the firm backside that flexed in the dark denim. His long, powerful stride forced me to quicken my pace to keep up with him.

My gaze lingered on the beautiful woodwork and modern fittings. I wasn't sure what I'd been expecting of this big, hairy guy more used to manual labour, but it wasn't this level of sophistication. The other guys I'd dated, white-collar men, who wore suits and had soft hands would seem better suited to this house. Boyd was clearly none of those things. Did that mean someone else had had a hand in helping him design the place?

Unnerved at the thought, I forced my attention back to Boyd. His too long, wavy hair and bearded face weren't something I'd previously have found attractive, yet now, all I wanted to do was curl up in his lap and stroke his beard. Although, his face wasn't classically handsome, the moment I'd laid eyes on him there had been something about the intensity of his caramel eyes that had spoken to me.

If I wasn't mistaken, there'd been a moment of connection between us in the locker room. I was positive he'd felt it too. When he'd knelt before me, he'd taken my breath away. That simple act had shown me more than anything that he was comfortable with himself and with what he was offering me.

His arm lifted and his forearm flexed as his hand raked through his hair, distracting me. That had to be why he'd used a picture of his forearm for his profile. His forearms were a thing of beauty that I wanted to feel wrapped around me.

Pleaseeeee.

A giggle got trapped in my throat as Boyd stopped and I *accidentally* bumped into his back.

He twisted around, his hands coming up to steady me. "Hey, Angel, take it easy. We don't want a visit to accident and emergency on our first date." His voice deepened and his caramel eyes gleamed with amusement as if he'd somehow figured out what my game was.

"I'm not normally so accident prone," I muttered, heat creeping up my neck as his gaze remained steady on me.

His warm hands stroked down my arms before he stepped back and scratched his neck. The overhead lights caught on his dark hair, causing it to gleam like polished wood.

"Is that right?" he asked, a genuine smile on his face. "This was kind of short notice so I'm hoping that I've got something decent in the fridge to make a meal for you."

Slashes of deep red darkened his cheekbones as he eyed me before glancing back to where I guessed the kitchen was. "Let's go and investigate. I can always ring for pizza instead."

There was indecision in his voice as he looked at me. "I'm sure you'll have something in your fridge I can eat," I said. "Oh, maybe I should have mentioned that I'm vegetarian. My parents went vegan a few years back but I couldn't make myself go the whole hog."

His lips twitched and then it hit me what I'd said. "Sorry, no pun intended," I said, grinning at him.

"I'm sure there wasn't. Let's go and investigate what I've got, but be warned I'm a carnivore and I can't see that changing—ever."

As I stepped into the kitchen, I tried to fathom out if he was warning me about trying to change him or something else. Then he turned towards me, his face beaming. *Maybe he was hoping to turn me into a meat-eater?*

As the thought popped into my head, I started to snigger.

His raised brow and his speculative look didn't help as I tried to stop myself from thinking about eating his meat.

"Did I say something funny?"

"No," I answered, trying to control my laughter. "I'm just thinking about eating meat."

His nostrils flared and desire I wasn't sure I was ready for shone in the depths of his eyes. As I exhaled, his body tensed. But then he shifted and moved across the room, drawing my attention to his kitchen instead.

The room wasn't huge but it was beautifully designed. The wood used for the cabinets was distressed in appearance and looked recycled. "Did you use recycled wood for your cabinets?" I glanced from the cupboards to Boyd as he stopped in front of a sizeable black fridge.

"Yeah, I did," he answered, sounding cautious.

"I love it. I've been searching for months for someone who does this kind of work. Would you mind giving me the contact details of the people you hired?"

His face got a strange look on it, but he nodded. "Remind me to give you their business card before I take you home."

He sounded a little distracted, but before I could ask if there was a problem he spoke again.

"Can I get you a drink?"

"What have you got?"

When he started to reel off a long list of soft drinks, I held up my hand. "I'll have a glass of wine if you have any, white preferably because red does silly things to me."

Did he think Littles only drank soft drinks?

He said nothing as he pulled out a bottle of white wine, the label showing it to be a sweet variety I happened to favour. I wasn't keen on dry white wines, they always tasted too bitter to me. He poured me a glass, walking over to the small, wooden table, which was also recycled, to lay it down.

"Why don't you have a seat?" One of his hands fidgeted at his side as he glanced in my direction with some uncertainty.

As I walked towards him, I tried to figure out how to put him at ease. I'd avoided talking about the other part of me when we'd messaged because I'd wanted to see his face to gauge his reaction. My mouth dried as I thought about it. Would he still want me once I'd explained my lifestyle to him? Why had I thought going on a date with a novice was a good idea?

My past relationships had always lacked something, though what it was I'd never figured out.

As I swept my gaze over his face, there was a level of concern in his expression that I'd never experienced before. There was something about him that called to me, and I wanted to give it a chance more than I'd ever wanted anything before.

With my chest tightening, I stopped a few inches away from him and tilted my head back to look him in the eye. Honesty being the best policy, I stared at him and started to explain who I was. "I'm what you'd call a Little. What that means is that there is a vital part of me that needs a caregiver. A Daddy that allows me the freedom to let my inner child come out to play. Someone who wants to take care of me, keep me safe and set boundaries for me." I chuckled. "Even when I say I don't want the boundaries. It's not something I can switch off, or change. I embraced that part of myself a long time ago. But it doesn't mean I act that way all the time. That I'm not an adult with grown-up needs. It just means that there are times that I have to set those needs aside to nurture myself, if that makes sense?"

I'd noticed a furrow deepen between his eyes as I'd spoken, but he hadn't interrupted or shown any disgust so I kept on talking, hoping he'd understand that even though there was a part of me that was childlike, I was still a man. "I'm still a man, nothing changes that."

I stood there feeling exposed as he remained silent. I wasn't sure that being so open was the right thing to do. My guts twisted into knots as the silence lengthened and Boyd continued to stare at me, his face not revealing what he was thinking.

About to grab my wine to help with the dryness in my mouth, my hand fluttered back to my side as Boyd spoke. "Thank you for being so open. I can't imagine how hard it must be to reveal something so private, so personal. You can trust me."

Opening my mouth to speak, I quickly closed it again and nodded at him when he held his hand up, indicating that I should let him finish.

"I know it's easy to say you can trust me, but I mean it, you can. And I'll be honest with you. It's a little difficult to get my head around how it all works…"

He rubbed his beard, the rasping noise the only sound as I held my breath, waiting for him to continue. Was it too much for him? Had I forced too much information on him all at once?

"I can almost hear your mind buzzing from here," he said, humour dancing in his eyes before they turned serious again. "I just need a little time to process everything. Okay? I want to get to know you, to understand why I'm drawn to the idea of wanting to give you... what you want, what you need."

Those words turned my insides to jelly as his face remained serious.

"Okay," I answered with as much conviction as I could muster. *What harm could there be in that?*

Chapter 7

Boyd

Clamping the piece of wood that required cutting to the workbench, I lifted the saw and started to cut where I'd drawn the line. I hoped that keeping busy would stop me from going over and over the evening I'd spent with Sawyer, two days earlier.

How's that working out for you?

My hand tightened around the handle of the saw as I considered how unsuccessful that had been.

I wasn't sure about the 'Daddy' aspect of what he'd talked about, and no matter how many times I'd tried to imagine him calling me Daddy, I couldn't envision how it would make me feel. *Is that so? Then why did it burn a hole in your gut when he called Nathan, Daddy?*

My jaw clenched as my teeth ground together.

There was something about Sawyer that triggered a need inside of me to take care of him, more than I'd ever felt with anyone else I'd ever dated. Was that part of it?

What about Glenn? You took care of him, paid his bills and supported him so that he could stay at home and build his own business.

Was that the same?

I wasn't wholly convinced it was, because the dynamic between Glenn and myself had been very different. We were both versatile and I knew damn well Sawyer would never want to be dominant if things progressed between us. There was also a significant age gap between us. He was only twenty-three, whereas I was coming up to forty. Would the age gap make a difference? The question I'd found myself ruminating over the most was how I should deal with a person, who, in essence, had two different sides to him? A ripple of apprehension slid down my spine at the thought of the minefield it could turn into.

We'd only just started to scratch the surface of what it all really meant to him, or to me. With each new piece of information he gave me, I found I wanted to know more. Our work schedules had left us unable to message for the last two days. Thankfully, tonight, he wasn't working and he'd agreed to another date. He was coming to my home again, only this time he'd suggested cooking for me. My apprehension was replaced with fluttering excitement at the prospect of seeing him again.

At the sound of a loud wolf whistle, I lifted my head to stare across the room at the culprit.

"Boss, have you got a sec? I need a hand to align this bloody booth. I'm sure the fucking measurements were exact but now I can't get the fucker to sit right," Brett hollered from the other side of the bar.

"Can't you act like a normal civilised human being and just come and talk to me?" I was so used to Brett's behaviour that my complaint carried very little heat. I dropped the saw onto the workbench and walked across the dusty floor. My gaze swept the room and I gave a heartfelt sigh. Even with the men doing double shifts to crack on with the work that could be done, we were running a few days behind schedule.

We'd been hit by yet another snag. This time it was the specialist wooden flooring I'd ordered from Sweden. Somehow, it had ended up in Scotland, and then when it had finally arrived, it had been the wrong colour. We'd had to return the whole shipment and reorder, leaving us with a very tight deadline.

The life of a contractor was never easy, but over the last few weeks I'd started to wonder why I fucking bothered. Raking my hand through my hair, I halted and eyed the wooden booth that still required leather upholstery. That was something else that had been delayed because the company had informed me that we'd requested a change of date. The universe was clearly trying to fuck with me and I had no idea why.

"Okay, what seems to be the problem?"

Brett wiped his sweaty brow and scowled at the wooden booth. "The measurements were perfect so this should fit into that corner, but it doesn't. The far end is jutting out. I've tried everything and nothing seems to work."

I grabbed the measuring tape off the counter and started to work through the figures he'd written down, as well as the dimensions of the booth he'd made. They married perfectly. I eyed the wall and my heart sank. I stepped closer, dread filling me. Brushing my hand down the wall, I looked at Brett. "Did you do anything to this wall?" If I wasn't mistaken, the wall cavity was bulging and it felt wet.

"Nah, why would I do something to the wall? What's wrong with it?" he asked as he stepped closer, his gaze narrowing to where I was touching the plaster.

"I don't know what the fuck is going on here, but someone is definitely trying to sabotage this bloody job!" I growled through gritted teeth. "This wall feels wet and it's bulging, so that's why the booth won't fit."

Brett's eyes went wide as he looked around the room at the other men working there, his face darkening with suspicion. He'd been my foreman for more than ten years and I trusted him implicitly. The building trade could be a cutthroat business, but I'd always been fair and loyal to my employees, which meant I kept my men. But there were always a few transient workers on every job I did, men that didn't stick around for one reason or another.

Mentally flipping through the men I'd employed for this specific job, I tried to figure out if I'd had any run-ins with the newbies. "Someone is fucking with us and I've no idea why, but we need to find out before it gets any more out of hand. I'll go up into the roof to see what's what. Can you stay behind tonight so we can go through the plans to check if anything else is amiss?" I swallowed a sigh at the thought of having to cancel my plans with Sawyer.

"Yeah, I can stay. No problem. I'll come with you to look at the damage," Brett offered, his voice distracted as he continued to stare at the men with distrust.

I punched his arm. "Try not to be too obvious, man." I laughed without humour. "It's alright, I'll go up and have a look and you keep your eye on things down here." With that, I headed to the stairwell that led up to the space above the bar. I crawled into the tight area and got my bearings as I tried to figure out whereabouts the wall was situated.

On my knees, I edged across the rafters, my gut twisting at the sight of several empty buckets, the cause of the pool of water above the damaged wall. *Fuckers! The shitty bastards. I hope they rot in hell!*

As I stared down into the tiny gap where the insulation was, all I could see was wet slush. The several buckets of water added to the mix had turned the paper insulation into a sodden mess. I crawled back out and stood in the stairwell. With very little option, I yanked my phone from my back pocket and called Nathan.

He picked up on the third ring. "Hello."

Not beating about the bush, I got straight to the point. "Nathan, it's Boyd, can you come to the second-floor stairwell that leads to the space above the bar. I have a problem."

"Yeah, give me two minutes." Nathan sounded pissed, but didn't ask any questions, a fact which I was grateful for because I wasn't sure who was with him, and at this point in time I wasn't sure who could be trusted.

A few moments later, there was the sound of heavy footsteps and I looked over the railing to see Nathan coming up from the lower floor. His face was a stoic mask as he came up the final flight of stairs.

"What the fuck is wrong now?" He demanded.

"Someone is fucking with this job and I have no bloody idea why?" I raked my hands through my hair as I stared at Nathan's distressed face. "There's been several fuck ups that could be passed off as just that. But now someone has taken it to the next level and dumped several buckets of water into the wall cavity causing the insulation to turn to mush and soak into the plaster. The wall is all out of alignment, which is what alerted me to the problem."

The more I said, the darker Nathan's expression turned. A thundercloud didn't look as menacing as Nathan did at that moment.

"Why would someone want to mess with us?" His eyes narrowed, his voice seething with anger.

That was the question I couldn't answer. "I've no idea. We didn't have any problems when we built The Playroom, so this has come totally out of the blue. You don't think it's connected to that Devon guy, do you?" I asked tentatively.

On New Year's Eve, Nathan's boyfriend Lenny and one of the club subs, Ferron, had been held captive in the basement by Ferron's ex, Devon. It turned out that he didn't like the fact that Ferron had dumped him after he'd beaten the crap out of him. But as far as I was aware, Devon was still in prison awaiting trial, which was supposed to happen sometime in June.

"No… I don't think so. Devon's business partner has disappeared, but I think that's more to do with the press hounding him for answers about Devon rather than anything else. Although, I suppose you never know. I've had Phil Knight overhaul our security, but I didn't get him to look at the second floor because it wasn't finished. Do you want me to call him now and see if we can get something rigged up to try and catch the bastard in the act?" Nathan was practically snarling by the time he'd finished talking, his face a deep red.

With no other solution, I nodded. "I think we need to do something quickly. I've got Brett staying late after the guys have finished tonight. Do you think your guy Phil will be free to come at such short notice?"

"There's only one way to find out," Nathan answered as he pulled his phone from the pocket of his hoodie. A few seconds later, I stood listening as he spoke to the person on the other end of the phone, who I assumed had to be Phil.

"Yeah, tonight if you can. It seems we have a saboteur in our ranks." There were several "yeps" and "hmms" and then Nathan ended the call and tucked his phone away.

"He'll be here around six-thirty. Will that work for you?" Nathan asked.

"It's fine for me, and as I said, Brett has already agreed to stay. I'll go and see if I can salvage the wall. I have a feeling I'm going to have to drill a bloody hole in it to get the insulation out and then redo the whole blasted thing again." I sighed dejectedly, Nathan patting my shoulder.

"We'll find the bastard and I won't hit you with the penalty clauses if we go past the deadline for opening."

His generous offer left me speechless for a minute, so I just nodded and offered a small smile.

"Show me where the damage is." As per Nathan's request, we headed back up into the tiny space and I showed him the state of the wall cavity.

We spent twenty minutes working to secure the space so that nothing more could happen up there and then I left to go back down to the bar.

After checking the time, I signalled to Brett as I walked back into the bar. "Let the men go early. Say it's a reward for the double shifts." He gave me a nod before wandering off around the room to talk to them.

As it wasn't that unusual to let the guys have an early finish from time to time, I hoped it wouldn't arouse suspicion. There were a few cheers, the noise level increasing and then decreasing as the room emptied. By the time everyone had left, I was already creating a mental list of the current jobs that would need to be checked in order to ensure that nothing else was amiss.

As I walked over to one of the finished booths, my phone vibrated in my pocket. But before I could check the message, Brett hollered over, "Boss, shit! I think I've found another issue."

Cursing up a blue storm, I stomped across the room and walked around the bar. "What now?" I ground out through clenched teeth. My temples were starting to throb as I eyed Brett's crestfallen expression. He pointed to the lower shelf and it took a minute before I could see what the issue was.

My gaze narrowed on the back of the shelf where there should have been several pipes fitted for the specialist beer that would be housed in a cavity we'd already created for the kegs to sit in.

"Where are the pipes? Didn't they get fitted last week?" I rubbed my aching jaw as I shifted my gaze to Brett. *Was I going mad?* I was sure they'd been there last week.

"They *were* fitted," he stressed as his face turned an ugly shade of red. "The guy came from the company last week. Due to their specific requirement to pipe the beer, we had to book him six weeks in advance because he works freelance for the company. He travels all over the world due to the stuff being exported internationally." Brett's explanation caused my gut to twist into tighter knots.

"Goddamn it!" Nathan growled, reminding me of his presence.

I turned my attention to him. "I couldn't have put that any better myself. This fucking stinks. We need to check to see if the pipes have been removed from the premises, because if they have your cameras might have caught who took them, right? They're at the front and back of the building."

"What about the garage, do they cover that?" Brett asked, his eyes lighting up with menace. Nathan's face was grim as he nodded. "Then we'd surely catch sight of the bastard?" Brett added with a hopeful smile.

"We'll do a search first. Then hopefully Nathan's security guy will be here and we can go through the video footage and see if we can find anything. We know what date the guy fitted the pipes so we have a rough idea of when they might have been tampered with."

With that, we went off in different directions to start a search of the entire second floor. My phone rang, but distracted by the search, I let it go to voicemail.

I was a sweaty, dirty mess by the time I finally sat down with Phil, Nathan and Brett. Nathan had found the pipes stashed behind an old container in the storeroom and although, I was pleased we'd found them, I was pissed that we still had no evidence to indicate who'd removed them in the first place.

"Where does this leave us now?" I asked them.

"I think we need to set up several cameras tonight and connect them to the mainframe so that Nathan can see what's going on from his office. You'll need someone you trust to monitor them when you're not there. I think it's probably the only way to catch someone in the act. From what Brett has told me, there are too many men to keep eyes on them all." Phil glanced at me. "Brett mentioned things going awry with your orders. Can you talk me through them? I might be able to set up an email account that you can use so that I can monitor your emails and trace if anyone is messing with your orders."

By the time Phil had finished speaking, my heart rate had settled and the knots that had formed in my stomach were starting to undo. The throbbing in my temples continued, but I felt a smidgen better now that we had a plan in place.

My phone rang and everyone stopped talking to look at me. I shifted on the seat to dig it out, and without looking at the caller ID, I hit the speaker button. Before I could get a word out, there was an angry shout.

"What do you think you're playing at? I've been waiting outside your bloody house freezing my backside off for ages. You know that's an arsehole thing to do, right? You can stick your date where the sun doesn't shine. A fine Daddy you'd make!" With that, the phone went dead.

I stared in horror at the blank screen, the sound of Sawyer's tearful voice ringing in my ears.

"Shit! *Shit!* I forgot to ring him and cancel." I explained to no one in particular, avoiding making eye contact as I jumped out of my seat.

My hands shook as I tried not to think about Sawyer's reference to being a good Daddy as I quickly pulled up his number.

Chapter 8

SAWYER

The bright blue sky was fading to a dusky pink as I cycled along the track that I'd discovered would take me directly to Boyd's home. I'd got up early that morning and done a dry run to check where the house was before I'd headed to work. I wasn't always good with directions so I liked to figure out where places were ahead of time.

Due to the darkness and how captivated I'd been by Boyd's home when I'd visited the first time, I'd not realised that there were only four houses in the large estate. Boyd's was situated on the most prominent plot and tucked into a corner shielded by trees and shrubs which gave him complete privacy. He'd mentioned that he'd been interested in the piece of land I'd bought for my home, but when I'd questioned why he'd not bought it, he'd diverted the conversation to something else.

When I'd thought about it later, I'd wondered if he'd not wanted to talk about it because he couldn't afford it. I seldom talked about how wealthy my grandparents were. It wasn't something I was comfortable discussing because people tended to question my family's choice of living in a commune when they were loaded.

As I didn't dip into my trust fund that often and lived off my wages, I didn't see that it was anyone else's business. The one time I had used it, was to buy the land and set aside the funds to build my own ECO home. I'd figured out pretty quickly that there was no way I'd ever be able to afford it on my wage. In fact, without my trust fund, I'd still be living in the commune, sharing a bathroom with thirty other people. Not that I'd minded. It was, after all, what I'd grown up with. It was just the lack of privacy that was a ball ache and I'd finally had enough of it and left.

I'd hated not being able to be myself without twenty sets of prying eyes watching my every move. My sigh was lost in the wind as I rounded the last bend and left the track to turn down the road leading to Boyd's home. As the house came into view, my heart sank at the lack of car in the driveway. Maybe he'd parked it in the garage?

I gasped out a breath as I cycled up the driveway and stopped at the garage door. Hopping off my bike, I leant it against the wall and strolled up to the door a little breathless. As I rolled my shoulders, the backpack full of pre-prepared food

I'd managed to coax out of Lenny, Carl's new trainee chef, slid down my arms. Given my distinct lack of cooking skills, I'd wanted to slap myself upside the head when I'd offered to cook for Boyd.

In a panic, I'd all but begged Lenny to make me something, explaining my date with Boyd to him. As Lenny was dating Nathan and seriously loved up, he'd seemed only too happy to help me.

Was it wrong to pass off someone else's food as your own?

By the time I got to the door, my hands were shaking. Instead of knocking, I shifted my weight and stood on my tiptoes to look through the glass window into the house. My brow furrowed at the absence of light, or any signs of life. Was I too early?

I shook my head at my own eagerness as I checked my watch. I had a habit of arriving early. It had been ingrained in me as a child and it was something that had stuck. I moved back a step and knocked hard, just in case Boyd was at the back of the house. I hopped from one foot to the other as the seconds ticked by and there was still no answer. Dropping my heavy pack to the ground, I rooted in my pocket for my phone. Had he messaged me to say what time he'd be home?

With no message, my guts twisted with anxiety.

Had he forgotten I was coming tonight?

You're early. Give him a chance for fuck's sake.

Chewing my lip, I typed out a message and hit send. There was no harm in him knowing I was there a little early.

We'd exchanged phone numbers on our previous date, Boyd leaving me with a kiss to the forehead after dropping me home. I touched that same patch of skin and sighed.

All the time we'd been sending messages back and forth, I'd worked on not coming across as too clingy. Now, as I waited for a response, I huffed out a frustrated breath.

He's probably driving so he can't answer his phone. That's all it is. You know full well what the traffic is like in London.

Feeling a little reassured as I calculated how far Nathan's building was from Boyd's home, I turned and eyed his garden in the evening twilight, looking for a distraction. He wouldn't mind if I wandered around his garden, would he?

I hesitated, then shrugged as I stepped off the porch and went to have a nose around the grounds. As I'd not had time to explore that morning, I was curious to see what he liked. My feet faltered as I turned the corner to go around the side of the building, my eyes widening at the abundance of colour. The scents of herbs and plants I couldn't identify wafted around me carried by the breeze. Inhaling, I stepped into what appeared to be a small oasis. There was a significantly sized water feature in the middle of the garden, which could never be described as a pond. It was more like a lake with a wooden bridge that allowed you to walk across it. Drawn by a desire to see if there were any fish in the water, I strolled over to the lake.

I lingered as the setting sun cast shadows over the water and for the first time in days, I felt the tension drain from my body. As the chilly breeze picked up and the sky darkened, I wandered around the garden trying to identify the plants and herbs.

There didn't seem to be any order to the planting, but it still created a kind of flow and order that had probably taken an age to achieve. By the time I'd returned to the front of the house, it was dark enough for the security lights to have come on. I checked my watch again and my eyes widened at how long I'd spent enjoying the garden. Where the heck was Boyd? He should have been home by now.

He's forgotten you.

My eyes burned as I tried to swallow past the ball of tears trying to choke me, but the thought persisted. *He wouldn't forget me! He likes me and was interested in getting to know me.*

I argued back with my Little, the urge to stamp my foot hard to resist as the temper tantrum tried to take hold. My hands shook as I pulled out my phone to see if there was any message yet that would explain why I was still stood outside his home—alone.

See, he doesn't want you. Why else would you be stood here like a fool on your own?

I sniffed at the lack of message, heat spreading up my neck as I attempted to keep a hold on the temper snapping inside me.

Ring him and tell him he's a dick, go on.

With the cold seeping past my jacket and jeans and chilling me to the bone, I dialled Boyd's number too upset to reason with myself.

The moment the call connected, I screeched tearfully into the phone. "What do you think you're playing at? I've been waiting outside your bloody house freezing my backside off for forever. You know that's an arsehole thing to do, right? You can stick your date where the sun doesn't shine. A fine Daddy you'd make!"

Ending the call, I grabbed my pack and slung it on my back. All thoughts of how happy I'd been when Lenny had handed the food to me, withered and died. My stomach felt like I'd eaten a ball of lead and I struggled to swallow the bile rising up my throat.

I ran to my bike and slung my leg over the saddle as my phone started to ring. Ignoring it, I peddled down the drive and back out onto the road, heading for the track I'd cycled down only an hour and a half earlier. How had everything gone from being bright and sunny to dark and dismal in such a short time?

Boyd's a bastard, that's why.

Why hadn't he just messaged me to say he didn't want to meet? Tears slid unwillingly down my cheeks, turning icy as the cold wind hit them. Swiping at my face, I peddled as fast as I could, branches catching at the sleeves of my jacket and tugging at it. My chest tightened and I wheezed as I struggled to keep my balance and see past my tears, but I didn't stop. The need to get home and hide overrode everything else. The ride home seemed to take forever as my misery dragged me down.

As my home came into sight, a sob escaped, and then another. There had been a small part of me that had hoped Boyd would somehow be there to magically make everything better. "Arsehole," I muttered as I all but threw my bike to the ground after I got off it. Not bothering to lock it away, I rushed into my home. Too distressed to do more than throw my pack on the floor, I headed for my bed to grab the box from underneath it. I couldn't think about anything other than the need for my blankie and dummy.

I hesitated at the sight of the new outfit I'd bought for myself that had arrived that morning. The playsuit was pale pink with bright blue bows on it and had an opening to allow for a nappy change. My mind in turmoil, I stripped out of my clothes and got dressed in my playsuit. By the time I was curled up on my bed with my blankie and my dummy clamped between my lips, an element of calm had returned, even though I was still hiccupping every now and then.

My eyes ached and I buried my face in the fleecy blanket. Why had I thought Boyd was different?

Because he is, you don't know what happened to make him late. You just overreacted like you always do.

How do you know that he's different?

The two voices continued to bicker, neither giving an inch. I sniffed and lifted my hot face from the blanket and stared up at the wooden ceiling.

What am I going to do now?

Nothing.

I sighed and snuggled down in the bed, letting the warmth of the blanket cocoon me. Weary from crying, my eyes drifted shut.

Chapter 9

Boyd

I avoided thinking about the reactions I'd seen displayed on Nathan, Phil and Brett's faces, grateful that none of the men had said a word as I'd explained I needed to leave. They didn't try to stop me, not that it would have made any difference with my hands still shaking after Sawyer hadn't answered his phone when I'd tried to return his call.

I broke several speed limits, thinking about how upset Sawyer had sounded, and with all sorts of horrible images of him having an accident running through my head. The drive across London was dreadful as usual, giving me time to play what he'd said over and over again in my mind.

My knuckles turned white as I gripped the steering wheel. Had I lost my chance with him? Was it over before we'd really had a chance to see where it could go between us?

Reaching my home, the security lights revealed an empty driveway with no sign of Sawyer. Not that I'd really expected him to be there, but I'd wanted to check first just in case. Cursing myself seven ways to Sunday for letting myself get so distracted, I drove the couple of miles to Sawyer's home. Praying he'd let me explain what had happened, I parked at the end of his drive so that I didn't alert him to the fact that I was there.

My palms grew sweaty as I stared down the length of his drive and gave myself a pep talk. Leaving the car, I walked down the rocky path, noticing Sawyer's bike lying on the ground. There was something not right about it. Sawyer, from what I could tell from our previous conversations, had a lot of respect for his possessions. Acting on gut instinct, I ran to his front door and tested the handle. When the door opened soundlessly, I stepped inside, unsure what had possessed me to walk right into his home without knocking.

The lights above the bed haloed Sawyer, who was snuggled in a sizeable, fleece blanket. My feet became rooted to the spot as my gaze was drawn to his mouth, a mouth that held an adult version of a child's dummy. He looked so vulnerable, his face flushed and his dark lashes lying against his cheekbones as his mouth moved to suck on the dummy.

Had I done this? Had I made him need to seek comfort?

My ears buzzed and my heartbeat raced, forcing me to grip onto the doorframe. Was I ready for this? Was this really what I wanted?

His eyelashes fluttered open and his sleepy gaze met mine. Any doubts I might have had were buried under a wave of affection as his lips clamped around the dummy. He tensed and his hand came up, his gaze holding mine hostage as he removed it from his mouth.

"You're letting in the cold," he whined sleepily, his lips forming into a pout.

The knuckles of the hand clutching the dummy turned white as the sleepiness disappeared from his eyes. The air caught in my lungs as his posture turned defiant and his chin jutted out. My hands balled into fists as I tried to figure out what I should do, or say.

"I said, you're letting in the cold. Either come in or leave but you're letting all the heat out. I was trying to get warm after being left out in the cold for so long." His voice, so different to normal, held a decidedly soft edge to it.

I sucked in a breath and took a step into the room. *Don't fuck it up. Don't fuck it up.*

With the door closed behind me, I stood there, uncertain of my next move. What I wanted to do was enfold him in my arms, but I wasn't sure whether that would be welcomed.

"Are you just going to stand there?" he asked, his eyes imploring me to... to what?

Fuck it! Shoving aside my confusion, I went with my instincts. Once I'd reached the bed, I bent over slowly to make my intentions clear. When he stayed still, I wrapped his blanket around him and lifted him up. The scent of herbs, that I was starting to realise must be something he used on his skin, filled my senses as I tucked him into my chest. I turned around so that I could sit in the space Sawyer had been lying in.

Warmth invaded my chest as his arms wrapped around me and he nuzzled his face into the crook of my neck. His breath tickled my skin as he snuffled and got himself settled. The stress from the drive to get here melted away as I sat with my arms full of the warm bundle. A warm bundle that didn't seem to want to talk, his face staying buried in my neck.

I tried not to dwell on how out of character this behaviour was for me. Was it because it was Sawyer that I felt like this? I couldn't pinpoint it, not when he made me feel all kinds of... of what?

God knows. But whatever I was feeling, it was playing havoc with my emotions. They seemed intensified as his small hand lifted to play with my beard and his quiet sighs had me holding my tongue to stop myself from spoiling the moment.

I prayed that I was giving him what he needed, what we both needed as I appreciated the gentle touches. I slid my hand up his back, gently rubbing it as the silence lengthened without being strained.

His head rose sometime later, his lips forming into a smile that seemed to light up his whole face. The air seemed to leave the room as I stared back at him. "You're so beautiful, Angel." As I spoke, his head tilted to one side, the hand behind my neck moving to the dummy he'd been holding to pop it back between his lips.

My brows drew together as my stomach dropped. Had I said something wrong?

Explain why you were late, you idiot. Maybe that will help.

Heeding the voice of reason, I took a deep breath. "I'm sorry about tonight. I should have messaged you—"

The dummy was spat out. "You didn't message me. I checked," he cried, his lips trembling.

"I know, Angel, I know. I'm sorry. I forgot because something happened at work and distracted me. I swear I was going to tell you that I'd had to cancel, but Brett came to me with a problem that escalated into something more, and then things turned to shit pretty quickly after that." I tried to keep control of my impatience as I explained what had happened. "I'm sorry, Angel, I really am. I was going to postpone. I'd never leave you stood outside like that." As I finished talking, I thought about the key I never used for my back door. Was it too soon to give Sawyer a key?

Yes, no, maybe?

My gut told me to ignore the latter two so before I could give myself a chance to talk myself out of it, I offered something that it had taken Glenn a year to get from me. "I have a spare key to my back door if you want it? I can give it to you so you'll never be stuck outside again."

His brows disappeared under his fringe as his eyes widened. "You want to give me a key to your place?"

An ache spread through my chest at the tentativeness in his voice. Had I fucked up so badly that he doubted my sincerity?

"Yes, Angel. I want to give you a key. That way the *next time* you come over, you can let yourself in and make yourself at home." I made sure to stress the next time, needing to be clear that I wanted there to be one. His face turned thoughtful.

My gaze swept the tiny room, taking in the threadbare, lumpy sofa, the rickety table and chairs and the small, cramped bed I was sat on. "I'm sure you'll find it more comfortable in my home."

His expression turned mournful as he followed my gaze. "This place was only supposed to be temporary, but the builders in London are crap." His gaze flew to mine and he babbled, "Present company excluded, I'm sure."

At his contrite tone, I kept the smile off my face with difficulty. "Is that right?" I brought my face to within inches of his until his warm breath touched mine. "Did you ring the company I recommended and get a quote for your building works?"

His brows pinched but he nodded.

When he'd come to my home the other night and assumed that I'd employed someone else to do the work, I'd been amused. Tickled by the idea that he had no idea what I was capable of, I'd given him my business card. I was going to surprise him when he rang up for a quote. The last few days had been so busy that I hadn't spoken to my office manager, Gloria, to find out if there'd been any new enquiries.

"I spoke to a lady and she said she'd get someone to contact me to sort out a suitable time for a walkthrough in order to get a quote."

His body quivered on my lap as he answered, and I couldn't help but respond to it. "I'm sure they'll give you a good deal."

The sound of his stomach gurgling stopped me from saying more as I eyed his fleece covered belly. "Did you not have anything to eat?"

A shadow crept into his eyes and dulled the happiness they'd held a moment ago. He stared at the bag on the floor that I'd not noticed. My stomach dropped as I realised it probably had the stuff inside it for the meal he'd wanted to make for me.

"Is the food in that bag?" I asked, indicating towards it with my head as he looked back at me.

"Yeah."

That one word sounded like it held the weight of the world in it, so I gave him a big smile before carefully shifting him off my lap. "Then let's see what we've got so I can feed you before your tummy decides to tell me off again," I joked, trying to bring a smile back to his face.

He giggled and clutched at the blanket as I stood and strode over to the bag. The scent of herbs and spices tickled my nose as I opened it, causing my own stomach to remind me I hadn't eaten either. Pulling the tubs out, I eyed the full table and the one empty chair.

"It's alright, I'll do it. I'm used to working with my cranky cooker."

I turned to glance at Sawyer as he spoke. My eyes narrowed as he stood by the bed, the blanket that had hidden what he wore now lying in a heap on the bed. With my heart battering against my ribs, I struggled to hear what Sawyer was saying when all I could focus on was the pink and blue adult-size Babygro he wore.

The dummy and the blanket hadn't fazed me in the same way that seeing him dressed as a child did. It brought images to the forefront of my mind of my sister as a baby, toddling around the house when she was two looking utterly adorable. Did he wear a nappy under that suit?

Feelings I wasn't sure how to cope with rode roughshod through me, and my hands fisted tightly around the tubs I held. Tension seemed to fill the small room as I remained transfixed by Sawyer.

I got the distinct impression I'd betrayed my thoughts when Sawyer stepped back to the bed and lifted his blanket, slinging it around his shoulders. His eyes looked anywhere but at me as his face paled.

"I think it's getting late and maybe you should go home. I've got work in the morning."

There was a finality to his tone that forced me to acknowledge my panic at him asking me to go. But I wasn't sure I was ready to face up to everything that was a part of Sawyer's life yet. My hands trembled as I stepped over to the chair and placed the tubs down on the table.

Any hunger I'd previously felt was buried under the ball of anxiety now clawing at my guts. With great effort, I turned and faced Sawyer, unsure whether this would be the last time I'd get to look at my Angel.

His downcast gaze and sagging shoulders were too much for me to resist. I was across the small space in a heartbeat, cupping his face and bringing his head up so that I could look into his eyes. "Can you give me some time to think about... everything? This is a lot to take in."

Tears sheened his eyes and for a moment I thought he was going to say no, but then his head moved a fraction in a slight nod. "Okay... I'll... give you time." He licked his lips, the action drawing my gaze to them. "I only ask that if you come back, you know for sure that this is what you want." His voice broke and tears slid down his cheeks onto my fingers. The unspoken part about how I'd break his heart if I didn't was there in his teary eyes.

The air whistled past my lips before I could clamp them together to stop myself from offering false promises. Instead I nodded, choking back a sob that rose so suddenly that it left me defenceless against the onslaught of emotions. I swallowed as I released his face and stepped back. My hands itched to return and soothe the deep furrows that marred his sad face.

Knowing now was not the time, I fled out of the door before I did something ill advised. I kept my eyes focused on my car, even as my head and heart warred with each other over what they wanted. My head wanted to process everything, but my heart wanted to take hold of the man and never let him go.

That thought scared me more than I wanted to admit as I got in my car and drove off, not once looking back.

JP Sayle

Epilogue

SAWYER

I stared glumly at my phone as I tried not to think about how many days it had been since Boyd had all but run away from me, from the reality of what was a vital part of me.

"Sawyer… Sawyer, do you want the rest of that pasta?" Theo asked, his face peering down at the plate in front of me.

"Nah, you can have it. I'm not very hungry." That was the understatement of the year. I couldn't remember the last time I'd felt like eating. The plate was whipped away as Theo plonked himself down next to me.

"Cheers! I'm bloody starved. I thought the lunch rush was never going to end. I hate it when we have those small parties in the private dining area, they never seem to want to leave." He huffed out a loud sigh before shovelling a huge forkful of pasta into his mouth. The fork, that if I wasn't mistaken, I'd just been using to eat.

"You do know that fork wasn't clean?" I baulked at the thought of shared saliva.

"Yeah, and? I'm sure you don't have cooties or anything else I could catch." He studied me for a few seconds as if looking for something that might alert him to any diseases I had.

Once he'd finished his perusal, he shrugged, and I couldn't help but chuckle. "What are you like?"

"A loveable fool," he quipped back through a mouthful of half-chewed pasta.

"Shut your mouth, I don't need to see what you're eating, man!" I rolled my eyes at him when he opened his mouth wider. "You're gross. I'm sure that's why you're single."

The light of humour that had been dancing in his eyes faded as he looked down "Maybe," he answered, before his gaze returned to mine. "What's your excuse?"

There was a seriousness to his question that I didn't often associate with Theo. He was all about clowning around and avoiding any topic of conversation that was in any way serious.

My gaze narrowed on him and I found myself answering truthfully. "People struggle with what I'm into." Recalling the look on Boyd's face when he'd seen my outfit, I responded glumly, "When they're faced with the reality, they don't tend to stick around."

Hadn't the lack of contact from Boyd this last week proven that? I sank lower in the seat and sniffed.

"I'm sure that you'll find a Daddy—"

I lurched forward in my seat. "I thought I said never to mention that at work," I ground out through clenched teeth. When I'd gone to Adam's stag do at Lenny's home, we'd had a few drinks and a game of truth or dare had resulted in me sharing more about myself than usual. Now, as I stared at Theo, I wondered if he'd been blabbing to the other staff.

He shifted closer to me. "Listen, I've said nothing to no one, just as I promised. It's just that you were so happy last week and I thought maybe you'd met someone. Then you got all miserable and testy and I couldn't help wondering if something was wrong? You can talk to me. I promise I won't say anything to the others." He patted my knee, his face wearing an earnest expression that I found it hard to resist.

"I did have someone... but he's not sure about everything... about me." I inhaled before whining, "It's been a week and nothing. No message, no call. Nothing. I wish he would just let me know that it's over." Tears clogged my throat as I closed my eyes to avoid seeing the sympathy on Theo's face.

"If it's been a week and he hasn't messaged or called, then doesn't it show that he's taking this seriously?"

Trying to think past my misery, I let what he'd said sink in. Was that why Boyd hadn't been in touch? Was he taking the decision seriously?

While I was mulling Theo's suggestion over, my phone rang. Picking the phone up off the seat where I'd left it during my conversation with Theo, I answered it, despite not recognising the number.

The sound of a woman's voice filled my ear. "Hello, is this Mr. Rowland?"

"Yes, it is," I answered, trying to figure out why the voice sounded vaguely familiar.

"This is Gloria from Convener's Construction Company. I'm sorry for the delay in getting back to you to sort out a date for one of the men to come around and discuss your needs," she tittered, making me wonder what the heck was tickling her.

"Oh, yes, that's right," I replied, doing my best not to let the wave of sadness rolling over me suck me under. The call was just another reminder of how I'd got hold of the number for the construction company.

"Are you still interested, Mr. Rowland?"

There was something a little odd about the question, but I couldn't grasp what it was. "Erm, yes, yes I am."

"That's wonderful. What date and time would suit you?"

My heart rate took off as I heard a voice in the background asking Gloria a question. Was Boyd there? *You're imagining things now.*

I strained to hear, but there was nothing except the sound of breathing on the other end of the phone. I rolled my eyes at my overactive imagination as I chatted about dates and times. Thinking the universe was out to get me as she offered several different times that didn't work for me, I was about to give up when she asked if I would be free that evening. "I won't get home until about five-thirty. It will be starting to get dark. Will that be a problem?"

There was a long hesitation that had me pulling the phone away from my ear to see if it had cut off. At the sound of her voice, I pressed it back to my ear.

"Yes, that should be fine. This will be more of a fact finding meeting to see what you have in mind."

By the time I hung up, Theo had finished off the remaining pasta.

His gaze shifted from the plate back to me. "That sounds positive. Does that mean you might actually have found a builder to finish off your home?"

The guys had all come out at one point or another to look at where I lived. I was never sure if it was to see if I practised what I preached, or if they were just curious. "It looks like it, but I'm not going to count my chickens just yet." I sighed, recalling all the other disastrous builders I'd had.

When Adam popped his head around the door looking for Theo, I checked the time and grumbled, but got to my feet anyway.

A buzz of excitement carried me through the rest of my shift and all the way home. After storing my bike away, I checked the time, my stomach fluttering as I strolled over to the half-constructed house. In the evening dusk, the roofless house appeared sad and forlorn, much like its owner.

The past week had weighed heavy on me, and what Theo had mentioned earlier about me being miserable and testy was probably right on the money. It was exactly how I felt and nothing seemed to take the edge off, not even wearing my favourite all-in-one.

Maybe getting someone to finish the house would help me to keep my mind off Boyd?

The sound of an engine drew my gaze to the end of the driveway where there was a large black van with Convener's Construction in silver writing down the side of it. It was being driven slowly over the rocky ground. As it got closer, I put a bright smile on my face, hoping that it was convincing.

My eyes widened and my mouth hung open as the van stopped and I got a good look at the driver. What the fuck! Was Convener's Construction, Boyd's business?

Of course it's his business. Why do you think he's here?

To see me?

The flicker of hope that sprang up was hard to push down as Boyd got out of the van and strolled towards me. His hair was windswept and his caramel eyes held mine captive as if they couldn't bear to look anywhere else.

His expression was cautious once he was stood in front of me. "Hey. A little birdie tells me that you're in the market for a construction company to finish off your house?"

Although his tone was light, I could hear the underlying anxiety he couldn't quite mask in it. "A little birdie, is it?" I asked, playing along for now, wanting to see what this was all about.

"Yes, a little birdie happened to mention that you needed a builder who knew his stuff when it came to ECO building." He grinned at me and my heart sank.

Was that the only reason he was here, for business? Did he only want my money? Quelling the pain in my chest with a deep breath, I willed the tears clogging my throat and making my eyes ache to stay put. It seemed like Boyd and I just weren't meant to be.

Can one man overcome society's view of what is classed as 'normal' and accept his hidden need to take care of the Little side of Sawyer?

Sawyer is miserable after Boyd walks out of his life, saying he needs time to think. Now he's back, but Sawyer is more confused than ever by Boyd's behaviour.

Then Boyd offers him a place to stay, after deeming his home unsafe.

Willing to live in close proximity to Sawyer, Boyd hopes this will show Sawyer that he can trust him with his little side. Only there is a sinister presence working to discredit Boyd's business and stop him from finding happiness at all costs. Will Boyd be able to figure it all out before he loses what's most important to him: Sawyer?

The Little Side of Me, (book two) The Flamingo Bar Series, is a close proximity, gay romance with an age gap, and age play. This is the long awaited HEA and the conclusion to The App: Littles, where you first met Boyd and Sawyer.

Warning: The author recommends that The App: Littles should be read first in order to fully understand the backstory.

Each story is crafted by my boys but I couldn't do that without the support of Mandy, Julie, Tina and Guy. A team that a girl couldn't live without!

Prologue

Sawyer

I stared glumly at my phone as I tried not to think about how many days it had been since Boyd had all but run away from me, from the reality of what was a vital part of me.

"Sawyer...Sawyer, do you want the rest of that pasta?" Theo asked, his face peering down at the plate in front of me.

"Nah, you can have it. I'm not very hungry." That was the understatement of the year. I couldn't remember the last time I'd felt like eating. The plate was whipped away as Theo plonked himself down next to me.

"Cheers! I'm bloody starved. I thought the lunch rush was never going to end. I hate it when we have those small parties in the private dining area, they never seem to want to leave." He huffed out a loud sigh before shovelling a huge forkful of pasta into his mouth. The fork, that if I wasn't mistaken, I'd just been using to eat.

"You do know that fork wasn't clean?" I baulked at the thought of shared saliva.

"Yeah, and? I'm sure you don't have cooties or anything else I could catch." He studied me for a few seconds as if looking for something that might alert him to any diseases I had.

Once he'd finished his perusal, he shrugged, and I couldn't help but chuckle. "What are you like?"

"A loveable fool," he quipped back through a mouthful of half-chewed pasta.

"Shut your mouth, I don't need to see what you're eating, man!" I rolled my eyes at him when he opened his mouth wider. "You're gross. I'm sure that's why you're single."

The light of humour that had been dancing in his eyes faded as he looked down "Maybe," he answered, before his gaze returned to mine. "What's your excuse?"

There was a seriousness to his question that I didn't often associate with Theo. He was all about clowning around and avoiding any topic of conversation that was in any way serious.

My gaze narrowed on him and I found myself answering truthfully. "People struggle with what I'm into." Recalling the look on Boyd's face when he'd seen my outfit, I responded glumly, "When they're faced with the reality, they don't tend to stick around."

Hadn't the lack of contact from Boyd this last week proven that? I sank lower in the seat and sniffed.

"I'm sure that you'll find a Daddy—"

I lurched forward in my seat. "I thought I said never to mention that at work," I ground out through clenched teeth. When I'd gone to Adam's stag do at Lenny's home, we'd had a few drinks and a game of truth or dare had resulted in me sharing more about myself than usual. Now, as I stared at Theo, I wondered if he'd been blabbing to the other staff.

He shifted closer to me. "Listen, I've said nothing to no one, just as I promised. It's just that you were so happy last week, and I thought maybe you'd met someone. Then you got all miserable and testy and I couldn't help wondering if something was wrong? You can talk to me. I promise I won't say anything to the others." He patted my knee, his face wearing an earnest expression that I found hard to resist.

"I did have someone…but he's not sure about everything…about me." I inhaled before whining, "It's been a week and nothing. No message, no call. Nothing. I wish he would just let me know that it's over." Tears clogged my throat as I closed my eyes to avoid seeing the sympathy on Theo's face.

"If it's been a week, and he hasn't messaged or called, then doesn't it show that he's taking this seriously?"

Trying to think past my misery, I let what he'd said sink in. Was that why Boyd hadn't been in touch? Was he taking the decision seriously?

While I was mulling Theo's suggestion over, my phone rang. Picking the phone up off the seat where I'd left it during my conversation with Theo, I answered it, despite not recognising the number.

The sound of a woman's voice filled my ear. "Hello, is this Mr. Rowland?"

"Yes, it is," I answered, trying to figure out why the voice sounded vaguely familiar.

"This is Gloria from Convener's Construction Company. I'm sorry for the delay in getting back to you to sort out a date for one of the men to come around and discuss your needs," she tittered, making me wonder what the heck was tickling her.

"Oh, yes, that's right," I replied, doing my best not to let the wave of sadness rolling over me suck me under. The call was just another reminder of how I'd got hold of the number for the construction company.

"Are you still interested, Mr. Rowland?"

There was something a little odd about the question, but I couldn't grasp what it was. "Erm, yes, yes I am."

"That's wonderful. What date and time would suit you?"

My heart rate took off as I heard a voice in the background asking Gloria a question. Was Boyd there? *You're imagining things now.*

I strained to hear, but there was nothing except the sound of breathing on the other end of the phone. I rolled my eyes at my overactive imagination as I chatted about dates and times. Thinking the universe was out to get me as she offered several different times that didn't work for me, I was about to give up when she asked if I would be free that evening. "I won't get home until about five-thirty. It will be starting to get dark. Will that be a problem?"

There was a long hesitation that had me pulling the phone away from my ear to see if it had cut off. At the sound of her voice, I pressed it back to my ear.

"Yes, that should be fine. This will be more of a fact-finding meeting to see what you have in mind."

By the time I hung up, Theo had finished off the remaining pasta.

His gaze shifted from the plate back to me. "That sounds positive. Does that mean you might actually have found a builder to finish off your home?"

The guys had all come out at one point or another to look at where I lived. I was never sure if it was to see if I practised what I preached, or if they were just curious. "It looks like it, but I'm not going to count my chickens just yet." I sighed, recalling all the other disastrous builders I'd had.

When Adam popped his head around the door looking for Theo, I checked the time and grumbled, but got to my feet anyway.

A buzz of excitement carried me through the rest of my shift and all the way home. After storing my bike away, I checked the time, my stomach fluttering as I strolled over to the half-constructed house. In the evening dusk, the roofless house appeared sad and forlorn, much like its owner.

The past week had weighed heavy on me, and what Theo had mentioned earlier about me being miserable and testy was probably right on the money. It was exactly how I felt, and nothing seemed to take the edge off, not even wearing my favourite all-in-one.

Maybe getting someone to finish the house would help me to keep my mind off Boyd?

The sound of an engine drew my gaze to the end of the driveway where there was a large black van with Convener's Construction in silver writing down the side of it. It was being driven slowly over the rocky ground. As it got closer, I put a bright smile on my face, hoping that it was convincing.

My eyes widened and my mouth hung open as the van stopped and I got a good look at the driver. What the fuck? Was Convener's Construction Boyd's business?

Of course it's his business. Why do you think he's here?

To see me?

The flicker of hope that sprang up was hard to push down as Boyd got out of the van and strolled towards me. His hair was windswept, and his caramel eyes held mine captive as if they couldn't bear to look anywhere else.

His expression was cautious once he was stood in front of me. "Hey. A little birdie tells me that you're in the market for a construction company to finish off your house?"

Although his tone was light, I could hear the underlying anxiety he couldn't quite mask. "A little birdie, is it?" I asked, playing along for now, wanting to see what this was all about.

"Yes, a little birdie happened to mention that you needed a builder who knew his stuff when it came to ECO building." He grinned at me and my heart sank.

Was that the only reason he was here, for business? Did he only want my money? Quelling the pain in my chest with a deep breath, I willed the tears clogging my throat and making my eyes ache to stay put. It seemed like Boyd and I just weren't meant to be. His next words seemed to confirm my questions.

"Do you want to show me the plans you have and talk through the work that's already been started?" His expression remained friendly but there was nothing that indicated if this visit was about more than just business. With each passing second, my heart sunk further to my feet and I gave up trying to figure out what Boyd turning up meant.

I waved towards the half-built house. "Come on, I'll show you what the last builder did before he pissed off." My shoulders slumped and I walked across the uneven ground.

Chapter 1

BOYD

Stalking out of my office, I headed to my work van. I didn't tend to drive it often as I preferred my Nissan Navara truck, but when I went to price up new jobs, I always took the van to identify myself.

If my fingers were trembling as I hit the fob to open the van, I pretended not to notice. I swallowed a disgruntled sigh and kept staring straight ahead. I could all but feel Gloria's eyes boring a hole in my back. I'd bet my whole crew's monthly wage bill she had her nose pressed up against the glass watching me.

As I hopped into the cab I glanced at the window and, sure enough, there she was. Her grey eyes were almost silver in the light as they filled with glee and she gave me a thumbs up. A sigh escaped me as I shook my head, started the engine, and drove out of the yard and onto the main road.

The woman was a bloody menace. She liked nothing more than to stick her nose in my business, stating it was just motherly concern for me. It may well have been, and I really appreciated it, but it was nothing if not embarrassing to have her call Sawyer, then explain he could be...

Well, I wasn't sure yet what he could be, but she'd figured out there was more to the silly story I'd given her than I'd let on. She was better than a bloodhound sniffing out a scent, and she could wheedle information out of anyone. I'd swear, even those men that trained in the SAS to keep secrets would weaken under her interrogation.

Clearly, I'd lost my marbles, asking her to call Sawyer in the first place. It must be that because it wasn't the only moment of madness I'd had. Hell no, I'd gone and jumped off the deep end. But there it was, I'd wasted god knows how many hours figuring out how to get to see Sawyer today.

The last week had felt never-ending. There had been no more disasters at the Flamingo Bar, that we'd found out about. That, however, didn't help with the suspicion that came from waiting to see what disaster would befall us next. And that, it appeared, had made Brett antsy to the point the men on the job site were starting to complain about his short fuse. He'd always been quick to flare up, but this was like he had a permanent rocket attached to his arse, the way he kept flying off the handle.

Topping it all off, Sawyer had become the constant companion to my thoughts. The leather needs fitting in the booths. What is Sawyer doing? Did the wood arrive for the shelves? Is Sawyer looking for another builder? On and on they went, only, I didn't have answers for the latter, and it was driving me to distraction.

The plan to take some time to think over what it all meant to get involved with Sawyer was harder than I'd anticipated for two reasons. First, I missed him more than I'd expected to. It had been a little shocking at how fast he'd managed to tuck himself inside my heart. A heart that ached at odd times for the loss of the contact we'd had.

I blew out a noisy breath as I glanced in the rear-view mirror, before indicating and switching to the lane that would take me towards Sawyer's. Then my mind drifted right back to the second reason I'd struggled. It was probably more important than the first because it revolved around my lack of knowledge around Littles. The lack left me at a loss at how to assess if him being that way was something I'd cope with long term. No matter how much my heart wanted him, my head kept throwing up a picture of him in a toddler outfit.

If the sight of him dressed in an adult baby grow sent me into a tizzy, how would I cope with more?

More what? You won't know if you keep hiding! You're a grown arse man, aren't you?

I cursed under my breath at the very same thoughts that had driven me to go all around the houses to ensure I would get to see Sawyer today. I couldn't even say what had possessed me to get Nathan and Carl, the co-owners of the Flamingo Bar, involved in the elaborate scheme to keep Sawyer in the dark about who he was meeting this evening. The fact I'd cut out of work early after I'd got Nathan to talk to Carl, who was the chef at the restaurant Sawyer worked at, to find out Sawyer's work schedule, showed how desperate I was. And did I like it? Not one fucking bit!

Give over! How happy were you when it all worked out?

As my head pointed out the obvious, I slouched in the truck seat and was so distracted that I nearly missed the turning for the road to Sawyer's land. Hitting the brake hard, I stuck my hand out the window in apology at the blare of the horn behind me. Indicating to turn left, I drove onto the dirt road. I cursed anew at how my van shook over the rocky ground, rattling my bones.

Then I caught sight of Sawyer in the fading sunlight. His rainbow coloured hair haloed his head in brightness. He wore an old pair of ripped, baggy jeans and a thick woollen jumper the colour of heather. His expression after he'd slammed his mouth shut was hard to read as I stopped the van a few feet from him. Inhaling shakily, I got out of the van and worked on keeping my anxiety at bay.

Several minutes later, as I walked through his half-built house, I got the feeling that opting for casual friendliness had been a bit of a miscalculation.

Sawyer's demeanour had swiftly changed. His shoulders had slumped, giving me the impression that he wasn't happy to see me. Had I left it too long?

"—this, as I said, is totally messed up. The contractor decided to do something with the boards to make the existing frame sturdier." Sawyer took hold of a beam and wobbled it. "But as you can see, all he did was make it worse."

I attempted to think over what he'd been saying before I'd lost track. Coming up empty, I sighed silently, mentally slapping my forehead for not paying attention. "Back up a bit and go over the first part again." I gave him a smile and prayed he didn't figure out I'd not been paying attention.

When a scowl formed on his pretty face, and his lip poked out in the most adorable pout, I struggled with the need to give him a hug. Instead, I tagged on, "It's just so I can clarify what you mean so I get it straight in my head."

"Whatever man," he muttered, his booted feet clacking on the wood as he swung around and stomped off.

I gave chase, catching hold of his arm as I opened my mouth to speak. Before I could utter one word, he swung back around so fast I was surprised he didn't lose his footing. His arms came up into a defensive posture. What the fuck was this about?

"Let go of my arm."

Hearing the steely thread in his normally soft, lyrical voice, I lifted up my hand and held it out in a gesture of surrender. All the while, my heartbeat worked to deafen me as it raced fast enough to make my ears buzz. "I swear I'd never hurt you, Sawyer. *Never*," I stressed, needing him to believe me. Men who hit out are nothing but weak bullies and arseholes, and I would never have put myself in either category.

His gaze searched my face, and I held my breath, until he dropped his arms back down to his sides. "Sorry, it's just some guys...well, let's just say I don't like to be manhandled and leave it at that."

I wanted to argue, but the stiffness in his body as we stood staring at each other said now was not the time. The tension crackled between us and I wasn't sure how to break it. I glanced about and my gaze landed on the blueprints he had retrieved. My eyes narrowed and I bit my lower lip.

Could taking on the job show him I was trustworthy?

Without overthinking it, I found myself speaking as I shifted my gaze back to him. "Do you still want me to give you a quote for the building work? I think this is a project my company could more than manage for you." Sweat gathered in the middle of my back as he remained silent for what felt like an age but was probably no more than a minute at best.

"Okay, you can quote me, and we'll go from there."

I tried to ignore the sad tone in his voice as he went back over what he'd been talking about, making sure I kept my full attention on him this time.

By the time I climbed into my van, dusk had fallen. As I went to shut the door, I heard Sawyer's shed door creak open then close. Only then did I glance at the tiny place he called home and release a frustrated moan.

It had taken nearly three hours to go through what had turned out to be the shittiest workmanship I'd ever seen. The cowboys that had taken advantage of Sawyer were top of my hit list. If I ever found the fuckers, I'd report them to the working standards commission for ripping him off for thousands of pounds.

When Sawyer had bemoaned the builders he'd come into contact with, I'd thought he'd exaggerated. After an hour going over the existing work, I'd seen that, if anything, he'd underplayed the shoddy workmanship.

It had taken that hour before he'd started to relax around me. Finally, my beautiful angel boy had shown himself as he giggled and joked with me. As he relaxed, he revealed more than I think he knew. There had been a yearning when he'd mentioned having a home of his own, about the vision he had in his mind. And by fuck, I wanted to give it to him. His need had left me defenceless, my heart left unprotected as I'd listened to him talk about the ethos behind his home. An ethos that matched my own perfectly, and I'd come to the realisation I wanted to give Sawyer what he wanted, but with one added extra: me.

All I needed to do now was figure out how to achieve that.

Simple, right? Then why did it feel like I was about to prepare to climb Mount Everest with no gear or training on how to breath at that altitude?

You fucked up, now fix it!

Chapter 2

*S*AWYER

With the quote clutched in my hand, I strode into my lawyer's office. The scent of leather and expensive perfumes made my nose twitch as I walked up to the large white counter. It was manned by a snooty looking woman dressed in what were probably designer clothes. I did my best not to cower under her dismissive gaze.

When I glanced down and caught sight of my mud stained clothes, I swallowed the sigh of frustration. *Bugger!* I'd forgotten to change after helping the builders clear the crap left lying around the garden into several skips. The last couple of weeks had given us nothing but rain, which for this time of the year was unusual, and explained why I looked like Peppa Pig when she jumped in muddy puddles.

"How can I help you?" Her tone clearly indicated I'd come to the wrong place as her glacial eyes stared at me.

"I've an appointment with Mr. Norris at twelve thirty. I'm Mr. Rowland."

Perfectly manicured nails in bold red tapped at the keyboard in front of her. Moments later, her eyes widened at the screen before she glanced back to me and I swallowed a chuckle.

"Yes, yes I have you in the diary."

The fact she didn't sound at all convinced prevented me from holding on to the laughter. I leant against the pristine, modern counter and gave her a cheeky wink. "It's fine, I get it. I don't look like the typical guy who has a high-priced lawyer." I shrugged when her face became flushed. "I know the way, if you'll let them know I'm on my way up, that would be cool." With that, I nodded and strolled over the white tiled floor, wondering how they managed to keep it clean.

I'd been a client of Mr. Norris for the last couple of years, ever since I came into my inheritance. Unfortunately, that meant I'd had to visit the building quite a lot. It was one of those modernist ones that was all sharp angles, with gleaming white, black, and chrome surfaces everywhere you looked.

The first time I'd come to see Mr. Norris, I'd had nightmares about it for weeks afterwards. The very idea of spending hours staring at white walls, black floors, and chrome counters all day would do my nut in.

The two other people that joined me in the chrome lift sidled back against the walls like they might catch something from me. The imp on my shoulder pushed at me, so I stepped closer to the man in the three-piece, pinstripe suit. He looked like he was holding his breath, so I gave a discreet sniff.

Oh man, I stank worse than week old garbage. This time my sigh escaped, and I took a step back, not wanting anyone to get a good whiff of me.

By the time I got to Mr. Norris's office, I'd blocked out the odd looks and several head turns because they weren't that unusual. Only today, I wasn't sure if it was my hair, my clothes, or the smell that was drawing attention.

My feet made no noise as I strode over thick black carpet to the office at the end of the white walled corridor. I was surprised when Mr. Norris's secretary, Shelia, glanced up from her desk as I arrived, until I remembered I stank. The warmth in the building wasn't helping my cause as I started to sweat under my coat.

Her suit today was a deep yellow, paired with a shirt in the same colour, the whole outfit making her look like a jar of mustard. Only, the lid on the top was a puff ball of dyed brown hair. As always, her smile was friendly, even when her eyes took in what I was wearing.

I gave her an apologetic smile. "Hey Shelia, I got a little caught up today so I'm not at my finest."

"Now Sawyer, how long have we known each other?" Her head tilted to the side, her puffball hair not moving a millimetre out of place. Her lips twitched, shortly followed by her nose.

"Yeah, yeah. You know I've no time or energy to waste on clothes."

"That may be so…but water and soap, they really do need time and energy," she countered back, as quick as a flash.

Not at all offended, as we'd bantered like this since we'd got to know each other, laughter rippled out of me and I nodded. "You got me there. I didn't realise how bad I smelt till I got in the lift." I shrugged. "Not much I can do about it now. I'll just have to hope that Mr. Norris has no sense of smell, or gets done quickly, so he doesn't have to put up with my smelly arse."

"He's ready to see you, so go on through," she encouraged as I blew her a kiss.

"You just want rid of me, but that's okay, I'm in a rush today." And I was, because Boyd was coming to do a site inspection later and finalise the paperwork. It was why I'd been forced to make an appointment to see Mr. Norris, so I could get the money transferred into my account. Boyd's firm required a ten percent up-front fee to start the work.

I was going to get my dream home because, this time, it was going to be different. Excitement buzzed through me and I tried to pretend it had nothing to do with Boyd's visit and everything to do with thoughts of finally seeing my house finished.

I gave Shelia a wave as I politely knocked on Mr. Norris's door, then entered when he called "Come in."

He was an imposing man with a stern face that often made my little side feel like he was being told off, not that the other side of me didn't feel the same. I gave him a smile he didn't acknowledge as he pointed to the thick, leather padded seats in front of his large, black desk. The polished wood had not a thing out of place and gleamed, showing there wasn't even a speck of dust on it.

How do people manage that?

My place was always dusty. Okay, I didn't go a whole heap of cleaning because what was the point when I lived in a shed?

"Have a seat, Mr. Rowland. Do you have the paperwork I requested?" His voice was deep and authoritative as he got straight to the point.

I'd got used to his brusque manner, which fitted with his appearance. An appearance that seemed to blend in with the white and black colour scheme of the building. He sometimes reminded me more of an undertaker, but I kept that thought to myself after I'd slipped up and mentioned it to my mother when we'd first come to the office together.

She'd given me one of her disapproving looks, so I'd shut up and remained silent throughout that first meeting where she'd decided he'd continue to look after my inheritance. My grandparents wanted me to have freedom but were still worried about me being taken advantage of after living in a commune most of my life, so mum had been nominated as one of my Trustees. They thought that I'd be gullible and, at times, I'll admit I could be. So even though I'd complained about having hoops to jump through to get my money, I also understood it was because they wanted to protect me from unscrupulous people.

That, however, didn't seem to work when it came to bloody builders, which is why I was here today, having to see Mr. Norris to ask for more money. The money I'd originally requested was mostly gone, to builders who apparently saw that I had mug written on my forehead.

Shaking off the negative thoughts, I placed the file I had with all the quotes on his desk, within his reach. His dark eyes observed me for a moment before he lifted the file and opened it as I took the seat right in front of him.

My hands twisted together nervously in my lap. "That is all the costings for the remaining building to be completed. I've tried to figure in any additional costs but left out the quotes for soft furnishings. I'm not sure what I'll want in that regard until I see it complete and walk through it." I had ideas but I didn't want to rush into anything. With the exception of a bed, I wanted a big bed that didn't have a lumpy mattress.

"I've checked the file you gave me before you came and some of these costs you've quoted here have already been accounted for in previous payments into your bank."

His tone wasn't accusatory as such, but that's how it sounded to me and I swallowed hard. "I explained that in my email to you. Those other builders were fu...were not good." I caught myself from swearing as his brow rose and heat filled my face. This was why I hated coming, the man's ability to make me feel like I was clueless was unavoidable and my little wanted to stamp his foot.

"Yes, Mr. Rowland, I got your email. But there was very little detail in it. Part of my role as your lawyer is to try and protect you and your assets."

I barely resisted rolling my eyes at him and counted to ten in my head. "Okay, let's go through the file and I'll explain what happened."

Two hours later, Mr. Norris's office was more than a little whiffy as I'd got hot under the collar at all his questions. Whatever satisfaction I might have had from all the funds I needed being transferred into my account in the next few days, was lost under the heavy balls of anxiety that had formed in my gut. My little was not happy and just wanted to curl up with my blankie and hide from the world.

Adding to my woes, as I retrieved my bike I frantically searched my jacket and came to the realisation that I'd left my phone at home in my rush to get to the appointment. Tears blurred my vision. *Bugger!*

With no way of contacting Boyd to let him know I was now running late, I cycled through London like a bat out of hell, aware that I'd probably miss him. It had been four days since I'd last seen him and right now, with the need to have someone take care of me, I wanted more than anything for it to be Boyd.

Stupid, stupid, really bloody stupid. I chastised myself while I weaved through the traffic, pretending not to hear the several horns blasting at me. Sweat dripped down my back and it gathered at my hairline under my cycle helmet, sticking my hair to my head.

The muscles in my legs burned, as did my lungs while I struggled to suck in some much needed oxygen. My heartrate had probably hit an all-time high by the time I got to my driveway and saw it was empty. "Fucking...shit!" I wheezed as I came to a stop and leant over the top of my handlebars, my feet trying to hold up my wobbly legs and exhausted body.

The cool afternoon air didn't take long to chill my body as it whipped through the holes in my threadbare jeans. Shivering as the sweat dried against my skin, I lifted my leg and dismounted my bike. I drew in a couple of deep breaths, enjoying air that was not full of exhaust fumes, and steadied myself before attempting to put my bike away.

With my bike locked away and my body begging for a shower, I turned towards my home when the sound of an engine was followed by the sight of Boyd's truck appearing a moment later, heading down my drive.

My heart rate, that had started to slow, picked right back up while I shoved my shaking hands into my jacket pocket. The movement caused a waft of scent to rise and I groaned aloud. "Buggering to all hell!"

Why did I have to stink like a skunk?

Chapter 3

BOYD

The day had turned to utter shit and the power drill hammering at my skull proved it. Right now, I would have sold my soul for a couple of paracetamol just to make it fucking stop. If there was ever a day I wanted to go back and start again, this was top of the list. First there was another fuck up with an email order and Phil, unfortunately, hadn't been available to take my call to talk about tracking down the fucker that was playing silly beggars with me.

It had taken two hours of my precious time to get through to someone in the company to explain there'd been a mix up with my order. That had been followed by taking an hour to talk Brett off the ceiling and that didn't account for the time I'd had to spend with the men he'd pissed off by losing his cool.

Then, right out of the blue, my ex, Glenn, had called to ask if he could meet to talk. For some reason, he'd thought I'd drop everything and come running. I could still hear the shock in his voice when I told him we didn't have anything to discuss, so what was the point in meeting? That had resulted in an ear blasting I'd really not needed and had been the final straw on the camel's back when it had led to me being late to meet Sawyer.

Four days I'd not seen him for, not that I was counting. Alright I was, and it didn't escape my attention how much of the time, even when we were apart, that I spent thinking about him. My plan to try and get back to where we'd been before I'd needed time to think was slow going. I'd discovered quickly that if he had time off, I was working, and vice versa. *How do you try and date someone without them figuring that's what you're doing?*

You stop acting like a moron and just ask Sawyer out is what you do.

I heaved a put-upon sigh and paid attention to the traffic. Thankfully that, at least, was being co-operative, so I was only going to be half an hour late.

My head continued to pound as I pulled into Sawyer's drive, hoping that he'd got my message to explain why I was running late. My breath caught in my chest as I saw him stood in the middle of what would eventually be his driveway. His face was red and gleamed in the glow of the late afternoon sun. His rainbow hair was stuck to his forehead as he clutched at his helmet. My brow furrowed. Had he been out cycling?

For the first time that day, I chuckled, as my gaze swept over his attire. Sawyer looked like he'd been in a mud fight with someone and come out the loser. I was reminded that the men had been clearing the site, ready for the deliveries to start arriving in the next few days. Had he been helping? Then why was he clutching his bike helmet?

Unable to think past the throbbing in my head to recall what Sawyer's schedule was today, I switched the engine off and climbed out of the truck. I rubbed at my temples while I glanced over to the half-built house and was pleased to note all the crap lying around the site was gone. I tried not to dwell on all the building material that we'd found to be substandard and had needed binning. Or how upset Sawyer had been as I'd explained we couldn't use a good chunk of what the other builders had bought because it was, in a word, crap.

"Are you okay?" Sawyer asked, his voice sounding a little breathy.

Switching my attention back to him, I went to automatically nod then stopped myself as my temples reminded me, I wasn't. "I've a headache that is pounding harder than a bloody jackhammer inside my skull. You wouldn't have a couple of paracetamol, would you?"

His mouth pinched, and he got a look of concern in his eyes that made my heart skip a beat. There were days I really felt we'd never get back to where we'd been before. Then there were moments like now, when he looked at me like that and it gave me renewed hope.

"I think I've a box somewhere. I don't tend to take pills. I usually use herbal remedies, some ginger, mint, and a few other things in a tea might be better for you." He hesitated and nodded towards the shed he called home. "Do you want to try some?"

I wasn't sure if he was recalling the last time I'd been inside his home and what had happened, but I was. My stomach knotted at how much I'd fucked up by leaving, so I quickly nodded.

He swung towards his home. "Okay...but don't get too close—"

"I've said before, Sawyer, I'd never hurt you," I jumped in, not moving to follow him.

He swung back around to face me as his hands went to his hips and his small chin jutted out at me. "I wasn't meaning that."

He sounded so put upon that I struggled to stop myself from laughing. Aware I'd failed when he rolled his eyes at me, I held up my hands in surrender. "What did you mean then?"

"I'm stinky, and that was before I cycled like a maniac to get back here for our meeting. Which, it seems, you were late for too." His brows rose in question.

Clearly, I couldn't stop reminding him of the last time I'd failed to call him, and then what had happened as a result of that. *Way to go arsehole.*

Instead of saying what I thought of myself, I explained, "But I sent you a text to explain that I was going to be late because I got caught up." I brushed over the fuck ups of the day, especially when I noticed my headache was lessening just being in Sawyer's presence.

His gaze shifted to the ground and he started to kick at a stone. "I forgot my phone in my hurry to get to the lawyers office."

His contrite expression when he looked up from under his eyelashes caused my heart to stumble in my chest. "Then it's perfect timing for both of us, right?" I gave him a smile and hoped he'd see I meant it.

There was the slightest of hesitation before a smile spread over his face. "I'm not sure you'll be saying that after being in the tiny confines of my home with my stinky body." With that, he turned and stalked off towards his home.

"I'd be happy to be anywhere with you," I muttered under my breath. His feet faltered and for a moment I thought he'd heard me, but when he didn't turn around, I released the breath I'd held. Unsure if I was disappointed or not that he'd not challenged me, I walked after him.

Inside the cramped room it only took a minute for the stench of sweat, dirt, and something a little more pungent to fill the small space. Sawyer seemed oblivious as he went and heated a pan of water to make his headache remedy.

With the memories still in the front of my mind of the last time I'd been in this tiny room, my gaze travelled to the messy, single bed. The same blanket Sawyer had been wrapped in last time I was here was sat on the end of the unmade bed. I must have been staring for some time because the next thing I knew, Sawyer was pushing a chipped mug of scented, steaming liquid under my nose.

"Here, this should help. Me, on the other hand being all stinky, will probably not help." He sniffed the air, his nose wrinkling adorably. "I'm going to have a shower. Are you okay waiting for me? It will be decidedly less torturous to your nose if I wash before we sign the paperwork." He sounded uncertain as he looked up at me, the cup still clutched in his hand.

Instinctively, I reached out and cupped his cheek, my thumb stroking the soft skin. "Angel boy, I'll wait as long as you want." The moment the words left my lips, I realised how true they were.

His whole body stiffened. The knuckles of the hand holding the mug turned white. A flash of what appeared to be hope crossed his face before he shielded his eyes by lowering his gaze.

Had I lost my chance with him?

At the very idea, my heart dropped into my boots, quite literally. About to remove my hand from his cheek, his free hand came up and touched it.

Please give me a chance. I held my breath willing him to somehow hear my silent plea.

"You...you still want me to be your Angel boy?" he whispered, sounding a little disbelieving.

"Yes, more than anything. I'm sorry I fucked up. I've been trying to give you some space so you could see I'm not normally a dick." I chuckled at how his face brightened at me calling myself a dick. I wanted him to understand I was serious, whatever it took. *What about the clothing he likes?*

One step at a time.

As I pushed the question to the back of my mind for now, I took the mug from him. Lifting the cup a little higher, I got a whiff of the ginger and mint he'd mentioned. There were also several fragrances I couldn't pinpoint. It reminded me of homemade baking smells when my mother baked at Christmas.

"You should drink it, before..." He coughed and his cheeks got bright spots of colour on them. "I...I need some help in the shower...Daddy."

Oh fuck. Apprehensive expectations about how I'd feel at him using that term of reference between us disappeared. The onslaught of emotions that flooded through me was quickly followed by a wave of desire that left me reeling. All the blood that a second ago had been in my head, fled down my body so fast it left me giddy.

Clutching at the cup, I attempted to swallow past my now dry throat. I didn't think as I drank the hot liquid down in one big gulp. Suddenly I was the one coughing as the hot liquid scalded the back of my throat, instead of wetting it liked I'd hoped.

As my eyes watered, he stepped to the side and patted at my back. "Well that was silly...Daddy."

Fuck, there was that word again. Why did it make my heart feel like it was trying to do somersaults in my chest? A wave of heat spread through me while I attempted to stop coughing, making it hard to focus on an answer. Sawyer's small, warm hand rubbed up and down my jumper and, though it was quite thick to ward off the cold, I could still feel the heat of his hand against my skin, burning me.

"I...you want me to help you shower?" It only added to my mortification when I sounded more like a squealing pig, rather than a sensible grown up.

"If you want to." This time he didn't use the term Daddy and, judging by the look of uncertainty he wore, I could see I was somehow fucking things up again.

I placed the cup down on the crowded table next to me and stepped closer to Sawyer. This time, I took hold of both of his cheeks and prayed I wasn't about to make an even bigger fool of myself. "Daddy would love to help give you a shower."

His whole face lit up, and any doubts that still lingered that this might be a mistake were smothered by his joy.

He squealed and stood on his tiptoes, offering his lips. The gesture was so sweet I couldn't resist kissing the tip of his button nose before gently kissing his warm, sweet lips.

"Oh, Daddy," he breathed against my mouth before stepping back, his face brimming with happiness.

Selfishly, I hoped that he'd never looked at anyone else the way he was looking at me right then. He didn't give me a second to think about it though, as he tugged me through the only other door in his home, which I'd previously suspected was his bathroom.

As I stepped in behind him, I re-evaluated the word bathroom. This was more like outdoor plumbing but with a roof over it. I eyed the chemical loo and the large bucket that sat under what I assumed he called a shower. It was nothing more than a rigged hose and what appeared to be a small heater the water must pass through to warm it.

"What on earth? Look at that wiring! And Jesus, is that an extension socket hanging next to the water pipe?" My voice shook with fear at the thought of Sawyer electrocuting himself with his makeshift shower.

"It's okay, I got it checked out. I've been using this for nearly two years and nothing bad has happened to me." He shrugged it off, much as a child would when they didn't fully comprehend the real risk.

Only thing was, I wasn't quite seeing it the way he was, not with my protective urges roaring to life and painting all sorts of scenarios in my head. Should I put my foot down about this? Would this be what he'd expect from me if I were concerned for his safety? The pounding in my head that had started to ease, resumed with each unanswered question. *Stop overthinking and do what feels right.*

As I dithered, Sawyer bent to remove his boots. I put my hand on his shoulder. "You can stop right there. That shower is out of bounds until I can be assured it's safe to use. We'll go to my house where I know you'll be okay, and I'll have enough room to be able to wash you properly." I kept my voice gentle but ensured there was an authoritative tone, so he knew I wasn't taking no for an answer.

I braced, thinking I might be in for a fight when he slowly stood up and stared at me. His mouth opened and he got a gleam in his eyes, then his lips closed, and he stepped into me. Wrapping his arms around my waist, he buried his face in my chest.

"Okay...Daddy."

Doing my best not to inhale the overpowering scent of dirt, I held him close. We stood like that for what felt like an eternity with my lungs screaming at me to take a breath. But my need to hold him won out.

When he finally lifted his head, he gave me a thoughtful stare. "Are you going to get someone to check the shower out...or will I have to do it?"

"I'm going to do it. It's too late today, but I'll get one of my plumbers and an electrician to check it out tomorrow." While I spoke, I went through the list of men on the different sites to see which one I'd trust with this job. I eyed the makeshift space again and shuddered. There was no way this was going to be fixed in a day, hell maybe even a week.

"How do you feel about camping out at mine until I'm happy with the setup here?" The question popped out before I could stop it, but once I'd said it, I realised I didn't want to take it back.

His eyebrows disappeared under his colourful fringe as he eyed me like I'd lost my mind. And maybe I had, but the more I thought about it, the more I liked the idea of him being close and getting to spend time with him. "I've a spare room that you can stay in, so you'll have your own space. There is no pressure here. All I'm after is knowing you're safe."

He wilted in my arms and dropped his chin so I couldn't see his expression. What had I said now?

I went through it in my mind. Had he wanted to share a room with me? Or was it something else? No closer to an answer, I brushed my hand through his still sweaty hair and encouraged him to look at me. "Have I said something wrong?"

At the question, his eyes widened. "Can I...bring my box?"

"Box, Angel boy? I'm not sure what you mean. But I'm sure we can take whatever you want to mine."

His face lost a little of its colour as he stepped back and took hold of my hand, leading me back into the main room. He said nothing as he released his grip and went to the bed. A wary expression crossed his face when he glanced at me briefly before crouching to pull out something from beneath the bed.

The air in my lungs refused to budge when it registered what he meant. The box was about two feet long and the same in depth. It was covered in bright stickers and as he removed the lid, my heart took flight at the array of things that were tucked inside.

His hand hovered over the baby grow he'd worn all those weeks ago, that was tucked in with several other outfits. There were soft toys, dummies, puzzle books, colourful pens, jigsaws, and other toys, all neatly arranged.

This was the reality we'd been heading towards, and even though I'd given it considerable thought, and had spoken through group chat on a couple of the sites on the internet with people who were Littles, I wasn't prepared for the feelings that flooded me, making it impossible to move. When he finally lifted his head to look at me, the vulnerability I could see cut me off at the knees.

The three steps it took to reach him felt like I'd crossed a desert at high noon. Sweat slid down my back as I got down onto my knees beside him. I took hold of his icy hand and squeezed it gently, praying that I'd get this right. "Do you want to show me what you've got inside your box?"

His nod was tentative, but he didn't hesitate to reach in with his free hand.

One step at a time!

Chapter 4

Sawyer

A groan of pleasure rumbled up my chest as I snuggled deeper into the warm bed, then my eyes popped open as it registered that it wasn't my lumpy mattress I was lying on. The remnants of sleep fled as the events of the night before came back in a flood. *Holy shit, I'm in Boyd's spare room!*

That might not be the room I wanted to be in, but it was the next best thing after last night. Oh boy, oh boy, we'd gone through my little box. I wriggled around, unable to keep still at how he'd not once shown any distaste. He'd let me talk for ages before we'd packed everything back in the box to leave.

And though I was a little pissed he didn't trust the system I'd rigged up for my shower, it had been quickly overridden by how concerned he was for me. I'd spent a long time after I'd gone to bed trying to recall if any of the other men I'd dated had shown such worry for my safety. There'd been none that I could remember and that just made the moment all the more special.

A smile spread over my face as my hands rubbed over the soft cotton of the duvet and I squinted at the room. The heavy curtains covering the windows only let in the barest of light, making it difficult to make out the room, not that I needed to see it. I'd spent some time last night exploring the room when he'd left me to go and throw together a quick meal for us. *Don't forget bath time.*

How could I forget that? Warmth flooded through me as the memory of the evening surfaced.

Boyd led me into the en-suite attached to the room he'd said was mine for as long as I needed it. The bathroom was fully tiled. There was an Aztec patterned border around the top of the walls and other tiles interspersed around the room. The plain tiles were in a soft palette of colours, taken from the larger, pattern bearing tiles. There was no bath, but a large walk in glass shower, a double sink in white, and a toilet. All the fixtures and fittings in the room were brass. Had he upcycled the fittings?

My thoughts were interrupted as Boyd spoke.

"Do you want me to strip you, Angel?" His voice held a hint of apprehension that hadn't been

there as he'd chatted before we'd come into the bathroom.

"Yes please, Daddy," I didn't hesitate, wanting him to know that I was happy with his suggestion. Fuck, I was more than happy. The moment of terror I'd had was long gone after I'd called him Daddy to see what he'd do. I'd not been sure it was the right move, but my instincts had taken over. Now, as he moved and started to strip off my smelly clothes, I was over the moon that I'd pushed for his reaction.

"Lift your foot for me?" asked Boyd as he crouched in front of me and unlaced my boots.

Doing as he asked, I tried not to think about how I smelt as he peeled off my clothes.

At the lavish care he was showing me, my body warmed, and blood travelled to the area level with Boyd's head. I tried not to squirm when he finally tugged my underpants down my legs, revealing exactly how much I was enjoying his gentle touches.

He said nothing as he stood and went to the shower. Opening the door, he reached in and switched on the tap, the air quickly becoming steamy from the force of the spray. This was not going to be the small trickle of water I was used to and suddenly I couldn't wait to get into the shower.

The commune had a good-sized shower, but the water had been restricted because of the *number of people living in the building. Showers had always been a quick affair. With the prospect of having my first proper shower that wasn't about getting clean as quickly as possible, I stepped closer to Boyd, my arousal forgotten.*

His gaze moved to me and his eyes crinkled. "You're looking forward to this, aren't you?" His voice was full of amusement.

"You bet your arse Daddy. I'm going to wallow in that water and not worry about rushing like I had to at the commune, for fear of getting told off."

His smile dipped a little.

"It's alright, I didn't mind. I didn't know any better." I shrugged, trying to show him it didn't matter.

He stepped out of the way and indicated for me to get in the shower.

I hesitated. He did say he was going to bathe me. Why wasn't he getting undressed? My teeth raked over my bottom lip as indecision warred with what I wanted. "Aren't you going to get in with me, Daddy?" I could hear the plea in my voice, my little coming to the fore, wanting what Boyd had promised.

"Are you sure?" His caramel eyes became a deep rich colour as he stared at me, need evident in his tight expression.

"Yes, Daddy." Only when he started to take off his boots did I step into the shower. Turning to face the room, planning to enjoy the show, the hot water sprayed my back. The heat soaked into my tired muscles and I registered how tense I'd been as the water pelted the tight knots in my shoulders. I groaned in delight and shut my eyes at the decadence.

At a whooshing sound and a blast of air hitting my skin, my eyes opened, and I groaned anew. My body thrummed with arousal at the sight before me. Boyd's body was a thing of beauty. His taut muscles rippled as he moved closer to me. The water plastered the dark hair to his chest, arms, and legs. His semi aroused cock hung down from a dark patch of hair that was a little unruly and showed he wasn't bothered with manscaping. Usually I preferred a man to be a little less hairy, but as I stood there, I couldn't find a thing wrong when it was Boyd that was wearing all that hair over his body.

I glanced up at his face and the chin covered in a soft, trimmed beard. Recalling how it made my skin tingle when he'd kissed me, my cock thickened imagining how his body hair would feel against my bare skin. Suddenly, I couldn't wait, and I took the step that separated us. The second I pressed up against him, he gently wrapped his arms around my shoulders. He didn't push for more and let me *rub myself against his wet, hairy flesh. My skin tingled with thousands of tiny sensations as I moved, much like a cat would against a rubbing post.*

The sound of several taps came from the other side of the door and I glanced down at the tent that had formed as I went over the memories from the shower. Boyd had done as he'd promised, washing me from top to toe, but he'd ignored my arousal. Although I'd been a little frustrated by that, I'd also never felt more cherished in my entire life, so I'd not grumbled at the time. Now though, with my cock leaking against the brushed cotton, I wanted what I'd not got last night.

With that running through my mind I shouted, "Come in." I sat up and forward to conceal what was happening under the covers.

Boyd's head popped around the door, but in the dim light, I couldn't see his expression. "I just wanted to let you know I've left you some breakfast in the kitchen. I've got to head out now. I'll message you once the guys have sussed out what you need for your bathroom."

The way he said bathroom indicated he thought it was anything but that, but I didn't take offence, because he was right. It could hardly be called that when compared to his.

"— we can figure out the rest then, okay?"

Shit what had I missed? "Erm, sorry can you say that again, I'm not f—"

The lights flicked on and the room was suddenly flooded with light. I rubbed at my watery eyes, trying to figure out what the problem was as Boyd came fully into the room.

"Are you okay?" he asked, not giving me a chance to finish talking. His voice was full of concern as he sat on the edge of the bed, his gaze roaming my face. His hand came up and he touched my hot cheeks. "You're hot and flushed, do you feel sick?"

I chuckled and his eyes narrowed on me. "No, silly. I'm not feeling sick," I fidgeted when he continued to touch my flushed face as if he were trying to make me out to be a liar. "I was...I...well...I was thinking about last night." I glanced down at my lap and eased back a little so he could see what my issue was.

His nostrils flared as his eyes travelled down to where the cover failed to conceal my problem. The care he was showing me right now didn't help in the slightest.

"Did you get hard from thinking about Daddy touching you?" His voice was so soft, it was a stark contrast from the strain on his face.

"Yes," I whispered, more heat flooding my face, making it more than obvious the effect he was having on me. The scent of his body wash and deodorant filled my nose as I inhaled.

His hand brushed over the top of the cover as his gaze held mine. Desire, and something else I couldn't name, was etched into his expression. But it was his eyes that held me captive as the pressure on the cover touching my cock increased.

"When I read up on what it means to be a Daddy," he paused and licked his lips, "there was mention that in some relationships, that the Daddy gets to dictate if his boy can come. Is that the same with a little and his caregiver? Would you like that? Is it something you're used to?"

My cock jerked and the caramel colour of his eyes darkened as he got my unspoken answer. But he waited for me to speak, showing how much he understood communication was vital between us.

"Yes, I like it. But I usually go with what my partner wants," I admitted freely.

A frown appeared as he stared at me. "Whatever happens between us, Angel, it should be what we both want. As I've said, I've done some research, but I'm the novice here and the last thing I want is to pressure you into something you're not happy with."

I groaned in delight and my cock again bucked into his hand, showing its appreciation, and I was reminded of how he'd offered for me to train him. *Jeez!*

"I like my Daddy to be in charge and to look after me."

Boyd's eyes lit up and I squirmed as he shifted closer to me. His lips brushed against mine in a soft kiss once, twice, and a third time. My mouth opened, wanting more, but he pulled back.

"What are you working today?" he asked as his hand remained unmoving in my lap.

"I've got the lunch shift today, so I'll be finished around four," I answered, sounding more than a little out of breath.

"I'll aim to skip out early tonight and we could eat together, maybe watch a movie or something." His lips were back to hovering over mine as his eyes locked with mine. "Then afterwards, I can give you a bath and take care of you properly." His voice thickened and he gave me another gentle kiss, his beard tickling my skin.

I groaned as he pulled back and then stood up. He gave me a wink as he looked down at my lap again. "No touching, Angel boy. I'll text to let you know what time I'll be home. I've left you a key on the counter next to your breakfast. Make sure you eat it all up." With that, he blew me a kiss and spun around, heading back out of the room whistling a happy tune.

Well damn! How was I supposed to be pissed at him leaving me aroused when my heart had never felt so full?

Chapter 5

$\mathcal{B}$OYD

The good mood I'd carried with me as I'd left Sawyer all flushed and aroused, had lasted about three hours before work intervened.

"What do you mean we haven't paid the last two invoices?" I growled into the phone, doing my best to keep a lid on my temper as I listened to Greg, the owner of the firm we used for plumbing supplies, refuse to let me order the list of things I needed.

"I'm sorry, Boyd, but your account shows that you owe over fifty K and our normal limit is forty. We let it slide as you're such a good customer, but I've sent three reminders and you've ignored them."

"Hang on a damn minute. Firstly, I'm bloody sure we've received no such demands, and secondly, I have a monthly standing order with your firm because I use you for all my plumbing supplies." I rubbed at my temple and eyed the huge pile of paperwork on my office desk that I'd had no time to go through with all the fuck ups at the Flamingo bar.

"No, man, hang on, let me check but I think you cancelled that about six, maybe eight, weeks ago."

There was the sound of tapping and breathing coming down the phone as a sense of dread filled the pit of my stomach.

"Yep, there we go, it was seven weeks ago you sent an email to advise you were stopping the standing order."

He continued to talk but I was too busy doing the math in my head, working out when all my problems had started. It all tied together. This confirmed that for whatever reason, someone had beef with me. But why? I racked my brain, trying to come up with who I'd pissed off enough that they'd mess with me this much and came up empty.

"—so, unless you pay the outstanding balance, I'm sorry I can't take another order." There was regret in his voice as I tuned back in.

"Listen, I'm sorry, Greg, I'll sort payment now. If you hang on, I'll do a balance transfer directly into your account. I'll reinstate the standing order too and try and figure out how it was stopped, when it shouldn't have."

"Oh, that sounds ominous. You think the bank fucked up?" asked Greg.

"Nah, they wouldn't have sent you an email. No, there is something else going on and I've no bloody clue what, but I'm gonna find out." I cradled the phone between my ear and shoulder as I logged online into my business bank account. I scanned down the transactions and, right enough, there was the information for the standing order and the date I'd allegedly cancelled it. I cursed under my breath at not having kept a better eye on things.

Promising myself I'd take a closer look at the details later; I sorted the transfer of funds and then placed the order for the things we needed for Sawyer's home. It seemed like kismet that I'd decided to personally deal with all the ordering of supplies for his build as I put the phone down. Normally, I'd have left the list with Gloria, the office manager, and would have got her to do it. But because of all the crap that Sawyer had been through, I wanted to personally make sure that everything was perfect. *Yeah, like that's the only reason!*

A tap at my office door thankfully distracted me from another internal debate. Gloria stepped into the room before I had a chance to say come in.

"Boyd, I've typed up all the quotes on the other jobs as you requested. I've just got a couple of questions."

185

She sat on the chair in front of my desk and we went through all of the quotes. By the time she left me an hour later, I'd ascertained that if I were to keep on top of everything, and stop whoever was messing with me, I needed help.

Phil's original offer had been more like a friend doing a favour, even though I didn't know him that well. But as I eyed the stuff piling up on my desk, I gave a resigned sigh. With an expanding business, which was great, came additional work. It was then inevitable, either I worked extra hours or employed someone to help. The priority, as I saw it, was to find out who the fuck was messing with me. Because after today, it was clear whoever had a problem, it was with me and not Flamingo Bar.

I searched my desk for my mobile and, finding it under several bits of paper, I went through my contact list. I hit dial when I found Phil's number.

"SSA, how can I help?"

At the rather odd greeting, I removed the phone from my ear, checked the screen before putting it back to my ear after seeing it was indeed Phil's number. Then I remembered what his firm was called, Security Specialist Advisors. "Hey Phil, its Boyd here."

"Oh crap, I was supposed to return your call. My secretary left me a message and I got buried in some other work. Sorry, what can I do for you?"

His voice had an edge I'd not heard before, so I got straight to the point. "You know how you offered to see if you could trace who has been messing with my orders and IT system? I was wondering if I could hire you for this. It's just that I've had some more issues, only this time someone has gone into my bank account and cancelled a standing order."

"Fuck, they've taken it to a new level. Banks don't take too kindly to their accounts being messed with. Whoever has a hard-on for you is upping the ante by the sounds of it. I'm sorry I haven't been back in touch to help."

"Listen, they'd already done this before you'd offered, judging by the date, so no harm, no foul. But if you could help me now, I'd be grateful."

"I'll send you a contract to look over via email. No forget that if you've a snoop you don't want to alert them. Do you have a fax?"

"Yeah, do you have a pen?"

Five minutes later, I put the phone down and breathed a sigh of relief at Phil's assurance that he'd catch the fucker who was messing with my business. With that one job ticked off, I then rang the plumber and electrician I'd picked to go to Sawyer's to check over his makeshift shower. After I'd ticked those jobs off my list, my stomach reminded me that I might have sorted breakfast for Sawyer but I'd yet to have something to eat.

As I stepped into the main office, Gloria glanced up from her computer, a smile lighting her face. "You need something?"

"No, I'm popping to the deli for a sandwich, you want something?"

Her hand disappeared and reappeared holding a bag that she waved at me. "I've a salad. You know I'm trying to make sure I'm ready to slip into my bikini for my holiday." She giggled, and I worked on trying not to cringe at thoughts of my fifty plus office manager on the beach in a bikini.

"Yes, right, okay, I'll be back in twenty. I've my mobile if you need me." I left the office, working through the list of things I still had to do before I could leave tonight.

As I walked down the street, I glanced in a shop window and stopped at the sight of the large cream cakes sat on top of stands directly in front of the glass. My mouth watered and I found myself heading inside. The sweet scent set off my stomach and it snarled with hunger. Rubbing at my empty stomach, I waited for the two other customers to be served as I all but salivated over the counter perusing the choices.

I felt a nudge to my side but as I turned to apologise, the words died on my lips as Glenn gave me a beaming smile. Why did I have to come into the shop?

I kept my face a neutral mask and nodded politely as I recalled our conversation the day before. "Hi," I muttered, and turned to glance back at the woman behind the counter when she asked, "Who's next?"

"Please can I have a couple of those fruit and cream tarts, and could I have a couple of those delicious looking pastries with the chocolate on the top."

She bustled off to get what I wanted, and I did my best not to look at Glenn, even when I could feel the weight of his stare.

"Are you planning on pretending that I'm not stood right next to you?" he asked in a surly tone.

I sucked in a fortifying breath before shifting my gaze to him. "I'm not ignoring you. I've just got nothing to say to you." I prayed he'd let it go as the woman returned with my boxed cakes and requested six pound forty from me. Rooting in my jean pocket, I handed over a tenner and waited for the change as the tension in the air increased.

Any hope that Glenn would leave it be was lost as he followed me out of the shop. I'd taken no more than two steps when his hand landed on my arm. "Where do you think you're going? We have things to talk about. Our relationship—"

I tugged my arm away from his touch and interrupted him, "No, we have nothing to talk about." I ground out through clenched teeth as I eyed him from head to toe. His suit was expensive and one I recognised that I'd paid for. The shirt was pale blue and showed off his tanned face and hands. His short black hair was styled and, if I wasn't mistaken, gelled into place to stop the wind from messing it up. If I looked up the term professional man in the dictionary, this would be what I'd find as a description. I'd once found it attractive, yet, now it left me cold. Was it the way Glenn had behaved or was it that I just wanted something else now?

I didn't have an answer until Sawyer's bright happy smile formed in my mind and that was all I could see, could feel, as the warmth of it took away the chill Glenn had left me with.

I gave Glenn a pitying smile. "I'm sorry, but I've moved on. You were right to make the decision to leave. I hope that things are working out for you." I made a show of checking my watch before offering him an apologetic smile. "Listen I've got to go. It was good to see ya." Without giving him the chance to answer I swung around and headed back towards the office, not once looking back.

It was only as I walked back into the office that I recalled that Glenn seldom came to the outskirts of London. There weren't any trendy bars or fancy restaurants around this area for him to be seen in. Had he been following me? I nodded at Gloria as I walked past her desk, but I hardly paid her any mind as I got a strange feeling in the pit of my stomach at the question.

I placed the cake box down on the drawing table that normally held architect designs and sat under the window overlooking the yard where my trucks and vans were parked. Rubbing at my bearded chin, I stared out the window. Would Glenn mess with my business to get back at me?

Don't be daft. But even as my inner voice spoke, my stomach clenched.

Would he?

Stop it. You were together for four years. Why would he mess with you? I'd never given in that last time he threatened me. Would he be that spiteful?

I shook off the worry as best I could, as I got up and returned to my desk. Leave the questions to the pros, Phil will find the answers.

Let's hope!

Chapter 6

SAWYER

"Can you clear table three and get the bill for table six?" Theo asked as he came up to stand next to me at the bar. His face was a little flushed and he looked more than a little harried.

"Yeah, no problem. You okay?" The restaurant was, as usual, packed with diners enjoying their lunch. The scents of rich Italian food seemed to want to tease me and my grumbling stomach. It gurgled loudly and Theo chuckled as he leant on the bar before giving his drinks order to Damian.

"I'm alright," he answered after Damian walked off to get his drinks order.

I glanced at him and noticed dark circles under his eyes, but his closed off expression forced me to keep my questions to myself. Theo, I knew, would only talk about what was bothering him in his own good time. Three years of friendship had taught me that, so I let it slide as I lifted my own tray of drinks and went to do as Theo asked.

Due to how busy the restaurant was, I got no time to think about Theo or anything else until the lunch rush was over. By then, my feet were aching, and I blamed Boyd. I eyed the shoes that had started to hurt three hours earlier and scowled. Wearing someone else's shoes at work was maybe not such a good plan, not when you had to stand and walk around for five hours solid. But as I'd wanted to please Boyd and stay at his house, I'd forgotten my work shoes, so I'd had to borrow a pair off Adam, who was a half a size smaller than me.

As grateful as I was that I'd not had to try and explain to Seb why I needed to go home and get my shoes, all I wanted to do now was take the bloody things off and soak my sore feet. Moving like I'd spent the night in high heels dancing in a club, I limped through the near empty dining room, heading to the kitchen. No matter how much my feet hurt, the call of the pasta frittata Carl had promised me was too much to resist.

The noise as I stepped into the kitchen was hardly noticeable now, after years of training to block it out. At first, it had been a bit of a shock moving from the sedate dining room into a kitchen that was a noisy hub of activity.

I grinned at Billy as he held out a plate to me. "Here you go."

I all but snatched his hand off, making him chuckle as he picked up a cloth and started wiping down the large stainless-steel countertop he was stood behind. There were several people scattered about the kitchen laughing and chatting. A warm feeling spread through me as it always did at being a part of this close-knit community.

I'd missed that feeling when I'd left home and, while my parents hadn't been keen on me wasting myself waiting on tables, I'd found a niche that fitted me perfectly when I'd started working for Seb and Carl. I loved everything about it. There was an eclectic mix of staff and, whether it was intentional or not, Seb hired mainly gay men to work for him. I'd made friends here and found a way to survive away from my family.

"You plan on eating that or just staring into space with a sappy grin on your face," Carl boomed from across the room as he came out of Seb's office.

"I was just thinking what a great bunch of people you all are. But I take that back. *Some* of you are great," I stressed, grinning up at Carl. Then I jumped back as he came close enough to try and snatch the plate out of my hand. "Hey, that's mine," I whined, holding tightly to the plate.

I got no further when Theo stepped into the kitchen and called my name. I turned around and he pointed behind him. "There's a dude in a smart suit here to see you."

I frowned and tried to recall if I had any plans to meet anyone today. Coming up blank, I stepped towards Theo. "Did he say who he was?"

His hair flopped over his forehead as he shook his head. "Nah, just asked if you were here and could he speak to you. I've left him in the entrance way."

Glancing down at the plate I held, I gave a resigned sigh and turned to Billy. "Can you keep that warm for me while I go and find out who wants to see me?"

His answer was to take the plate from my hand and head to the bank of ovens. He opened one and placed my plate inside. "I'd hurry, otherwise it will dry out."

Not needing to be told twice, I darted past a bemused looking Theo and went out into the main restaurant. With no one left in the restaurant, with the exception of the guy stood in the entrance way, I offered him a polite smile. As he stared at me, I tried to remember if we'd ever met before. Not able to recall, I had to work to keep a pleasant smile on my face as I walked towards him. Because, although he was attractive, there was something a little mean in his expression that set my nerves tingling.

"Hi, I'm Sawyer. Did you want to see me?"

When the guy's gaze swept over me, followed by a look of distaste, I stepped back. My hands trembled at my sides and my unease continued to grow as he stared at me like a bug under a microscope, saying nothing.

Feeling more than a little out of sorts by this odd behaviour, I glanced back at the empty restaurant. Before I could shift my gaze back to the man, he'd moved so he was inches from my face. "I don't know who you think you are moving in on my man, but I'm telling you, you're messing with the wrong person." His finger drilled into my chest.

Shocked by the outburst, I remained rooted to the spot, my hands hanging uselessly at my sides.

"Get your fucking scrawny, ugly arse out of my home and crawl back to whatever sleazy rock you came out from under. I won't give you a second warning."

I'd hardly had time to process his words when pain exploded in my cheek and my head swung back from the impact of the painful slap to my face. Tears sprung into my eyes, but he was already moving as I stood staring in disbelief at the door as it swung closed behind him.

"Sawyer, Billy is fret... What the fuck, man?" Theo halted in front of me, his expression aghast. "What happened? Why do you have an angry handprint on your cheek?" Theo demanded as he took hold of my arms gently.

His face blurred as tears slide down my cheeks and I tried to figure out what the *fuck* had just happened. "I...I don't know," I choked out on a sob.

His arms instantly went around my back and he pulled me in for a hug. I buried my face in his neck, still trying to process what the hell had happened. Was the guy nutso? I wasn't living in his house; I was living with...Boyd.

Fuck, was Boyd a cheater?

Don't be daft. Why would he ask you to stay with him if he had a boyfriend?

Then who was the guy? Was it a case of mistaken identity?

Maybe?

With no chance to talk, and he'd never mentioned his boyfriend's name, it was damn near impossible to figure it all out. It had to be a case of mistaken identity, right?

Theo guided me into the locker room, and I went into the bathroom and splashed some cold water on my face, hoping it would help cool down my hot cheek and wash away any evidence of my tears.

"That's fucked up, man, if you've no clue why the guy hit you. What are you going to do?" Theo's tone was indignant on my behalf as he paced behind me.

Looking at him in the mirror's reflection, I managed to smile at him when he paused and glanced at me. "There isn't much I can do. I don't know the guy's name, or what he was on about. I think it's a case of mistaken identity." I shrugged, prepared to let it go and chalk it up to some cosmic joke.

"I'm not so sure about that. He called you by name. If it were random then how would he know where you work?" Theo's face was thoughtful as I turned around to face him. My hands shook as I felt the water drip off my chin, realising that he was right.

How did the man know my name and where I work?

I released a shuddery breath. "Yeah, you're right. He said I should move out of his boyfriend's home. I moved in with Boyd last night after he saw the state of my shower," I all but whispered, almost afraid to voice it aloud and for Theo to confirm my fears.

His eyes widened. "Wow, you're a fast worker. But after everything you've mentioned about Boyd, I don't get the vibe he's a cheater. Do you?"

I sagged back against the sink. "No, I don't get that impression either. And just so you know, I'm not that fast. I'm in the spare room. I'm staying while he figures out how to make my shower *safe*."

Theo burst out laughing. "The only thing that would make that safe is if you binned the thing. It's a fucking disaster waiting to happen. I said that to you when I first came to visit your place last year. I bet it's still the same patch up job, right?"

There was humour dancing in his eyes as he continued to chuckle when I waved away his comment. "Stop, it was perfectly fine, and it worked, didn't it? We're getting off the subject, what do you think I should do?"

"Ask Boyd if he has any crazy exes in his cupboard and go from there. If it turns out this guy is one of Boyd's exes, maybe he can warn the shithead off." The humour of moments ago was replaced with anger as Theo's eyes glowed. "I'd like to give the guy a taste of his own medicine. In fact, why didn't you do some of that fancy jujitsu on his arse?" Theo's head quirked to the side as he stared at me.

"I've told you before, it isn't about beating people up. That being said, I'd have stopped him if he hadn't caught me completely off guard. I was trying to process what he was saying, then wham and he was gone." I rubbed at my hot cheek and hoped it didn't leave a bruise. "I'll be ready the next time, if he comes back."

"Are you gonna talk to Boyd about this?"

"Yeah, I am. He'll be home around the same time as me. I'll talk to him then. Let's hope it's easy to sort out." I touched my throbbing cheek and my stomach twisted into several knots recalling the man's hostile expression.

A part of me wanted to run and do as the man wanted, but then I recalled Boyd's beautiful face as he sat patiently listening to me talk about who I was. How could I give that up?

Chapter 7

BOYD

At the sight of Sawyer's bike sitting at the bottom of the stairs leading up to my front door, my mood lifted. By the time I'd parked up and was opening the front door, there was a smile stretching across my face.

"I'm home," I shouted out, shutting the door behind me. I carried the bakery box and my leather holdall containing a pile of invoices I needed to go through, as I headed towards the scent of food.

Sawyer had revealed that the food he'd brought the night I'd got stuck at work had been prepared by Lenny and that he couldn't cook for shit, so as I entered the kitchen I was surprised to see pots on top of the cooker and steam rising with the scent of, if my nose was correct, a herby tomato sauce.

With Sawyer's back to me and his hands buried in soap suds, I placed the bakery box on the table. I paused and stared at the table that was set for dinner. The domesticity of it caused my heart to beat erratically as my overactive imagination conjured up what it would be like to come home to Sawyer every night. *Stop getting ahead of yourself!*

"I thought you said you couldn't cook," I joked, as I walked up to Sawyer. About to lay a kiss on the top of his head, I froze at the sight of his face when he twisted to look at me. "What the fuck happened to your cheek?" The holdall I held fell to the floor, unheeded in my need to check on him.

It took a second to register the change in his demeanour as he lifted his dripping wet hands out of the water and faced me. His bottom lip quivered, and his eyes filled with tears. "Someone hit me, Daddy," he cried in anguish.

His voice sounded somewhat different and something told me his little was fully in charge right now as I wrapped my arms around him. As I struggled to keep myself from trembling at the burning anger riding through me, I made shushing noises. I buried my face in his hair when he hiccupped and sobbed into my chest.

Only when he quieted did I lift my head and put my hand under his chin, carefully lifting it so I could see his face. At the sight of his red rimmed, puffy eyes, hurt sliced at my heart. "Who did this to you, Angel boy?"

"A man came to the restaurant," he explained. Then everything seemed to move in slow motion as he relayed what the guy looked like and what had happened in a small voice that increased my anger. It was all the information I needed to know exactly who had done this to him.

"—ugly arse out of my home and crawl back to whatever sleazy rock you came out from under. Then he said he wouldn't give me a second warning. Did...did you date this...person?" His eyes implored me to say no, even as I registered the resignation that was on his face.

"I wish I could say no, but yes, I did. His name is Glenn. We broke up about a month before I messaged you via The App." I sucked in a tremulous breath. "He called yesterday wanting to meet and I told him we had nothing to discuss. I bumped into him today when I went into a bakery to buy you a treat for tonight."

His gaze moved to the table behind me and though his face was still tear stained and his eyelashes were wet, he gave me a smile that melted my heart. "You bought me a treat?"

There was such wonder in his voice, my anger instantly drained away and I nodded. "That I did, let's hope you like what I bought for you."

"If it's a cake, I will, I swear Daddy." He bounced on his feet for a minute before I led him to the table to show him what I'd bought. Following his lead, I let the topic of Glenn drop for the moment and lifted the lid. He squealed in delight and clapped his hands.

While he rubbed at his damp cheeks, he glanced at the cooker. When he looked back at me, his expression reminded me of a dog I'd had as a child that begged for treats. I'd been defenceless then and I got the distinct impression I'd be no different now.

"Can I have one now, please, Daddy?" His head tilted to the side and his face softened as his lower lip poked out. "Pleassssseeee."

Oh god, how the hell was I supposed to resist that look? This new dynamic left me floundering for a few seconds as I struggled to fathom what reaction he might expect from me.

"Did you have something to eat during the day?" I asked, trying to come up with a plausible excuse to make him wait until after dinner.

His smile disappeared and I cursed when I got the impression he hadn't, and Glenn was to blame. My suspicions were confirmed when his face morphed into a mutinous scowl.

"I didn't Daddy, but that's not my fault so I should get to eat my cake first," he whined.

The need to give in was at odds with how I saw the role of responsible adult, especially after he'd made the effort to cook a meal for us. "Don't you want Daddy to eat the lovely meal you made for us? What about, we eat a small bowl of the food then have a cake? And if we're still hungry later, we can have some sweets while we watch a movie?" The second I mentioned I wanted to eat his meal, his face got a dreamy expression that was a whole lot more tempting than his sad, puppy dog eyes.

"Okay, but a small bowl and you'll eat fast." He sucked his lower lip in between his teeth. His eyes got a calculated look in them as he glanced back into the cake box. "We can watch a movie and have the other cake, then we won't be hungry." His smile was angelic as he beamed up at me like he'd solved all the problems of the universe.

I pushed the hair back off his face and gently cupped the unmarked cheek. "That sounds perfect." I kissed his upturned mouth. "Maybe after I've bathed you, you can pick one of your favourite outfits to wear."

His gulped and his eyes widened. He looked uncertain for a few seconds, and I wondered if I'd made a wrong step, then he nodded tentatively.

"I'd like that, Daddy."

The meal went without a hitch and, keeping to my word, we had a small bowl each as Sawyer admitted that he'd brought home some leftover sauce from the restaurant. It didn't matter to me; it was the thought that counted.

By the time he'd eaten his fruit tart, stating he wanted the chocolate pastry while we watched a film, the air was buzzing with a sexual tension I hadn't felt in a long time.

I pushed aside the nastiness of the day to pamper Sawyer. I left him so he could go and pick an outfit to wear while I went to fill the bath in my master suite. Finding several bath bombs I'd been given as a gift from Gloria at Christmas, I dropped one into the water and the room filled with a heavenly scent. It took a second to register that it smelt like fruit salad, and the swirling colours in the water looked the same as the somewhat vintage sweet.

When Sawyer stepped into the bathroom, a big grin on his face, I couldn't help but respond.

"It smells like sweeties in here," he said as he stopped at the side of the bath, clutching what looked like a pale lemon all-in-one. He hesitated for a moment before offering me the outfit.

Without overthinking it, I took it and placed it on the heated towel rail behind me. "Let's place it here, then it will be nice and warm when we get you dressed."

"Thank you, Daddy."

His shy smile as I turned to face him left me a little breathless. "You're welcome, Angel boy. Let's get you underdressed and in the bath."

He stood and waited for me to help him. By the time he was naked and in the bath, I realised how much I was enjoying doing these simple tasks for him, especially when he beamed up at me like I'd hung the moon for him.

As he started to splash and play in the water, it dawned that he might like some toys in the bath with him. Recalling the box of stuff in the room Amelia, my sister, no longer had use for when she stayed with me, I stood up.

"I'll be back in a minute." I ran my hand over his wet hair while he splashed and giggled up at me, appearing happy for me to leave him.

Leaving the bathroom, I quickly retrieved the box from the back of her wardrobe and lifted the lid. Inside were a collection of dolls, all of which were naked, and their outfits scattered in the box. There were cars I'd had as a child, which the two of us had made a ramp for.

My sister was so much younger than me that I'd often forget we were siblings. After our mother had died and my father was struggling with his grief, I'd taken on the role of parent, even when she'd rebelled against it. I didn't remember being difficult as a teenager the way Amelia was, but my father assured me I had been.

As I continued to root in the box, I noted several things that Sawyer might like to play with and put in his box. I placed them on the bed with the water pistol I found and some squeaky toys that also squirted water.

"Where are you Daddy?" came Sawyer's shout from down the hall.

I collected what I thought he might enjoy in the bath and hoped I wasn't making a massive mistake. When I walked into the bathroom, there was coloured water on the floor tiles and Sawyer was creating waves that were getting closer to the top of the bath.

I chuckled at the mess and, ignoring it, I dropped to my knees at the side of the bath, offering him what I held. His eyes lit with delight as he grabbed for the water pistol and examined it closely before dunking it in the water.

He giggled, and before I could figure out his intention, water hit my chest, soaking my T-shirt. The pistol was dropped back into the bath as I went to stand, my lips twitching. "Did you get Daddy wet?"

"Nooooo, the pistol did it," he chortled and fired again.

Water sprayed my jeans, adding to the wet patches at my knees. I pointed at him. "You're playing with fire."

His response was to grin at me and hit me a third time, this time with a spray of water to my face. I spluttered through my laughter as I wiped at my face. The bathroom was becoming a mess of rainbow colours from the water, but all I saw was the glee on Sawyer's face detracting from the bruise marring his cheekbone.

When the anger wanted to surface at what Glenn had done, I pushed it aside, vowing to deal with Glenn later. Instead, I gave Sawyer a wolfish smile and tugged off my wet top and threw in on the floor, tutting at him.

As my hand went to the button of my jeans, Sawyer got up on his knees and fired another stream of water at me. "Now you've done it. Daddy might have to spank you for getting him all wet."

The mock threat got a full body shiver from Sawyer, his eyes remaining full of laughter.

"Don't be silly, Daddy. You don't want to spank me. I's done nothing wrong. It's the pistol's fault."

His joyous childishness was contagious, so I finished stripping off and jumped into the bath, causing a huge spray of water to hit him and the floor.

He spluttered, then splashed at me. His laughter and the sound of splashing filled the bathroom. He pounced on me and I staggered for a moment as I laughed at him. His smile dazzled me, and my insides lit up.

Oh fuck!

Something I was nowhere near ready to name rose in a wave of longing so big I struggled to remain in the moment. Was this what had been missing from my life, from my relationships?

Chapter 8

Sawyer

With the box of nails clutched in one hand, I rubbed at my aching lower back. My week off from the restaurant had been anything but relaxing. Why did I think offering to help out with the build of my house was a good thing?

Because you knew Boyd was going to be here helping this week!

I had to fight to keep in a sigh as I searched the ground for the hammer I'd put down a minute ago when I was looking for more nails. Unable to find it, I glanced at Stu, one of Boyd's workmen.

Today he wore an off-grey, skinny fit T-shirt that showed off his rail thin torso. I'd mistakenly thought that he'd never be able to keep up with some of the other burly guys that worked for Boyd, but he'd shown me this week how wrong I'd been to assume anything. The man worked like a Spartan Warrior, and nothing seemed to faze him. This week working on-site, I'd known after just two days, I was the weakling. I'd wanted to cry like a baby at the aches and pains in my body.

Any thoughts I'd had that I was physically fit enough to compete with these guys had been proven wrong, so I'd resigned myself to doing some of the smaller tasks. "Did someone take my hammer?"

Stu glanced up from the piece of wood he'd been planing and shrugged. "I didn't see anybody take it." He was a man of few words and went back to what he was doing, paying me no attention.

"Okay then," I muttered, and stomped off to see if I could find another hammer. I'd barely got three feet when I heard a shout from the above landing.

"Sawyer, can you go grab one of the wooden struts that's lying against the wall over there for me?" Boyd asked, peering over the new banister he'd finished fitting the day before, while he pointed to what he wanted.

"Yeah, gimme a sec."

His face was a mask of concentration as he nodded and then disappeared from view. It was an expression I'd got used to when he was on-site. The Boyd at home was a very different man from the one at work, I'd found out.

At work, he was serious and had a tendency to let his anger out when something pissed him off. When he came home, there was a playful side to him that he embraced right along with the role of being a daddy. I'd not anticipated he'd be such a natural, and he never once made me feel like it was wrong to allow my little to surface.

So much so that over the last two weeks I'd been living in his home, I found, with his encouragement, that I'd spent a lot more time being little. I paused, recalling the previous night.

The second I stepped through Boyd's front door, I sighed. I was so tired and didn't have the energy to contemplate helping with dinner.

"That was a big sigh, Angel boy." His hand stroked my hair before cupping my cheek. "Do you want Daddy to make you something to eat while you go and do something fun like colouring?"

"Can we snuggle after with my blankie?"

A slow smile spread over his face. "Yes, we can do that, and I'll pick out a onesie so you can curl up on Daddy's lap and get comfy."

The note of sweet affection in his voice left me with a fluttering in my chest. He helped me settle at the kitchen table with my colouring pens and a new colouring book he'd bought me. After checking I was happy, he started to sort out our dinner.

The sounds of him moving around gave me a contented feeling that was becoming familiar. Several times I'd look up and catch him smiling at me indulgently.

Before too long, he'd set a meal in front of me and we ate in a comfortable silence. After he'd cleared away the dishes, he took me upstairs and into the bathroom to help me shower. The gentleness and loving way he cared for me was something I knew I was going to miss when I had to leave.

Don't think about it.

How could I not think about it? *The snarky voice answered, and I struggled to keep still as Boyd dressed me. Each and every loving gesture that allowed me to be myself made it impossible not to think about what would happen when I had to leave him.*

"Why the frown?" His fingertips traced the lines over my forehead after he finished fastening my onesie.

"Can I have one of my snuggle bears?" I asked, avoiding giving an answer when all I wanted was to be little.

His fingers lingered a moment as he considered me. "Yes. Go get it and your blankie."

His easy acceptance let me breathe a little easier. Once downstairs, he switched on the TV and went to the films he'd downloaded. He picked Aladdin, then placed me on his lap, laying my blankie over me and ensuring snuggle bear was tucked in.

I blinked the room back into focus as something clattered against wood. My heart twisted in my chest at the sweetness of the memory. In the past, there had always been barriers to me giving free reign to my little. Often, I'd only been that way when I was upset and my little took over. It was totally different with Boyd. There was no expectation, he went with what I needed, and boy it made it far too easy to see what life could be like if I lived with him on a permanent basis.

Stop right now. You want your own home. It's your dream remember.

Is it?

Not wanting to think about it too hard, I retrieved what Boyd wanted and went to the new staircase to head upstairs. My feet dragged as I gazed around at all the work that had been completed over the past couple of weeks since the men had arrived on-site. My hands gripped tightly onto the wood I held, squeezing tighter at the prospect of moving into my completed house and leaving Boyd behind.

After the two guys had been to assess my makeshift bathroom, and quoted a stupid amount of money to fit a new one and re-wire the shed to make it reach an acceptable health and safety standard, Boyd had offered for me to stay with him till my house was complete. At the time, I'd been overjoyed thinking I'd be with him for months after all the fuck-ups with previous builders. Sadly, I was mistaken, because Boyd's firm wasn't anywhere near like the other firms I'd employed to work for me.

Now, as the days went by and the house resembled an actual structure you could live in, I'd started to worry I'd only have weeks, rather than the months I'd hoped for.

"Thanks, just put it over by my toolbox," Boyd requested as I crested the top of the staircase and found him standing there waiting for me. His brow furrowed as he focused his gaze on me. "What's up?"

His voice was laced with concern and my stomach fluttered as he took the wood from my hands and laid it down.

"Nothin'." I kicked at a bit of sawdust while I lowered my eyes to the floor. From under my eyelashes, I watched him brush his hands down his jean-clad legs before he took a step closer and crouched in front of me. He made sure to catch my eye before he touched my cheek gently.

"What is it, Angel boy, has someone upset you?"

Although the question was asked lightly, his eyes got a warning light in them. The protective side I was coming to recognise came to the fore as he waited for me to answer.

I fidgeted, unsure how to respond without revealing the extent of my worry about moving out. The last thing I wanted was to seem too clingy after the issues he continued to have with Glenn, his ex-boyfriend.

Boyd had contacted him and warned him off the day after he'd struck me, but I wasn't deaf, and I'd heard the answer machine messages Glenn was leaving daily. The arse was like a thorn in our sides and I got it, Boyd was a catch, but that didn't mean I had to like it. I'd made sure to mention his description to the guys at work in case he popped up again, wanting to have another go at me.

The silence lengthened between and was only broken by the sound of the men's shouts and the subsequent clattering, thudding, and general noise of men working.

"Talk to Daddy. Come on, I can't fix it if you don't tell me what's wrong." Although he'd lowered his voice, I could clearly hear him, and my heart leapt in my chest at his words.

"I was thinking about leaving you," I blurted out, and then groaned when he clearly misunderstood what I meant as he masked his expression with a blank look.

I wrapped my arms around his neck and clung on as he went to stand. "No, no, Daddy, that came out wrong," I choked out past the ball of fear now lodged in my throat.

He stilled, but his arms remained at his sides. I clutched at the hair at his nape and gulped. "I...I don't want to leave you. I want to stay with you. I know it's too soon and that we've not...you don't..." I trailed off, my cheeks heating because I wasn't sure how to broach the subject of sex.

Boyd had been very affectionate and spent a lot of time touching me, taking care of all my needs with one exception, sex. Initially, I'd not paid it any mind because it was so great to be little with him and he was always making sure I was happy. And although I loved that, I'd been a little uncertain in the last few days as the need for more had become all I could think about. The close proximity to him day and night was doing nothing to help. I'd started to worry my little side was putting him off wanting to have sex with me.

"We've not? I don't? You need to be a little more specific, Angel boy. What do you mean?" He frowned, and the creases around his eyes deepened as he sounded more than a little exasperated.

Seeing no way out, I muttered, "Had sex."

His expression was unreadable as he stared at me for long seconds. Then my mouth was taken in a brutal kiss that left me hanging on to him for dear life. My lips parted as he plundered my mouth. His tongue tangled with mine. My groan was swallowed in his mouth as he shifted, and I found myself dangling mid-air before he cupped his hands one at a time under my bottom to get a better grip of me. My legs wound around his waist and my fingers dug into his silky hair as the world disappeared.

The lack of orgasm, that hadn't really bothered me up until now, roared to life as my back hit a wall and I used the hard surface to push closer to Boyd. The stark arousal pulsing through me clouded my mind to everything other than the need for Boyd. "Daddy, please," I whined against his mouth.

"Boyd, you up there?" came a voice I didn't recognise, breaking the sexual haze.

My head thudded against the wall as Boyd released my mouth. He was flushed, his hair was a mess, and his eyes held a dark desire that left me in no doubt that, if we'd not been interrupted, we'd have done more than kiss.

"I'll be down in a sec," he called out, his voice sounding more than a little strained, before resting his forehead against mine. "We'll talk about this tonight." He kissed my tingling lips. "And in the meantime, I want you to think about whether I should spank you for not being honest with Daddy." He met my gaze and shook his head, before lowering me to the ground.

The look of disappointment hurt more than any spank could, so I quickly agreed, hoping to appease him. He gave me one last peck on the lips before heading downstairs. My hands clenched together as he disappeared, and I leant against the wall when my legs found it difficult to hold me up.

Had I just fucked things up?

Chapter 9

BOYD

With my body still in a state of arousal, I did my best to concentrate and listen to Rod as he went through the next phase of filling the cavity walls with insulation. Now that the roof was on, and the building was structurally secure from the elements, the internal work had begun in earnest. I'd taken a week off from working on Flamingo Bar to come and help with Sawyer's house. Normally, I'd leave the work to Rod, the site foreman I'd picked, but with everything Sawyer had gone through with previous builders and the mishaps my firm was going through, I was taking no chances.

Phil had faxed me the contract and we'd come to an agreement. I'd texted him all the login information for my computers at the end of the week before. We had a planned meeting for Monday, to see what he'd discovered. My stomach knotted at the prospect of uncovering who had it out for me.

My arousal was dampened down by my worrisome thoughts, which was the only benefit of them. I swallowed a sigh and responded to Rod when his brow arched, and he got a look of expectation on his face. "That's great. When will the truck arrive with the insulation?"

"Should be Monday, now. I'd wanted to make sure we'd finished with the roof first." Rod glanced up and rubbed at his unshaven jaw. "Whoever the previous builders were that said they could do the work; they were talking through their arses. Shitty fucking cowboys."

I slapped at his brawny shoulder and scowled. "On that we can agree. I took the paperwork Sawyer had and I've reported the fuckers to trading standards. They ripped Sawyer off for tens of thousands. Even if they'd built a house for him, I'm sure the thing wouldn't have passed building regs." I sighed as I glanced about the large open plan room cluttered with workmen, tools, and debris.

"He'll get his house now. He's got a good eye and knows what he wants," Rod said, his voice full of humour. Stu hollered for him, so he walked away, giving me a salute as he did so.

This week, I'd seen Sawyer in a different light. He'd faced off with two of the men when they'd argued about the logistics of what he wanted. He'd shown he could stand up for himself and I'd applauded him. Then we'd gone home, and he'd gone into little mode the second we'd entered the house and I'd seen the toll it had taken on him. Spending so much time with him had been insightful, not only about Sawyer, but about me, too. And Sawyer's earlier questioning gave me something else to consider on top of the continued calls coming from Glenn.

The constant ache in my neck and shoulders left me in no doubt about how tense I was. The upset I'd felt at Glenn attacking Sawyer increased daily with the messages he was leaving at my home. No matter how many times I'd told him to stop, and that it was over, he wasn't listening. I'd not told Sawyer about the gifts he'd been sending to the office for me. I'd binned them all, but not mentioning it left a bad taste in my mouth.

Rubbing at the back of my neck, I went to check where everyone was up to before they left for the weekend.

The remainder of the afternoon was uneventful, but I was glad it was Friday. Excitement buzzed through me at the prospect of a whole, uninterrupted weekend with Sawyer. With his work pattern, it made it hard to plan days with him. When he'd said last week, he was on holiday this week, I'd been thinking all week about what we could do.

Yet now, as Sawyer sat huddled into his coat and remained silent throughout the fifteen-minute journey home, my excitement was waning. He clutched at the strap of the bag he'd brought our lunch in, the way he liked to clutch at his blankie.

After I stopped in the driveway of my home, I undid Sawyer's seatbelt when he waited. I exited the truck and went around the bonnet to open the door for him, helping him out. The cool evening air hinted that even though we were now in spring, winter still wasn't far enough away to not threaten us with a blast of chilly weather.

I kept hold of his hand as we walked towards the house, then he hopped from one foot to another as he waited for me to open the door and allow him to step into the house before me. The second he was inside, he headed straight towards the stairs. I sucked in a shaky breath. "Where do you think you're going?"

He halted at the base of the stairs and slowly turned around with the bag clutched to his chest, as if he were using it as a protective barrier. "I'm going...I was...ermm." He lifted his shoulders and stopped stuttering as I tilted my head and raised my eyebrows.

"What did I say back at your house? When we got home, we'd talk about you not asking for what you wanted. I'm disappointed that you didn't feel you could talk to me about your needs, Angel boy."

A heartfelt sounding sigh escaped from his lips as he hung his head, but not before I saw a pink hue colour his cheeks. The light coming from the window at the top of the stairs bathed the top of his colourful hair.

Taking in his defeated posture, my hands curled into balls at my side with the need to make him feel better. But I restrained myself for the moment, knowing we needed to talk first, for him to understand he had to talk to help me navigate what happened next between us.

If I'd accepted one thing this afternoon, it was that by being so focused on making sure I'd built a relationship that nurtured his little side, I'd fucked up by not seeing that he still needed more from me. Oh, I wanted to blame him for not talking, but I was equally to blame for not asking. Clearly, he'd been waiting for me to take the initiative, only I'd based my actions on what my previous boyfriends had wanted from me, so I'd held back.

After our little discussion today, it was as if someone had washed my windscreen after it had been covered in bird shit. Before, it was impossible for me to see out, but now I could see everything and I wanted, no needed, him to be up front with me so there was no misunderstanding between us.

The tension in the air increased as he remained unmoving at the bottom of the stairs, saying nothing.

"Follow me." My tone was authoritative, but I held my breath as I walked into the lounge. Only the sound of a thud, which I thought was the bag being dropped, and feet dragging on the floor allowed me to release the pent-up breath I held.

I sat on the large leather couch and patted the seat next to me.

He eyed his clothes, the sofa, then my lap, before he shook his head. "I'll make it dirty," he muttered.

"Okay then, sit on Daddy's lap."

As if that's what he'd been angling for, I'd hardly finished speaking and he was curled up in my lap, his head tucked under my chin.

I stroked the top of his head and let the weight and warmth of his body settle the ball of anxiety that had grown in my stomach from the silence in the truck. "I'm sorry that you didn't feel able to ask me for what you wanted."

He sighed but said nothing.

"I've been thinking about everything this afternoon." He tensed before I got any further and I stroked my hand down his back. "Shush now. What I realised was that I'd assumed you'd take the initiative to show me when you were ready for the next step. I realised, maybe that isn't what you want?"

"Since I moved in here, you've encouraged me to be myself. In a way, you set my little free from the box I contained him in." He shifted so he could look at me.

There was vulnerability but also hope in his eyes, so I remained silent and waited for him to continue.

"When I figured out there was this part of me that liked being little and being taken care of, I accepted it. What I didn't do was let it have free reign, not really, because first there was the shared living. Then the boyfriends I picked were only interested in me being little when it suited them. So, the only real time I could just be me was when I was on my own. And although I enjoy it, it's not the same as having someone to give me structure. To take care of me and let me just *be* without having to worry about anything else." He scratched at his head, his face wearing a thoughtful expression.

I waited a beat to see if he'd finished before asking, "Have I focused too much on your little, and not enough on your other side?"

He chuckled. "If you give attention to my little, are you not giving attention to all of me?"

I tilted my head to look at him while I considered what he'd said. Was I making it too complicated? Was I muddying the water by trying to separate out the two sides of him? Or was it something else?

Glenn had called me perverted. Had I let that stop me from what would happen naturally between me and Sawyer?

A gentle brush of Sawyers fingertips to my forehead pulled me from questions I wasn't sure I had answers for, or not ones I wanted to acknowledge right then.

He gave an exasperated snort. "Daddy, you're overthinking it." His face got red splotches on his cheeks. "When I'm little, do you get...aroused?" He bit his lip and met my gaze with eyes filled with dread.

"Angel, I only have to be near you to become aroused," I answered honestly, wanting to remove any doubts he had. It appeared that while I'd been pushing aside my own needs, doing my best not to give in to my baser instincts, I'd made him think I didn't want him. When, in fact, all I'd been doing was dreaming about all the things I could do to his delectable body. Fuck, bath time had become a torturous session on how far it could stretch my control. Especially as, most of the time, I'd somehow end up in the bath with Sawyer.

His face brightened and he leant forward, his mouth puckering for a kiss.

I got to within mere millimetres from his lips and stopped. His breath gushed out and brushed against my parted mouth as his eyes pleaded with me. "Maybe it's time Daddy showed you exactly what he'd like to do to his Angel boy. But first, I think we should talk about the spanking."

At his moan, and bottom wriggling against my lap, my cock took notice and started to plump in appreciation.

"Spanking," he squealed, sounding more delighted than horrified.

"Yes, you knew Daddy was a novice at this. Yet, you remained quiet about something that was important to you. It made you worry, and Daddy hates the thought of that. So that means I have to teach you a lesson, so it doesn't happen again."

His eyes got so wide they seemed to consume his face.

My hands trembled as I helped him to stand up. *Please let this be the right move.* "Daddy's going to take off your clothes. Then I'm going to spank you. If you take your punishment like a good boy, Daddy will reward you after bath time. Are you willing to take your punishment?"

His whole body juddered. "Yes, Daddy," he mumbled, his hands fidgeting at his sides as he struggled to meet my gaze.

"That's a good boy." I stood and stroked my hand down his hair, gaining a little whimper, before I removed it to start undressing him.

His whole demeanour changed. It was subtle, but I'd come to notice when his facial expression would soften, the same with his posture. His little was now in charge and I acknowledged the tug to my belly at what I was about to do, then I focused on the arousal that was fizzing under my skin excitedly. It easily overpowered the doubt or worry that this was wrong.

How could this be wrong when it made my heart soar, knowing the care I gave fulfilled needs in my man? And he was a man. There was no denying that, regardless of his little persona. He was a fully grown man with different needs, needs I could meet, as well as the ones inside me that I'd ignored for years. Sawyer had allowed me to embrace who I was without judgement. How could I not...*love...him*?

It's too soon, surely? What has it been six, seven weeks? *You can't fall in love with someone in that time, can you?*

Without a clue how to answer that, I stripped Sawyer while I struggled to stop my hands from shaking. *Think about it later.*

That's a good idea, go with that.

Chapter 10

Sawyer

There was something different about Boyd as he removed my clothes. Was he more confident? I wasn't sure if it was that, but there was something remarkably different, I could sense it. It was like he'd finally accepted who he was and what we were doing.

The thought fled at the brush of his fingertips over my naked backside. When he'd talked about punishments, I understood why he felt I needed a spanking. Secretly, I wanted it, wanted him to show his authority, even if the idea of getting a spanking caused nerves to dance along my skin, making me want to fidget.

His hand lingered on my skin as he eyed the sofa, then the big window that overlooked his garden. His brow pinched before he looked back at me. "I think maybe we'd be better taking this upstairs."

Without any further explanation, he took my hand and then, as if thinking better of it, he dropped it. About to complain, I was lifted off the floor.

"Wrap your legs around Daddy and hold on."

The sexy rasp of his voice, and the show of strength, heated my blood and my body responded. The firm press of his rough palms to my naked arse as he walked through the house and up the stairs, did crazy things to my insides.

By the time we got to his bedroom, pre-cum was smeared over his scruffy work jumper. Boyd was hardly out of breath as he sat on the edge of his bed. He met my gaze and the intensity in his eyes left me breathless with desire. He helped me to stand without saying a word. My cock bounced and drew his attention. He traced a finger up the solid length until he reached the tip. His fingers slid over the slippery head and I groaned at how good it felt. At bath time, he often touched me, but somehow this felt more intense, with him showing me exactly how excited he was.

The air crackled with tension and made my skin buzz by the time he tugged me over his lap. He positioned me so that he could trap my erection between his spread thighs. I whimpered when he traced his fingertip down the crease of my arse.

"You've such beautiful pale skin, but I think it will look gorgeous when it's red." He sounded almost like he was talking to himself. There was no time to reply as I jerked forward at the first stinging slap.

The sound was more shocking than the heat of the spank, but I wailed anyway. "Ouchhhhh."

"You can shout as loud as you like, Angel boy, but Daddy's not going to stop until he's satisfied you understand the importance of talking to me about your needs." The next spank was harder than the first, and my eyes filled with tears as my arse cheek started to burn.

"Daddy, I'm sorry, I understand now, I do," I cried out, but to no avail. Heat spread over my body as Boyd alternated between both my cheeks.

I lost count of how many times he spanked me, my cock jerking and rubbing against the soft material of his worn jeans. Tears slid down the sides of my hot face as I mewled and cried, lost to the pain and the desire that merged into one large ball of need. Tingling sensations started to tickle the base of my spine and I pushed back into the next spank, then thrust forward to gain much needed pressure on my cock.

The surging desire drove me back and forth, my body tightening as I felt my balls getting ready to release their load. As if Boyd read my intention, his hand lifted and he spread his thighs further apart, removing all pressure to my cock.

"Noooooo, why? Please, I was gonna come," I complained in a teary voice.

Boyd's hot palm rubbed over my tender backside, and he chuckled. "I know, but this is a punishment not a reward, remember?" His voice deepened. "But you were such a good boy for accepting your punishment, after I've bathed you, Daddy will give you a reward, like he promised."

"It better be a good reward, Daddy," I grumbled as I was lifted onto shaky legs.

He brought me into his body and held me gently. "It will be."

His eyes were so full of...was it love? Oh god, please let it be that. I opened my heart, hoping he could see what I was coming to understand.

He continued to stare into my eyes for long seconds and, for a moment, I thought he might declare his feelings, then he kissed the tip of my nose and the moment was lost.

Warm fingers squeezed my tender arse. "Come on, let's get in the shower, then I'll put some cooling cream on your bottom."

My heart leapt with joy at his concern for me as he led me into the bathroom. Once we were in the shower, my throbbing backside took the edge off my arousal, now my cock was not getting any attention. I rubbed at my bottom, hoping it would help ease the tenderness.

"I'll do that. Turn around and put your hands on the wall."

The husky demand was easy to obey, and hot water sluiced down my body as I placed my hands on the cool tiles.

"Spread your legs, Angel boy."

Doing as he requested, a bubble of excitement built in my chest as his breath touched my arse cheeks. *Oh fuck, oh fuck.*

The chant continued as Boyd lapped lazily at my hot skin before he kissed the tender flesh as if he were kissing me better. My flagging arousal pulsed back to life at the tender treatment. Then his wet hands parted my arse cheeks and he blew on me. A shiver racked the whole of my body, and my hands struggled to remain in place on the tiled wall when his tongue licked a path down the crease of my arse to my quivering hole. At the first touch of his tongue pressing against me, adrenaline shot through my body and I jerked back, desperate for him not to stop. His warm chuckle brushed against me before he licked around the puckered skin, teasing me mercilessly. His whiskers tickled my heated flesh and added to my delight.

My hand slid off the tile and headed straight to my cock.

"No, Angel, no touching. Put your hand back," he rasped before I'd got to my needy cock.

"Daddyyyyy, I want to touch," I complained, my hand still hovering close to my dick.

"Who's in charge here?"

The simple question got me to put my hand back on the wall, albeit reluctantly. "You are, Daddy," I muttered, not sounding contrite at all.

"Oucchhhhhh." The sound of the spank was loud in the shower, as was my squeal as it rang against the glass of the shower stall.

"If you don't behave, I'll stop what I'm doing. We can go back to how Daddy normally bathes you and later, instead of sharing a bed with Daddy, I can tuck you into your own bed."

He sounded so utterly serious that I looked over my sagging shoulder. I met his serious expression and it pinched at my heart. "I'll behave, Daddy, I promise, no matter how hard it is for me." I gave him my best earnest expression, hoping that would help.

His lips twitched, and I could see he was struggling to hold onto his serious face and my heart felt lighter. "Face the wall, so Daddy can finish washing your bottom."

Never one to look a gift horse in the mouth, I twisted my head to face the wall and promptly exhaled in a noisy rush. There was the noise of a lid opening and a squirting sound before his mouth latched on to one cheek and he sucked hard at the flesh. I felt the tug all the way through my arse right to the tip of my leaking cock. My fingers curled against the wet tile in an effort to stop my hands from moving. The ache between my legs intensified as his lips travelled back to my pucker. His tongue swirled over the sensitive skin, alternating between lapping and pushing the tip against my hole.

About to scream in frustration, his hand moved from my hip bone and slid over my lower abdomen towards my cock. The air in the steamy shower seemed to disappear as he pushed the tip of his tongue past the tight rim of muscle in my arse and took hold of my cock, stroking firmly from base to tip. The noise I'd heard now made sense, as his lubed palm glided up my aching cock in time to the thrusts of his tongue deeper into my arse.

"I ohh...ohh...jeez...gods...oh bloody hell, more, Daddy. I swear I'll be a good boy. Please let me come," I cried, my whole body straining against the need to just let go.

The pace of his hand increased as I ground my arse against his face, needing something more. His tongue sank deeper inside me, stretching the ring of muscle until it burned so good my eyes rolled into the back of my head.

"Come for Daddy," he growled as he pulled back and eased two lubed fingers into my channel. His fingers were tentative at first, then he found my prostate, and my hips got a mind of their own.

I rocked forward mindlessly into Boyd's firm grasp, and back onto his fingers.

"That's it, Angel, fly for Daddy."

"Awwwww fuckkkkk." Cum jettisoned out of my body in hot spurts and hit the tiled wall in front of me as he pegged my prostate. I watched my cum slide down the tiles with the water. Pulse after pulse hit the tiles, as my body took over and my mind emptied of all the worry I'd had that Boyd might not find me sexually attractive. The water hitting my over sensitive flesh, combined with the feel of Boyd's hands on my body, seemed to drag out my orgasm until I could barely stand.

My legs trembled with the effort to stay standing, then Boyd carefully removed his fingers from my arse and released my cock, tugging me down as he shifted so I could sit in his lap. Water poured over our heads and I blinked several times to focus my gaze on him.

He gave my lips a soft kiss. "You were beautiful, Angel boy," he whispered against my mouth. His tongue licked at the seam of my lips and I could taste my own musky flavour. Whatever thought I'd had that I was knackered was disputed by my cock twitching as Boyd deepened the kiss. I opened my mouth and our tongues met in a heated caress. I swallowed his moans as his cock pushed up against my wet skin, sliding against my hip.

Expecting him to want more, I was surprised when he released my mouth and helped me stand, ignoring his own arousal while he slowly washed me. He gave himself a cursory wash before we left the shower and he spent time drying me.

I eyed his groin as he stood and rubbed the thick fluffy towel over his torso. "Daddy…" I trailed off when I looked up at his face. Restrained desire was there in the depths of his caramel eyes and in the strain of his tight features. It was a heady combination, especially when I realised, I'd put that look on his face.

"We need to have something to eat, then afterwards we'll snuggle in bed. If you're not too tired, then Daddy will see about letting you suck his cock." His jaw bunched as he finished drying himself, barely touching his arousal as if it were too painful.

"Thank you, Daddy." My pulse skipped excitedly at the thought of touching him. But at the reminder of what my reward was going to be, I struggled not to bounce on the spot. *Oh, my giddy aunt, I was going to be sharing Boyd's bed.*

Then, as if Boyd's prediction was coming true, a wave of tiredness washed over me, and I hid a yawn with the back of my hand and prayed the week's manual labour wouldn't spoil the evening.

Chapter 11

BOYD

A groan escaped from my parted lips as wet heat surrounded my painfully hard cock. My sleep addled brain was not quite awake enough to grasp if what was happening to me was real or a dream.

The feel of lips mouthing my cock felt real, and I prayed I'd get to come before I woke up. At the next firm suck to the head of my cock, small hands slid up my thighs, and over my rippling abdomen, until they reached my nipples.

"Fuck, shit, oh god, please, don't stop," I called out mindlessly when the mouth popped off my cock.

"I'm not going to stop but I thought you were trying to suffocate me, Daddy," a muffled voice stated indignantly,

I blinked open my eyes and the dimly lit room came into focus. It was then I noticed my hands were pushing down on the duvet under which I could feel Sawyer's head. Shit, not a dream. I groaned in distress at the thought of trying to suffocate Sawyer and pulled back the cover to reveal his flushed face hovering over my groin.

"I'm so sorry, Angel, I thought I was dreaming," I said, sheepishly. As I'd predicted last night, Sawyer had crawled into bed and curled up next to me, falling asleep within seconds. Although he was used to working hard, manual labour was a different kettle of fish than standing and running around all day.

My head blanked as Sawyer's nose became buried in the hair at the base of my cock, and he inhaled deeply.

"You smell so good," he muttered before his tongue lapped at the hair then moved to slide up my cock. His small fingers barely touched as he clasped the base of my cock, and he rose up on his knees. I caught a glimpse of his own arousal as he sucked the head of my cock back into his mouth.

"Angel...Angel," I wheezed, and tried again to get my brain to function while Sawyer did something magical with his tongue and the slit of my cock. "Twist your body round so I can suck your cock, too."

My cock vibrated with the moan he released before he started to shift without taking my cock out of his mouth. He was panting around my erection by the time he swung his leg over my head and presented himself to me.

I chuckled when he wiggled a little, his cock waving in my face.

There were several slurping noises, before he muttered around my cock, "Suck me too."

With his mouth and tongue all over my cock, it was difficult to concentrate, but I grasped his meaning. Licking the palm of my hand, I took hold of his flushed cock and stroked it firmly. He mewled, and I felt saliva slide over my balls. My arse clenched as I struggled to focus. His cock throbbed in my hand, so I drew it towards my lips, only after I sucked my fingers until they were dripping wet. With his cock in my mouth I moaned as his flavour flooded my taste buds. I moved my soaking fingers to his pucker and used my spit to slick his hole. His thighs trembled and clenched closer to my head as I sucked him fully into my mouth.

Each firm suck I gave Sawyer's cock, he matched, until we were completely in sync. At the same time, I fucked him with one and then two fingers until he started to undulate above me. His mouth left my cock as his whole body stiffened and his back arched. The cock in my mouth thickened and warned of his impending orgasm, then hot spurts of cum filled my mouth. I continued to suck on his cock and thrust into his arse. He muttered and cried nonsensical words before his quivering, sweaty body landed on mine. This time, he was trying to suffocate me.

I didn't get time to complain when he swallowed my cock down his throat. There was the sound of gagging and yet more saliva slid over my balls, but Sawyer didn't stop. With trembling arms, I lifted his leg as I gasped for breath once I'd removed his flaccid cock from my mouth. But I'd no time to catch my breath as Sawyer squeezed my balls and gave a firm suck to the head of my cock.

"Mother Fuckerrrr!" I shouted in a strangled moan as my body strained against the damp sheet beneath me. My thigh muscles contracted painfully as my cock thrummed with painful pleasure as it emptied into Sawyer's willing mouth. He slurped, sucked, and groaned in what sounded like utter delight, until I had to pull him off as my cock became too sensitive.

He laid his cheek on my thigh, and curled his body into mine, then looked up at me with a smug smile on his face. "Morning, Daddy."

As he licked enticingly at his puffy lips, I couldn't help but respond to his happiness. "That's a wakeup call that I could get used to." His expression became guarded for a second and I wondered what I'd said.

"Any time...you want, Daddy." There was a hesitation, but the offer sounded genuine.

I patted the bed next to me. "Come up here for me."

He did as I asked, but suddenly there was a tension in the air that hadn't been there a minute ago. I cuddled him into my chest and stroked the top of his head until he melted against me.

"Tell me what's wrong."

"I don't want to," he said, ever so softly, as his body language changed and he buried his face in the side of my body, hiding from me.

"Daddy isn't going to get mad, I promise. Just tell me what's wrong, Angel?" I kept my voice gentle, hoping it would help ease the tension that was now radiating from his stiff body. I worked to remain still, struggling against the bounding pulse that was buzzing through my body.

"I sleep in the other room..." he trailed off as he continued to avoid looking at me.

And it suddenly dawned on me what the problem was. Last night was the first time we'd shared a bed and I'd said it was a reward. Did he assume I'd want him to go back to his own room tonight? *What else would he think?*

I gave myself a mental slap for being such a dick and not figuring out what the issue was earlier.

"Can you look at Daddy, please?" Although a question, I used the tone that said it wasn't up for debate, and the air rushed out of my chest when he obeyed. All I could see was dread, and it hurt to see him so unsure of himself. "Do you want to switch bedrooms? Stay in here with me?"

His head bobbed so fast, a tear slid down his cheek.

I rubbed at it with my thumb and sucked it into my mouth. There was a salty taste, but also the all familiar hint of herbs. His skin tended to smell of herbs, and when I'd smelled the bath products he had in non-descript bottles, I'd understood why. When I'd questioned him, he'd explained he made all his body products to help reduce his carbon footprint. I'd even purchased one of the crystals he used as deodorant to see if it was really as good as Sawyer bragged about.

"Then we'll do that after breakfast." I ran my fingers over his head. "You can look for the perfect spot in here to keep your little box."

The smile that appeared at that suggestion could have rivalled a full moon for brightness.

"Thank you, Daddy." He tugged at my arm before he sat up and got off the bed. He eyed me as I remained lying down. "Come on, we need a shower and breakfast, then…" He stopped talking as his gaze moved about the room.

Although the curtains were shut, they let in a little of the morning light, but not enough to allow him to see the room clearly.

As if he'd just registered that thought, he skipped to the window, naked as a jaybird, pulling open the curtains. He spun back around, his lips pursed as his hand came up and he played with a strand of his hair.

He looked utterly adorable as his nose wrinkled and he pouted at me. "You don't have any space under your bed," he stated in a dramatic voice.

The base was solid, but it had drawers on either side, though you couldn't see them because of the cover. I shifted onto my side and lifted the duvet to reveal the side of the bed. "There's a drawer here that might be perfect?"

At that, he was over the carpet in a flash and down on his knees, examining the large empty drawer. I could see that whatever we did today, it was going to include moving his meagre belongings and his box into my room. As that reality sunk in, I waited for the anxiety to follow. When nothing happened and the warm feeling inside my chest remained, I released a tremulous breath at what I'd suspected but hadn't been ready to accept. I was in love with Sawyer. *I love him.*

It had taken me two years to ask Glenn to move in with me, and another year before I'd really declared how I felt. Had I been kidding myself? I'd never felt this deep-seated happiness I had with Sawyer, that was for sure. I'd spent so much time trying to please Glenn, I'd somehow lost sight of what was important to me. Had he used my need to take care of him against me?

I'd let him use me.

"—then we can put the box in storage." Sawyer's excited chatter pulled me from my thoughts, and I swallowed past the bitterness coating my mouth and focused on what was important: Sawyer.

Chapter 12

Sawyer

Hearing Boyd call me from the kitchen, I dropped the colouring pen onto the picture I'd been drawing and got up off the floor to go and see what he wanted. We'd decided to stay in all weekend and just have fun, and we had.

Boyd had helped me move my things into his room the day before, and I'd spent an age making sure everything in my box was now tucked in the drawer under his bed. It had been a weird feeling putting my things into something other than the box. It felt kind of monumental, and I'd found myself wandering upstairs just to open the drawer and look inside.

Was it too soon to have all these feelings? To want to talk about them?

Stop it, we're little today and you're not supposed to be worrying about the big stuff.

I huffed in frustration, feeling conflicted with myself at wanting to be little and not shut off my head at the same time.

Walking into the kitchen I halted when I saw that Boyd had his coat on. Glancing down at my adult baby grow, my lip poked out. "I thought we were staying in?" I said in a sulky tone that got an eyebrow rise out of Boyd.

"We are, but with how busy we've been at your house, I forgot to do a food shop and get some essentials. We've none of the cereal left that you like and there's no fresh fruit or veg either. If I want to make the roast dinner I promised you, I need to go and get some shopping." He tucked his wallet into his back pocket, then grabbed the keys off the counter and walked towards me.

When he reached me, he kissed the top of my head and gave me a wink. "I won't be long. Maybe you'll be finished with your picture by the time I get back and you can show me what you've done."

His grin was contagious, and my insides warmed at being able to show him my completed picture. "Oh, Daddy, you're gonna love it." I clapped my hands together in excitement.

"I'm sure I will. Go on now, Daddy won't be long." He patted my bottom before giving me a quick kiss.

I waved him off at the door before rushing back into the living room, hoping I'd be able to finish the picture I'd made of his garden. I chewed the end of the pen as I looked out the window, then carried on with my colouring in.

Unsure how long I'd spent kneeling on the floor, I groaned when my bladder said I needed to pee. The doorbell chimed, and I froze in a half crouched position then glanced down at my outfit, chewing my lower lip between my teeth. *Bugger!*

There was no way I was going to answer the door dressed as I was, because I was damn sure that Boyd wouldn't want me outing him like that. I remained crouched, rooted to the spot, feeling more than a little ridiculous when I realised nobody could see me or get in the house.

As I stood tall, there was a scraping sound, as if someone were messing with the lock on the front door and I literally felt the blood leave my face. Was Boyd about to be burgled? Anger at the injustice of that surged through me, and before I could think about what to do, I looked about for a weapon, then remembered I didn't need one. Years of training to gain discipline, as my parents had put it, also gave me skills to defend myself and what was mine. And that meant Boyd's things too. So, instead of ringing the police, like I should have done, I crept as quietly as I could to the door, listening for more sounds.

The moment the front door opened and closed, the air seemed to disappear as I struggled to centre myself. *Remember your training, come on. Boyd needs you to do this for him.*

I inhaled and exhaled twice before I stepped boldly into the hallway. I didn't get very far before I went into shock. I wasn't sure who was more surprised, the man stood by the door, or me. The sudden blood rush I got caused a wave of dizziness as I eyed Glenn and the holdall he clutched in his hands. *What is he doing in Boyd's home?*

While my gaze swept him from top to toe, I suddenly felt completely inadequate. He'd clearly dressed for the visit. His outfit looked more suited for a runway model show than a trip to someone's home. The first time we'd met, I'd hardly had any time to take anything in. Now, as the guy stood eyeing me like I was shit on his shoe, I struggled to understand what Boyd would see in me. I was clearly nothing like this man.

Doing my best to school my features, I stood tall, pretending I wasn't stood in an adult size baby grow in mint green.

"What do you think you're doing coming into the house uninvited?" I asked, trying to inject as much confidence into my voice.

When Glenn laughed, I knew I'd failed, but I refused to back down.

Why was he here? How the hell did he have a key to get in?

"How can I be uninvited when I have a key?" He waved the key at me, and my heart dropped. "I think the question should be. What the fuck are you still doing here?" His gaze moved over me again and I saw the moment he registered what I wore. "Jesus, is that a child's outfit you're wearing. Christ, I knew there was something funky about you, you're a bloody pervert." Disgust coated his voice as he stared at me, his nose curling up like he'd smelt something bad.

Finding it difficult to swallow past the ball lodged in my throat, I blinked back the tears, not wanting to show how much his comment hurt. There were a lot of misconceptions about Littles, and I wasn't about to try and explain anything to this man. I tried to keep hold of my dignity and ignore his comment.

"I'll ask again, what are you doing here?"

He took several menacing steps towards me, the intent on his face clear, only this time I was ready for him. I relaxed my stance and took a deep breath, letting it fill my lungs, then I let it go as I pivoted to the left when he swung at my face with his fist. My movements were fluid as I dodged the next two flying fists and the foot aimed at my knee cap.

Glenn was now panting, and his face was a flushed mask of fury. The next punch glanced off my shoulder as I spun and shifted my weight.

"Fucking shithead," he screamed and lunged at me, only he caught air and went skidding towards the bannister, bashing the side of his face on the wooden post hard enough to make a loud cracking sound. His legs crumpled under him as he dropped to the floor.

I ran towards him and bent down to see if he was okay. Blood poured out the gash above his half open right eye.

About to go and grab a cloth, the door behind me swung open. In a split-second Glenn glanced from me to Boyd and screamed while lifting his hands in defence. "No more, please don't hit me again."

"What—"

"Oh my God, what the hell is going on here," Boyd shouted as he dropped the bags he was carrying and rushed over towards us. He gently moved me to the side, not letting me talk, and bent down to look at Glenn's bleeding face before he looked at me as if I was a stranger. "What on earth happened here, Sawyer?"

His voice trembled, and my heart felt like it was dying a slow death when he looked back at Glenn, asking, "Are you okay to stand? I need to see if I can get the bleeding under control before I take you to the hospital." His voice came out a strangled whisper, as if he were in agony.

I didn't wait to listen to anymore when Glenn gave me a triumphant smirk. Boyd didn't notice in his haste to help Glenn off the floor. I walked past the men and up the stairs with as much dignity as

I could muster. The pain hit once I entered Boyd's bedroom. It left me panting, as if I'd run a marathon in forty-degree heat. I laid my head on the door I'd shut to block out the voices below.

Did he think I'd hurt someone on purpose? Evidently. He moved me away from Glenn like I was the one that was a monster. A hiccupped sob caught in my throat. Did he believe I could be so horrible? *Think about how it looked and what Glenn had said?*

Yeah, but Boyd didn't ask me. He believed what Glenn said without question.

With the betrayal so fresh, I shut my reasonable side out.

Tears ran down my cheeks as I stripped off my clothes, needing to be anywhere but here. I went to the wardrobe to pull out what I'd only placed in there the day before. I did my best not to recall how happy I'd been as numbness filled my chest. I grabbed what I could and shoved it into the large backpack I'd brought my stuff in. I eyed the bed through my tears, knowing there was no way I could cart all my stuff on my bicycle. Opening the drawer, I grabbed my blankie, knowing I'd need it, and left the rest. I'd ask one of my friends to come and get my stuff when I went back to work. Theo would surely help me.

I slung my backpack over my shoulders and stepped back out into the hall, my heart thundering in my ears as I crept down the stairs and straight out the front door undisturbed.

You're being a coward.

No, I'm not.

The internal debate didn't help as I swiped at my nose with the sleeve of my jumper. *Go home, you knew this was only temporary.*

That rang through my head as I quickly unlocked my bike. Reality hit like a freight train, and I started to shake in the chilly afternoon wind. *Keep it together, keep it together,* I begged repeatedly as my heart felt as if it were being ripped out of my chest. I wobbled down Boyd's drive, and only once I lost sight of his home, and felt I was far enough away, did I pull over into a layby. I let out an anguished cry and wept as I lowered my head and rested it on my forearms, hiding my face.

Chapter 13

*B*OYD

I t had taken all my willpower not to leave Glenn at the kitchen counter and go after Sawyer, when I recalled the utter defeat on his face before he'd walked away. But the sight of Sawyer bent over a bleeding Glenn had been jarring, to say the least. Sawyer was the last person I'd expect to hurt another soul, he was always so gentle.

Then why is Glenn injured, and Sawyer has not explained what happened?

You didn't give him time to say anything!

Bile burned the back of my throat as Glenn got comfortable on the stool and I strained to hear what Sawyer was doing upstairs.

"I'm going to report him to the police for assault. He's a perverted menace." Glenn huffed and puffed indignantly, bringing my attention back to him.

The ugly expression he wore took my breath away and I was reminded again how awful he could be. I sucked in a shaky breath, willing myself to keep control of the temper that wanted to have me snap at him.

"I think you need to remember that you hit Sawyer first. He was probably worried you'd hit him again."

"Look at me, I'm bleeding. He's not got a mark on him," Glenn sneered.

My innards turned to water at the prospect that Sawyer could be done for assault if Glenn pressed charges. Before I could try and placate him, he carried on talking.

"I knew you'd take his side. I'm the hurt one and you don't seem to care." His cry was full of anguish before he buried his head in his hands.

"Then why am I in the kitchen helping you?" I muttered sullenly, feeling more than a little conflicted by the whole situation.

It took a second to register that Glenn was peaking at me through his fingers and that caused my nerves to dance under my skin when I looked into his eyes. The calculating look was something I was all too familiar with, as were the dry eyes he watched me with.

What was I missing here? I ran through what I'd seen and heard as I'd come through the door. Sawyer had been crouched over a bleeding Glenn, who had shouted out in distress. Had he only done that because he'd seen me? The knee jerk reaction at the scene I'd witnessed hadn't given me any time to think. Now, with Glenn sitting at the counter looking...smug, I got the impression that all was not as it seemed. But what had happened?

I retrieved a cloth and my first aid box from under the kitchen sink, thinking about how to get answers. Had there been any blood on Sawyer's clothes? Had his hands been bruised from lashing out? I didn't think the answer was yes to either of those things.

My hands trembled as I laid everything on the counter and sat on the seat next to Glenn's. "Let me clean you up and see what damage there is."

He said nothing as he leaned into my touch. His eyelashes lowered and his face became flushed while I tended to the cut. Doing my best to ignore his reaction to my touch, I examined the cut. A cut that clearly hadn't come from a punch, the way the skin was split in a vertical straight line in his brow. "How did you get this cut?" The question popped out as I considered where he'd been lying in the hall.

He hissed as I brushed the antiseptic over the wound. "You know how, that dick punched me in the face."

"Really? He's several inches shorter than you. The angle to cut you like this with his fist would be impossible." I didn't beat about the bush, because clearly things weren't adding up.

"It happened so fast, I can't quite remember." He shrugged nonchalantly, but his body had stiffened when I'd challenged him. "He just came at me, I couldn't tell you how he managed it," he ground out between clenched teeth. His eyes sparked with anger.

"What brought you here?" I questioned, changing tact. "In fact, did I see your bag in the hallway?"

His face flushed an angry shade of red as he looked away, his lips moving as if he was trying to think of something to say. I remained silent, the churning in my guts now rivalling a sea in the height of a storm.

Things just weren't adding up. I finished cleaning up his face and as I started to shift back, his hand moved to my thigh and he started to squeeze it. I shot off the chair, making it clatter while I glanced in the direction of the door, worried that Sawyer would appear and get the wrong impression.

"Stop that Glenn. I've told you it's over. You need to hear me. I'm with Sawyer now. We're happy together. As I said before, you were right to make the decision to split up. We don't have anything in common any—"

"Don't be ridiculous. Four years together show that we've plenty in common. You love me. Not some...man-child. Fuck, how can you want to be with a man that dresses like a bloody child? It's just a phase you're going through. It's probably all connected to that bloody bar you're working on. All you need is for me to come home. Finish that damn project and leave all that nonsense behind you. You'll see that I'm right."

Something nagged at me, but it was gone when it registered how utterly convinced Glenn looked as he spoke. How the hell wasn't he getting that we were over?

His hand ran through his hair as he got up off the seat and came towards me.

I held my hand up to ward him off. "I don't know how else to say this without hurting you, but I love Sawyer. He's it for me. What I feel for him...well, it's just everything."

The following silence felt like I was in the eye of the storm, and I braced. For what, I wasn't sure, but I knew it was going to be something bad.

"You love him?" he screeched, so loudly I was sure anyone within a five-mile radius would have heard him.

Expecting Sawyer to run into the room at any moment, I nodded. "I do, and you need to listen and hear what I say. I love Sawyer and nothing is going to change that."

When Glenn charged forward, his fists flying, I got an idea about what might have happened earlier. I side stepped and took hold of his shoulders as he careened past me. "Stop this, you'll end up getting hurt," I growled.

His chest was heaving as he glared at me. "You've already hurt me. You and that man-child you're obsessed with. You'll come back to me begging, you'll see," he spat at me with venom. Then he spun on his heel and stalked out.

I clenched my hands to stop them trembling as I followed him at a more sedate pace. It was only as the door opened that I noticed his car wasn't in the drive. Where had he parked? I shook my head at the whole surreal situation.

After the door slammed shut, I ran up the stairs and stopped dead in my tracks in the doorway of my bedroom. Where was Sawyer? I went to the bathroom, finding it empty. I ran to the room he'd been using up until Friday. My heart dropped to my boots at finding it empty. Oh fuck!

"Sawyer, Angel boy, where are you?" My shout went unanswered, and dread settled heavily on me as I stepped back into my bedroom. The air punched its way out of my chest so fast, and I blanched when I noticed the drawer under the bed hanging open. My legs became shaky and I struggled to walk to the open drawer. I shut my eyes and took a second to prepare before I opened them again and looked down. Thank fuck!

Sawyer's blankie was gone but the rest of his little things remained. Would he leave without his things? I turned and eyed the wardrobe with trepidation. Shoving my shoulders back, my fists clenched at my sides. The few steps it took to reach the wardrobe felt as if I was walking through quicksand. I opened the door and my heart bled. "Nooooo!" Tears burned my eyes and a sob rose in my throat when I saw the empty space where Sawyer's things had been.

What have I done?

Go and find him, now!

No sooner had the thought registered, I was running down the stairs and out the front door. The two bags of shopping remained sat on the floor as I flew outside, uncaring that I'd not put the fridge items away. I got in the car and my hands shook as I drove out onto the main road, following the route to Sawyer's and hoping that he hadn't gone through the wooded area.

I cursed up a blue storm until I spotted him, then I mewled loudly and clutched the steering wheel in a death grip. His body shook as his head rested on his forearms over the handlebars of his bike.

Look at what you did!

Parking behind him, I'd hardly stopped before I was out of the truck, my need to take away the hurt firmly in the driver's seat.

Sawyer appeared to be so lost in his misery that he didn't notice me as I approached him. I tentatively reached out. "Angel boy…" The words dried on my lips as his head lifted and tear drenched eyes met mine. It was impossible to stop myself awkwardly clasping him to my chest. Half expecting him to push me away, I groaned when he tucked himself into my chest and started to sob in earnest.

Words caught in my dry throat. "I'm so sorry…I really am. Please don't leave me…I love you," I croaked.

His gasp was followed by several hiccups as he pulled away from me, his expression showing confusion. "What about Glenn?" he whispered in a fearful tone. Fear I'd clearly caused by not giving him a chance to explain what had happened in the house.

"What about him? It's you I love. I'm sorry you were hurt by my thoughtlessness and over reaction. Please come back so we can talk about it, please?" I begged again while my pulse tried to deafen me.

He hesitated and then his hand came up to scrub at his wet cheeks. "You love me?" his voice quivered as his eyes continued to show disbelief.

"Yes, yes I do. But I don't think this is the place to talk about it. Please come back. Let's talk about what happened." I held my breath and released it in a hasty rush when he nodded.

Thank you, gods!

Not giving him a chance to change his mind, I helped remove the backpack from his shoulders and took it to the truck. Once in the back seat, I walked back to him with my heart pinching at him still sitting on his bike.

"I'll put your bike in the back of the truck and you can ride with me." Although it wasn't a question, I waited to see if he'd argue. Only when he swung his leg off the bike did the tightness in my chest lessen.

Resting the bike against the truck, I first helped Sawyer up into it and fastened his seat belt before I placed his bike in the bed of my truck. When I was sitting next to him, I took my first real breath since I'd walked into the house to find...what?

I shifted to face him and took hold of his cold hands.

When he looked at me, there was apprehension and sadness etched into his face. "I'm going to keep saying it till you believe me. I'm sorry, and I love you. Nothing is going to change that, not Glenn, not what you are, and not whatever happened today. Do you understand?" I infused as much love as I could into my words, meeting his gaze head on so he understood I meant every word.

This time, when he nodded, it appeared to be with a little more conviction, but I could still see sadness there in his eyes. I silently vowed to myself I would do my best to make sure I never caused him to look at me like that again. Because the one thing this had taught me was that my heart belonged to him and being without him wasn't something I could bear to think about.

Chapter 14

Sawyer

The drive back to Boyd's seemed to take seconds and didn't give me any time to pull my thoughts together. All I could see was Glenn's smug face and his immaculate clothing. The betrayal was the hardest part to swallow. How could Boyd take sides with Glenn? How?

He said he loves you.

Does he? Does he really mean it?

Back and forth my little argued while Boyd stopped the truck and got out to help me from the cab. The blustery wind whipped at my tear stained cheeks as I stood waiting for him to reach into the back and lift out my bag.

He remained silent as he let us back into his home and my gaze landed on the bag that Glenn had brought with him earlier. "Is Glenn still here?" I asked with resignation.

"No, he left after I told him *I love you*."

The stress he put on the latter helped a little to settle my pulse, but it didn't stop me questioning, "Then why did he leave his bag behind?"

I pointed to the floor where the bag sat, taunting me with memories of what had happened.

Boyd walked over to the bag and picked it up. He opened it and peered inside, his face a mask of anger. "It looks like he thought he'd be staying. I'll return it to him, so he gets the picture. He's not wanted here. Can you tell me what happened before I came home?" His voice was strained, and I couldn't tell if he was angry with me or Glenn.

My shoulders sagged and I dropped my gaze to the floor. "There was the sound of someone messing with the lock on the front door. Thinking you were about to be burgled, I came out to confront them—"

"*You did what?*" he bellowed, and I was sure the glass in the door shook.

I took a step back, my frightened gaze meeting his.

His chest heaved and my bag, along with Glenn's, was dumped on the floor. The next thing I knew, his arms were wrapped around me and his face was buried in my hair.

"What were you thinking? You could have been hurt, fuck...worse...murdered." He shuddered violently, and I could hear the anguish and distress he didn't try to hide.

"I'm sorry...I can defend myself," I muttered sheepishly, praying that my confession wouldn't make him jump to the conclusion I'd thumped Glenn.

He moved and his hand cupped the back of my neck. When our gazes met, any doubt I'd had about his feelings being real were washed away by the look of love he wore. "I don't care if you can defend the whole fucking country. You are never to do anything like that again. Do you hear me?" His lips twisted into a grimace. "For god's sake, what would I do if something happened to you?"

The depth of his emotion helped to heal the hurt he'd inflicted and gave me the courage to talk about what had happened. As I laid it out in graphic detail what had occurred from when Glenn had entered the house with a key, to his attempt to hurt me, and eventually bashing his head, Boyd became motionless.

"That fucking bastard." A scowl appeared as he glanced at the post Glenn had hit. A streak of blood marred the wood and confirmed what I'd said. When he stared at me, the scowl was replaced by sorrow. "Shitting hell! Why didn't I just ask you what had happened?" he ground out, his jaw bunching tightly. "Please forgive me."

I exhaled a tremulous breath and reached up to stroke his breaded cheek. "You hurt me. But I'm also to blame for not trying to explain what had happened. Leaving wasn't the answer, I get that now." And I did, after explaining what had happened. It was clear Glenn had played me and Boyd. "I know that the caring side of you would be concerned if someone were hurt, and so would Glenn. He used that, and my insecurities." I moved my hand, placing a finger over his lips as he went to interrupt.

"I was jealous and couldn't see why you'd want me, when you could have him."

"He's not half the man you are," he whispered against my finger. His eyes pleaded for me to listen, to believe him.

I removed my finger and he sighed.

"I love you because you are a beautiful human inside and out. And once I'd got over my shock of seeing Glenn on the floor, I realised there was something amiss. If you hadn't left, you'd have heard me tell him in no uncertain terms that it is you I love." I witnessed a flash of hurt cross his face before he looked away.

"We're a pair, aren't we?" I puckered my lips, waiting for him to look back at me. The second he did, he didn't hesitate, and his mouth took mine in a gentle kiss. I sighed into his mouth as he cupped my cheeks and deepened the kiss. One kiss melded into another until I was left breathless and aroused.

When his mouth nibbled its way to my ear, shivers skittered down my spine. He whispered, "Let's unpack your bag and put everything back where it belongs, Angel."

Joy flooded my chest as he released me to pick up my bag and then held out his hand for me to take. I took it and intertwined my fingers with his, hoping that the drama part of the day was over.

***

Back at work the next day, all I could think about was what had happened. With no Boyd to tell me I was being silly to worry, I couldn't stop the fears from surfacing. Boyd had been so concerned about Glenn having a key to the house that after we'd unpacked my things, he'd called an emergency locksmith and paid a small fortune to have all the locks changed.

The questions I had about what Glenn had said when I'd left them alone had been dodged, leaving me with an antsy feeling. Now, as I chewed on my thumbnail, I wondered if I should have pushed harder.

There was also the matter of Boyd's declaration. His feelings, I was sure, were real, but for some reason I'd held back voicing mine.

Was it because I was pissed about Glenn and what happened? I really wanted to think I was above holding grudges, but my little... Well, that was a different matter.

"You're very quiet today, is everything alright?" Adam, who'd managed to enter the room and sit down next to me without my even noticing, nudged my arm, causing me to jerk.

The scent of his expensive aftershave was all I could smell as I glanced at him. His eyes showed their concern as he stared at me. His face was tanned from his recent honeymoon and he looked relaxed and in love. He'd only been married for a few weeks, but it seemed married life suited him. Would he understand my worries?

"I've a lot on my mind." I looked away, not sure I wouldn't cave and spill my guts. Theo was on a day off today, so the plan to talk to him had fallen by the wayside. Although Adam and I were close, Theo was the person I normally confided in.

He nudged my arm again. "You can talk to me. I'm a good listener...well, most of the time." He chuckled, and as I glanced back at him, I caught the glint of humour.

"Boyd's ex turned up at the house yesterday. It all kicked off. We're okay now, but it was a little shaky there for a while." Hurt washed over me in a wave of misery, and I sucked back the sob that tried to escape. "Anyway, Boyd declared his love for me, but..." I trailed off. Had he told me he loved me as a knee jerk reaction to what had happened?

Adam's expression showed sympathy. "But what? Do you love him?" he asked tentatively.

That part was easy, I did. I'd laid awake for hours last night sorting through my feelings. It was easy in the dark, with the weight of Boyd's arm wrapped around me, to acknowledge how I felt. Yet, I couldn't stop replaying Glenn's disgust. It was fucking with my head and, somehow, I couldn't seem to just say 'fuck it,' what did it matter what he thought? Would Boyd say 'fuck it' if it were a friend that knew what we were doing together?

I didn't have the answer, and a part of me was too scared to ask him outright. It felt as if I was wearing a pair of concrete boots, my thoughts weighed that heavily on me. It hadn't helped that I'd noticed Boyd couldn't completely conceal that something was bothering him. Where does that leave us?

"You just gonna sit there and stare into space?" Adam tapped his watch, his head tilting as he offered me a smile of encouragement. "You've only ten minutes before you're due back in the restaurant. Spill, it might help."

Seeing that it couldn't harm, I twisted my body, so I was looking directly at him. I ran my hands through my hair. "You remember I confessed at your stag party I'm a...Little."

He nodded, his expression showing no repulsion.

"I was wearing an adult baby grow when Glenn rocked up." His eyes widened as I continued. "He threw some insults at me. Thing is, I'm struggling to shake them off. It was right after Boyd found me crying in the street that he confessed to loving me. What if it was just a knee jerk reaction to me leaving him?"

"Okay back up, you left him?" Adam frowned as he rubbed at the back of his neck.

"It was for like, all of probably ten minutes." Realising there were big gaps in Adam's understanding, I explained more fully what had happened.

"—so you see, I'm worried that he only said he loved me because he is feeling guilty for taking Glenn's side."

"Right, first off, I've only met Boyd once at the new bar, but he doesn't strike me as someone who'd say something he didn't mean. I also know you, and you're really good at sizing people up. I'm pretty sure you're letting Glenn's dickish behaviour cloud your judgement. Unless there's something else you're not telling me?"

I sighed and recounted what had happened the first time Boyd had seen me dressed as a little.

"Hang on, are you saying he doesn't want you to act little? Because if that's the case, bin him."

I couldn't help but chuckle at how indignant Adam got on my behalf. "No, he...he asked for some time to think about what it all meant. Things progressed between us when he asked me to move into his house."

"Fuck, he's a fast worker," Adam stated, his eyes full of wonder.

"Nah, it wasn't quite like that. He saw the state of my bathroom and wasn't at all happy with me staying in a 'death trap,' as he put it."

"He's right," said Adam, giving a dramatic shudder.

I rolled my eyes at him. "It was only when I moved into his place that things between us really changed. He's really caring when I'm little." I sucked in a deep breath before stating in a rush, "I love him, I'm scared he'll wake up and realise it was all just a fad, and I'll be left with a broken heart. My parents never really bothered to show their love for me. Boyd, god, the way he is with me. Shit, he has the power to crush me." As I confessed to the power Boyd held over me, I acknowledged the part of me that was terrified that I wouldn't be enough for him.

All humour fled from Adam's expression as he placed his hand on my thigh. "Parents...well, I can empathise with you there, mine aren't going to win any awards for parent of the year."

I cringed when I recalled they hadn't come to the wedding. "Shit, I'm sorry for bringing that up."

"No, it's fine, Carl shows me every day how loveable I am. That being me is okay. My question to you, does Boyd do the same for you?"

I was nodding before I even had time to really consider Adam's question. My head and heart were in total accord.

"Then kick Glenn's arse right out of your head and let your heart lead you where it wants to go. Because once you let go, I promise you won't regret it." His eyes brightened as he spoke.

Was it that easy? I wasn't sure, but I was going to try, because the one thing I did know was that Boyd was worth fighting for.

Chapter 15

ℬOYD

"When is Phil coming?" Brett whispered, his gaze moving furtively around the room.

I didn't sigh, but it was a close call. He'd become so suspicious of everyone, it was hard to get him to listen to reason some days.

"Phil said he'd come at four when the men knock off. I got the impression he might have some news that requires privacy." I shrugged, not sure what he'd found. The original time for the meeting had been changed with a cryptic message this morning.

Brett glanced around the busy room before he met my gaze. "Whoever is fucking with us better be prepared for hell to rain down on them when I find out who the fuck they are."

"Hold your horses, Rocky. All we'll be doing is reporting it to the police. We don't need any more fucking drama."

"What drama?" Nathan questioned, moving silently towards us. It never failed to surprise me how such a big man could move so quietly.

I cursed and looked about. Had anyone else heard me speaking? Seeing everyone was busy, I answered Nathan in a hushed voice. "Phil might have some info on who is messing with us. He's coming at four this afternoon. You free then?"

His blond brows rose, and his expression became thoughtful. "Should be fine. I've nothing scheduled and Lenny is working at the restaurant this evening so I'm home alone." Nathan glanced about the room. "Want to walk me through and talk about what's outstanding." When he glanced back at me, his mouth was pinched.

"Yeah, we'll start in the kitchen. I think Lenny is going to cream his pants when he sees the new fitted ovens."

Nathan's face morphed into a stunning smile. "Lead on. He's been desperate to come down and see how it's progressing, but I've told him he needs to wait till it's complete so he can get the full effect."

We chatted as we walked through to the kitchen, Brett following and chipping in with the list of jobs that had been completed, and the ones that remained outstanding. Nathan didn't point out the obvious, that it was only two weeks to opening night and the outstanding jobs list was larger than any of us would like.

Thankfully, there'd been no new setbacks last week while I'd been working on site at Sawyer's, but I had an unnerving feeling that whoever was fucking with us wasn't finished. When Nathan left later with a promise to be back at four, I went to tackle the tilers to see why the restrooms weren't finished.

Time seemed to pass in a flash and the next thing I knew, I heard my name being called by Phil. I placed the electrical screwdriver down and checked my watch. *Fuck, it can't be four already!* I swiped at my sweaty brow as I walked over to the completed bar he was leaning against, holding a thick file in one hand.

His pewter eyes surveyed the room and then came back to me. His dark hair was cropped in a military style and showed off his strong features. There was something about him that screamed 'don't mess with me' and, not for the first time, I wondered what he'd done while he was in the military. He was well over six feet and though not overtly muscular, he appeared physically fit. His tendency was to wear black and today was no different. His black jacket matched the canvas trousers that had numerous pockets.

"Will the men be leaving soon?" asked Phil when I stopped in front of him.

I glanced back, seeing that the men were showing no signs yet of packing up. Had Brett offered overtime? My brow furrowed when I searched the room and didn't immediately see Brett. I scratched my chin.

"They should be packing up, hang on." I took a couple of steps into the centre of the room and hollered, "Packing up time, guys." The sounds of drills, saws, hammers, and talking ceased for a brief second before the men started to gather their tools and tidy while the sound of talking increased.

When I glanced back at Phil, Brett appeared from the back room behind the bar, his face grimy with dirt and what looked like grease. "What have you been doing?"

Seeing his lips pursing and a glint of anger appearing in his eyes when he looked at the men behind me, I kept quiet, not wanting to deal with his anger in front of the men.

As the room emptied, I led Phil to a completed booth and indicated he should take a seat just as Nathan appeared. Within minutes we were all sat, and the room was finally quiet. Tension rolled off Brett, who'd opted to perch on a workbench he'd pulled up.

"What's happened?" I asked resignedly.

Brett growled low in his throat and ran his hands through his filthy hair. "Someone poured fuck knows what down the drains. It blocked them good and proper, and it was only when the tiler alerted me to the fact he couldn't get the sink to empty, that I went to have a look." He got up and stalked in front of the booth, agitation showing in every step he took. "We were planning to run the water through the heating systems tonight and the overflow pipe would have been sat flooding the fucking place."

"You're fucking kidding me!" Nathan's voice sounded deadly as he glared at Brett.

"Fuck's sake!" I ground out through clenched teeth. My jaw throbbed with how hard I was working to keep control of my anger.

Phil opened the file he'd held and tapped at the paper, bringing our attention to him. "Your guy on site wreaking havoc is Fredrick Gale. From what I can see, he's been with you about a year. He's been texting and receiving emails from Glenn Maidstone—"

"You've got to be fucking kidding me!" The strangled voice sounded nothing like me as my heart violently hammered against my ribs.

Brett's face went a vibrant shade of red as Nathan remained stoically silent.

Phil continued as if I hadn't interrupted him. "The correspondence started about six months ago. It would appear Glenn met Fredrick on one of your work nights out. They've been texting ever since. The emails started not long after. It appears Fredrick has a bit of a gambling problem and was an easy target..."

As I listened, I didn't need to do the maths for when Glenn had started to enlist Fred's help to sabotage my business. The timeline fitted perfectly from when I started to do some research on the internet to spice up our sex life. A snippet of the conversation we'd had when Glenn had left me floated through my head, making total sense now. He'd thrown out an insulting barb about my searches on the internet. Why hadn't I questioned his snooping? He'd no need to use my computer, as he had his own.

The silence around the table penetrated through my misery and I glanced at the men staring at me.

"You okay?" Nathan's face showed more concern than I deserved.

"Not really. It's not every day you learn that the guy you dated for four years has been secretly working to discredit you. To try and ruin your business. The same business that was paying for everything he wanted." The anger fought past the devastation and betrayal as I struggled to sit still.

I stared at Nathan. "I'm so fucking sorry, if you want to find someone else to finish the project I'll fully understand."

Nathan placed a hand on my arm and squeezed. "Why the fuck would I do that? You've worked your fucking arse off." His other arm swept the room. "This place is everything I wanted and so much more because of your input into the design and planning. Your ex is the issue, and whoever the hell Fredrick is. Deal with them. Then work on completing on time. That will be the biggest 'fuck you' to the pair of them."

Brett finally stopped pacing and grinned for the first time since we sat down, pointing at Nathan. "What he said but with one exception. I want to deal with Fred, the fucking little weasel. If he thinks he can fuck with me, he's going to find out differently."

"Stop, we do this the right way. We've enough shit to deal with without the police pressing charges and my best foreman ending up in prison," I stated firmly.

"Alright, but I get to tell him he's fucking fired when the police come to arrest him." Brett sounded far from placated, but I'd known him for years, so I knew he'd stick to his word.

"Let me go through these emails and the traces I've put in place. I've also created a dummy website for your business so when Glenn hacks in, he will only access that from now on. You shouldn't have any more problems." Phil stated as if it were nothing, while he pulled out several pieces of paper that I could see were copies of emails.

Had my search for something more caused all these problems? *Look what it gave you.*

A vivid image of Sawyer's face this morning popped into my head as he'd offered up his lips for a kiss before he'd set aside being Little to get ready for work. Would I want to change back to how things had been before? My breath caught in the back of my throat at the very idea.

No, what I had was worth fighting for.

"Let's do it. The sooner I get this monkey off my back the better."

Chapter 16

SAWYER

The double shift I'd opted to do on my first day back at work left me feeling drained. My chat with Adam had buoyed me but now, as I eyed the phone I held, I wasn't feeling as confident. Would Boyd come and pick me up? *Of course he would.* At the far too obvious answer, I rolled my eyes and hit dial once I'd found Boyd's number.

After the fourth ring, I was starting to worry, but then a flustered sounding Boyd answered. "Hello, Sawyer? Is everything okay?"

"Yeah, I'm fine, I'm just knackered and was ringing to see if you'd come and pick me up."

"Yes, of course," he answered. There was the sound of muffled conversation before he carried on, "I should be with you in about twenty minutes."

When he hung up, I got the impression something wasn't right.

"You gonna help with the set up for tomorrow? Some of us have places to be," Scott said from the doorway of the locker room.

Heat flooded my face as I shoved my phone back into my rucksack. I gave him a sheepish smile, knowing he'd also pulled a double so had to be feeling as tired as me. "Sorry, I was just ringing Boyd to see if he'd come and get me." I rubbed at the back of my neck. "I'm knackered."

"You've just had a week off, how can you be knackered?" Scott returned my grin, his face glowing as he threaded his arm through mine as we walked back into the restaurant to finish setting the tables for the next day.

I rested my head on his shoulder. "I worked on the house with the workmen. It's bloody hard graft building a house."

"But just think how it will be worth it when you move in," Scott enthused as he rubbed at my head before stepping away and releasing my arm.

The very idea of leaving Boyd's home left me with palpitations. With yesterday still playing on my mind, my feelings for Boyd had never strayed far from my thoughts. One thing was certain, after my talk with Adam, I was ready to confess how I felt.

"Come on lazy bones, the quicker we get done the sooner we can leave. Luke is coming to get me in"—he checked his wristwatch— "ten minutes."

His happy grin was back in place at the mention of his boyfriend.

I went to the trolley housing all the glassware, clean tablecloths, napkins, and cutlery. "How are things with you and Luke now?" Scott and Luke had a rocky start to their relationship but from what I could see, Scott had never been happier.

"I've moved into his and god, he's such a great Daddy. Some days I have to pinch myself to make sure it's all real." Scott continued to set up the tables as I stood staring at him.

"Did he ask you to move in?"

Scott glanced up, his hand pausing as he went to place a glass down. "He did, but it was kinda mutual. We couldn't bear to be apart and how else would he be able to go Daddy on me if I'm living somewhere else?" He shrugged as he placed the glass down, then his gaze moved to me. "Do you want to live with Boyd?"

At his tentative question, I nodded. "His house is amazing, and I know mine will be too when it's finished." My teeth raked over my bottom lip. "Thing is, my house won't be a home unless it's got Boyd in it." As the words came out of my mouth, it struck how true they were. When was the last time I'd visualised my home with me in it?

When I came up empty, I frowned at Scott. "I'm not sure...I want to move into it."

He gave me a sympathetic smile. "You'll figure it out. Boyd seems like a decent guy, and from what you've mentioned, he wants to make you happy. Talk to him. It's hard, I know, but opening up about shit really helps. Take it from me." He sighed and his eyes clouded with sorrow before it disappeared as quickly as it appeared.

Shit, why couldn't I just keep my mouth shut today? First Adam and now Scott! "Sorry," I mumbled when I remembered all the hassle Scott had been through when he'd found out Luke had done some crazy shit to his ex.

"Don't be sorry, stuff happens," Scott stated, clearly understanding what I was apologising for. "We're cool, and I've never been happier."

We finished laying the tables in a companionable silence. Scott skipped to the locker room to retrieve his things when Luke appeared. With a shout of goodbye, I waved them off before going into the kitchen. With ten minutes to kill, I figured I'd check if there was anything else I could do.

When Carl, the head chef, all but pushed me back out of the kitchen when Adam came in wearing a sexy smirk, I went willingly. There was no way I wanted to witness what the pair were going to get up to. Sometimes the noises that came from the locker room when they went in there together were hotter than an electrical paint stripper.

Clutching my bag as I left through the front of the restaurant, I locked the door behind me and went to retrieve my bicycle. I stood next to it and waited in the carpark for Boyd to arrive.

I inhaled the night air and was disappointed when all I could scent was car fumes. The flash of headlights hit me before Boyd's truck came to a standstill. I'd hardly taken a step before Boyd was out of the cab and wrapping his beefy arms around me. He clung on to me for a minute, burying his nose in my hair.

What was this about?

A sense of unease threaded through me when Boyd eventually looked at me. His face was drawn and there were deep lines of strain around his eyes. "Are you alright?" He'd only talked a little about the mishaps at work and I worried something else had happened.

He shook his head. "I need cuddles with my Angel boy first. Let's go home." At the casual way he referred to his home as if it were mine too, my heart swelled.

I left my questions for now and let him help fasten my seatbelt. On our way home, the silence between us continued. I rested my hand on his thigh, offering my support. When his hand settled

-

over the top of mine, giving it a squeeze, the knots in my stomach eased a little.

At the warmth inside the truck, the long day, and the lack of sleep from the night before, my eyelids became too heavy to hold open.

A waft of cool air and the scent of flowers tickled my nose. My eyelids drifted open as Boyd lent over me and unbuckled my seatbelt. He reached in, his arm going under my legs as his hand went around my back. I didn't protest as he whispered in my ear, "Hold on to me."

Doing as I was told, I rested my head on his shoulder as he stood straight and adjusted me slightly after he'd shut the door. The lights flashed and then darkness surrounded us.

As he reached the steps, we were temporarily blinded by the security lights, then he chuckled, and his hot breath hit my cheek.

"I should maybe have taken my keys out of my pocket first."

He gently lowered me to the ground, holding me steady with one hand as he rooted in his jacket for his keys. When he had the door unlocked, he picked me back up and I snuggled back into his chest. My eyelids struggled to stay open with the feeling of contentment at his care flowing through me.

"Can you stand while I get you undressed?"

"Yes," I mumbled, even though I wasn't completely sure. With my feet on the floor, I held his arm for a second till I gained my balance.

"I think we'll leave your shower to the morning."

I could tell from the way he spoke, his Daddy was firmly in charge, so I meekly agreed and I let him tuck me up in bed while trying not to think how sweaty I'd got through the day. The mattress dipped, and I realised I'd shut my eyes. With difficulty, I opened them.

Boyd's expression was strained as he gently rubbed his hand over my hair. "I'm going to have a shower as I'm grimy. I won't be long." He kissed the tip of my nose before going to stand.

"What happened?" I whispered, reaching out for him, fear working to snatch my sleepiness away.

His arm tensed under my fingers, but he shook his head. "You're tired, and now is not the time to talk about it. Nothing is going to change between now and tomorrow." His caramel eyes pleaded with me.

"Okay. But you promised me snuggles," I reminded him.

He gave me a smile that touched his eyes. "That I did. Give me ten."

He was quicker than that and, as I snuggled into his embrace, I closed my eyes and hoped that

whatever the morning brought, it wasn't anything
we couldn't deal with together.

Chapter 17

BOYD

Eyeing Sawyer as he sat opposite me, playing with the bowl of cereal I'd laid in front of him, I could see he was in Little mode. His lips were pouty, and his features held a softness I'd come to recognise. "Want to tell Daddy what's wrong?"

His spoon splashed milk and cereal all over the wooden table as it landed in the bowl with a clatter. "No."

His gaze remained on the table as he started to play with the spilt milk, making more of a mess. "Stop that, please."

The firm request did nothing. He continued to play, drawing patterns using some of the soggy cereal from the bowl. His eyes peered up once through his thick eyelashes and I had to bite my lip at the petulant expression he wore.

"I won't ask you again." Having never encountered this side of him, I considered what my options were as he made more of a mess and got his work shirt cuffs dirty.

Do I punish him? Do I ignore his behaviour? What did he expect me to do? The last question was the one I debated over as I got up off the chair.

He never stopped his playing as I crouched right next to him and took a gentle hold of the hand he was about to stick in the bowl. "I want you to go to the sink and wash your hands. When you've dried them, I want you to go and sit on the bottom of the stairs and think about your behaviour. I've asked you twice to stop and you've defied Daddy," I scolded, albeit gently.

His chin trembled, and for a moment, I thought he wasn't going to do as I asked. He didn't meet my gaze as he got up and went to the sink, his feet dragging on the floor. I let out the breath I'd been holding while waiting to see what he'd do, as he turned the tap on.

Taking the seat I'd vacated, I resumed eating my breakfast that tasted like sawdust in my mouth, pretending disinterest in what he was doing. In truth, I watched him out the side of my eye the whole time.

After he'd left the room, I silently got up and poked my head out the door, craning my neck to see if he'd done as I asked. A smile spread over my face at the loud, put-upon sigh he gave, indicating he was exactly where I'd sent him.

The smile dropped from my face when I returned to the kitchen to clean up the mess. Why was he acting out? Was this over last night? Was my avoidance this morning the real issue? The food I'd consumed churned in my stomach as it knotted.

When we'd got up this morning, I'd given him a shower but struggled to find the words to explain what Glenn had done. The more I thought about it, the less I wanted to mention his name ever again, especially after everything that had occurred on Sunday.

Phil had stayed for hours going through everything he'd found. To say I was shocked to my core was a bit of an understatement. That had been quickly followed by fury when Phil pointed out Glenn had been helping himself to my money and paying Fredrick with it. I'd been speechless, whereas Brett had more than made up for my silence.

Mortification at others witnessing my distress had left me with a heavy heart. All I'd wanted last night was to hold on to Sawyer and not think about the years I'd wasted on a man that wasn't worth my time.

In the light of day, I was still not sure how to face what he'd done to me, to my business, and ultimately, to Sawyer. *What a fucking mess!*

With the kitchen set to rights, I glanced about, realising I couldn't delay any further as time was ticking away and I needed to head out to work.

Fred was on my hit list, well Brett's, but only after I'd been to the police with the file I'd left hidden in my truck.

"Daddy, Daddy, I'm sorry," came Sawyer's tearful shout from the hallway.

Buggering to all hell!

I marched out of the kitchen and as soon as I got to the bottom of the stairs, I swept Sawyer up into my arms. He immediately buried his face in my neck as I encouraged his legs to wrap around my waist.

He sniffed twice. "I'm sorry…but you're naughty too, 'cause you're not talking."

My heart bled at his accusation as it hit its mark. My arms tightened around him. "You're right, and I'm sorry. It's hard for Daddy to talk about what an arse he's been."

He released a heartfelt sigh as he nuzzled at my neck. "I won't hold it against you."

Those few words melted my heart as I turned and sat on the stair that I'd lifted Sawyer off. With him straddling my lap, I looked into his beautiful face. "I love you."

His eyes sheened with tears and his chest heaved. "I love you too, Boyd."

The use of my name made his statement that bit more real, and I felt my own tears gather at the corner of my eyes. I'd not known how much I needed to hear those words until he'd said them.

"What did I do to deserve you?" I struggled to stop my voice hitching with the emotions steamrolling through me.

His lips spread into a wide smile. "You must have been very bad, that's what." His voice was full of mirth as his eyes sparkled and he brushed a soft kiss over my lips. "Tell me what's wrong." All the humour disappeared as he cupped my cheeks. "I'm a good listener."

The serious side of him was back and though I loved his little, I needed him to help share the burden, of which I had no doubt he would.

***

After leaving the police station, I watched in my rear-view mirror as the police van followed me. With all the evidence Phil had collected, the police had been more than willing to listen to me. After my painful conversation with Sawyer this morning, I'd decided to leave Glenn in police hands and keep well out of it.

I didn't need any more grief and, as Sawyer pointed out so eloquently, 'Glenn had made his bed, now it was time for him to lie in it.' He couldn't do anything more with my computers after Phil had worked his magic. He was also going into the office this morning to check over the work computers, just to make sure Glenn hadn't tampered with any of them.

A heaved sigh filled the cab as I snail-paced it across London in heavy traffic. By the time I'd got to Nathan's warehouse, I'd lost sight of the cop van. Getting out of the truck, the brisk April breeze tugged at my light jacket as I waited for the police to turn up.

I'd been texting Brett all morning, while saying a silent prayer he wouldn't lamp Fred before I got to the bar. When the police van parked behind my vehicle, I checked it was the same copper that I'd spoken to. He gave me a nod and waited for the female officer to meet him on the curb.

"Shall we go?" asked the officer in a gruff voice. His weathered features did not reveal any of his thoughts.

"I just want him off the job and out of my hair."

"He'll be arrested and charged today. He'll be arraigned to appear in court and, judging on what he pleads, will determine what happens next."

Sweat beaded on my brow by the time we entered the bar. I spotted Brett stood with Fred by the bar. Brett was laughing, but I could see the tension around his mouth and eyes.

If there was ever a freeze frame moment, it was when Fred glanced in my direction. His mouth hung open and his eyes widened at the two coppers flanking me. It took a second or two before his head spun from side to side as if he were looking for an escape. Brett didn't give him a chance to move as he gripped him by the throat and squeezed until his knuckles turned white.

Convinced it was only the officer that stopped Brett from throttling Fred to death, I breathed a sigh of relief when Fred was able to cough and splutter. The commotion caused all the men to stop working and watch as the drama unfolded, so I was relieved when the police finally left with a crying Fred. I felt no sympathy after reading the list of things he'd done to sabotage the job all for a bit of extra cash.

Brett growled loudly. "That's what happens to traitors. Remember that before you think about fucking with us." He pointed between me and him while glowering at anyone that looked at him.

There was loud muttering and Ricky, one of the tilers, stepped forward, a scowl on his face. "If you'd told us there was an issue, we'd have kicked his fucking arse first before the coppers took him."

The sincerity in his tone warmed my heart, though the menace I could well do without. "Thank you. There'll be no arse kicking please. The police will deal with him."

"Is this why Brett's been a knob?" shouted Mal, one of the carpenters, from the back of the room.

I roared with laughter and it felt good as Brett muttered about ingrates and put up his middle finger at Mal, who just shrugged.

"Okay drama over, we've a deadline to meet. There's overtime for anyone who wants it." That got several cheers and for the first time since Phil had revealed what had been going on behind my back, the tension that had caused my shoulders to stay firmly fixed under my ears, released.

Chapter 18

Sawyer

Pleased to be only doing a short shift and that Lenny was working the restaurant kitchen, I sidled up to him, keeping my voice low. "Would you be up to doing me a huge favour? I'll pay you."

Lenny's ginger brows disappeared under his fringe as he eyed me with interest. "Pay me for what?"

"Boyd has had a real rough few days, and I mean the fucking worst." Anger I'd been working on keeping hold of all day bled into my voice.

Something flickered over Lenny's face that gave me pause.

"You know, don't you?"

He sighed and nodded. "Nathan asked me not to say anything about it,"—he inched closer to me, lowering his voice to a whisper—"what with Boyd going to the police this morning."

My stomach jittered. "Yeah, it's a big shitty mess. I have no clue what Boyd saw in that piece of shit Glenn," I spat out in a harsh whisper.

"What are you two gossiping about like two old women?" Carl called from across the busy kitchen, making every head turn in their direction.

Lenny gave Carl a cheeky grin. "How I'm a better baker than the head chef," he quipped so fast, it took several seconds before the kitchen was filled with raucous laughter.

Seb popped his head out of his office a few seconds later. "I'm on the phone, can you keep the noise down, some of us have work to do." He gave everyone a hard stare before he went to take his seat. The glass walled office gave him the perfect opportunity to watch us as he went back to his call.

When Seb left the door open, Carl bellowed loud enough for even the now empty restaurant to hear. "Says the man that spends most of his day sat on his fat arse."

There were several sniggers and Carl shook his head when Seb got up and shut his office door, but everyone went back to what they were doing.

With the show over, Lenny took hold of my arm and led me into the locker room, away from prying eyes. "What do you need me to cook?"

He grinned, and I let out a giggle. "Thank you. Boyd has a thing for pasta, loves it. So maybe lasagne or meat filled ravioli. I don't want to ruin it so whatever is easiest and can be done before I head out in forty-five minutes."

Lenny glanced at the door before looking back at me. "I've been working on a new pasta sauce and it's got meaty chunks in it. The meat should melt on the tongue. I'll put two big helpings into a tub. There's some fresh pasta in the fridge I'll give you." He rubbed his hands together. "Now, let's talk payment."

***

I let myself into Boyd's house two hours later, relieved to see his truck wasn't in the drive. He'd said he wouldn't be late tonight, knowing I was working the lunch shift. Eagerly, I raced to the kitchen with my spoils and stopped when I noticed that he'd cleaned up my breakfast mess.

A wave of heat flooded my face as I remembered how he'd reacted to me acting out. I'd been anxious when the time had crept along as I'd sat on the stairs and he'd shown no sign of ending my punishment. My little had been in full control and I'd been apprehensive and unsure about him not talking to me.

He did talk and okay, you might have had to push, but remember he's a Daddy and you know he just wants to look after you.

The reasoning helped as I unpacked the food and followed Lenny's instructions on how to cook it. When I started to set the table, I heard the front door open. I continued what I was doing, rushing to make sure it all looked perfect for when Boyd came into the kitchen.

I was back at the cooker, putting the fresh pasta into the boiling water, as he came up behind me and kissed the side of my neck. "This is a lovely surprise, Angel boy. What did I do to deserve this?" He continued to nuzzle at my neck, his whiskers making my skin feel hypersensitive while his hot breath gave me shivers.

"I wanted to make you happy."

His chest shuddered against my back as he exhaled gustily. "You do," he whispered against my neck. "So fucking happy, sometimes I'm frightened it's all a dream and I'll wake up and you'll be gone," he confessed.

I stopped stirring the pasta, turning in Boyd's embrace, the food timing forgotten at the edge of uncertainty in his voice. His face was flushed as his caramel eyes revealed his vulnerability. I clasped my hands behind the nape of his neck and stood on my tiptoes. "I. Love. You." I punctuated each word with a kiss. "I'm not going anywhere."

I caught a look of doubt before he could mask it. Was he thinking about my house? Was now the time to mention that I didn't want to move out? I nibbled on my lower lip. *Do it, do it now!*

"I don't want to move out," I blurted out so fast, it took me a second to run through what I'd said to make sure it made sense.

"You don't? What about your dream home? You were desperate to create it, have a place of your own."

Boyd pointed out everything I'd stated I'd wanted, but he'd failed to mention the most important thing: him. About to answer, I was distracted by the hissing pot behind me. *Shit.* I released Boyd and swung back to the stove, trying to rescue the over-cooked pasta as I glanced at the clock on the stove.

"Bugger! Whatever you do, don't tell Lenny I over cooked the pasta," I muttered as I went to the sink to drain the water out of the pot. Boyd's laughter stopped me in my tracks, and I glowered at him.

"I promise I won't, but what's the worst he can do?" he said, his voice laced with laughter.

Stomping to the table where I'd put the plates, I started to dish out the now gluey looking pasta, eyeing it mournfully as I ladled a large helping of the sauce over the top to hide the mess. Any thoughts of sending a picture to Lenny, as I'd planned, disappeared while I scowled at the disaster on the plates. "He'll have my guts for garters, that's what. He'll never want to give me food again." I cried, thinking about the promises he'd made to try and teach me some basics so I could prepare food for Boyd by myself. "He's real serious about making sure you treat food with respect. I know it's weird, and he wasn't like that before he started to cook, but that's how it is."

"Have you finished having a meltdown?" Boyd's brows were arched as he spoke.

I looked at the table and back to him. "I just wanted it to be perfect after the last couple of days you've had." It came out sounding whiny and I worked to keep from slouching.

The smile he gave me brightened the room. He walked to the table, sat down, and patted the seat next to him. "It is perfect because you did all this for me. Come sit and eat with me before it gets cold." He sniffed the air above the plate. "Smell's divine."

Grumbling only a little, I did as he asked and took the seat he pulled out for me. I followed his example and tried the food, finding that though the pasta was a little over cooked, it didn't taste half bad with the delicious sauce.

We'd nearly finished before Boyd glanced in my direction. "Are we going to talk about what you mentioned before pasta-gate?" He'd gone for humour, but there was strain in his voice. He ate another mouthful of food as he continued to keep his gaze on me.

I contemplated for a split-second pretending I didn't know what he meant, then I looked deep into his eyes and gave in to the need to talk about what I wanted. "Is it too soon to talk about living together permanently?"

His hand stilled halfway back to his plate and his eyes widened. "You meant what you said earlier?" he asked hesitantly.

I placed my cutlery down and pushed my chair back from the table. I stood and started to pace, trying to find the right words as I felt the weight of his stare on me. "I've always had to share what I had with others for most of my life. My home, my parents, my things, but I didn't know any different when I was younger. Then I started to see that it could be different, that I could have stuff that just belonged to me. The idea for my house, a home that was mine, came from that." I stopped and stared him directly in the eye. "But you changed that, because what I didn't understand was that home is where the person you love is. It doesn't matter where that is, as long as you're with that person."

It wasn't until, a second later, Boyd's fork clattered down onto the plate in front of him that I realised he was still holding onto it. His eyes gleamed with love as he stood and came towards me, his arms outstretched. I didn't hesitate and jumped at him. He lifted me easily as I hooked my arms around his neck and my legs around his waist.

"Oh, Angel boy, I don't care either as long as we're together. It might be too soon, but who the fuck cares. All I know is that I love you and you make me happy."

His face was full of emotion as his lips claimed mine and I tasted hints of the sauce mixed with Boyd's unique flavour. I ground against him, my body reacting to his confession. His lips firmed as the kiss deepened and went from gentle to demanding.

Chapter 19

Boyd

The feel of Sawyer's frantic heartbeat against my chest affirmed that he was as excited as me. And if I'd needed any further proof, there was the arousal he was grinding against my stomach.

I'd been going slowly to make sure that we went at a pace that suited Sawyer. Right now, with him humping against me like a dog in heat and a powerful surge of desire spreading through me, I questioned why I thought it was a good idea. Refusing to give up his mouth, I blindly staggered towards where I thought the door was.

Any thoughts of food were forgotten in my need to get him on a flat surface and fast.

His mouth released mine as he huffed. "Careful."

I eyed the door frame I'd knocked him against. "Sorry, did I hurt...you?" I gasped as his hungry mouth sucked on my neck, just below where my beard finished.

"I'm fine! Hurry," he mumbled, before he licked up the side of my neck to my ear and nibbled.

Not needing any further encouragement, I marched as quickly as I could to the stairs. Sawyer hung on, his hips continuing to dance against me. My dick complained at being squashed painfully behind my jean zipper. I was panting and groaning as we entered the bedroom.

Sawyer's greedy mouth moved from my ear to my mouth the moment he noticed we were in the bedroom. His tongue teased the seam of my mouth and for a moment, I let him take control of the kiss. His tongue stroked against mine in a caress that I felt all the way down to my toes, which curled in my work boots. His fingers clenched and unclenched in the hair at the nape of my neck, holding me in place.

He moaned into my mouth as I massaged the rounded globes of his pert backside. His pelvis thrust harder against me as I took charge of the kiss. My mouth devoured his, one greedy bite after another. I swallowed every moan and groan while his body shuddered and melted against mine.

My lungs screamed for air, so I released his mouth noticing his breathing was as erratic as mine. His face was rosy and beads of sweat coated his forehead as he ran his hands down my back. He tugged at the jumper I wore, pulling it up my back.

When he struggled to get much further, I chuckled at his impatient huff. "I'll help, but I need to put you down." He wriggled impatiently at my suggestion and was slithering down my body making the situation in my pants worse as his cock bumped mine.

"Strip quickly…I'll strip too," he stated excitedly as his feet hit the floor. He bounced from one foot to another, tugging off his shoes and socks and throwing them on the floor. Then he started on his jeans.

His excited gaze met mine and he hesitated. "Why aren't you stripping?"

"I was enjoying the show."

He giggled at this, his face beaming up at me. He nodded towards my jeans. "Hurry, I need you naked."

Not needing any further encouragement, I stripped at a more sedate pace, watching him crawl onto the bed on hands and knees and wiggle his naked backside at me. He then turned and lay down, his gaze meeting mine in a challenge. My heart tripped over itself and all but landed in a heap at his feet. *Fuck, how had I got so lucky?*

His pale skin glowed against the dark cover. His hairless arousal bobbed before his hand slid down his body.

"No, you know the rules," I rasped through a dry throat.

His hands fell to the cover, his hungry eyes never leaving me as I retrieved the lube and condoms before stepping naked to the bedside. I felt like I was on fire and the only thing that would put it out was the man staring up at me with naked desire. "Spread your legs."

Goosebumps appeared over his legs and arms as he did as I bid. I crawled between his spread limbs and kneeled, balancing back on my heels. With the knowledge that I was already struggling to keep control and his safety my first priority, I cloaked my cock with a condom. My teeth gritted together at the sensations penetrating through the thin latex from my trembling fingers.

By the time I picked up the lube, his knuckles were white as he gripped the cover. *Please let me do this right, please.* That thought continued to run through my head as I lubed my cock then dripped lube over his cock and balls, uncaring of the mess I was probably making. He gasped as cool liquid slid over his bare skin, making it gleam in the evening light coming through the windows.

The lube bottle landed on the bed and was instantly forgotten about as I crowded over Sawyer. I lent down on one elbow and placed open mouthed kisses on his salty skin, slowly moving up his body until I reached his heaving chest.

He shuddered, quivered, and moaned at each kiss. His nipples budded with arousal as I sucked one and then the other into my mouth, swirling my tongue over the sensitive flesh. He thrust up and his cock bumped against mine and I growled low in my throat as sensations thrummed through my whole body.

"Oh gods...more...give me...more," he gasped, his hands now gripping the back of my head.

I swirled my fingers in the lube dripping between his thighs and took hold of his cock to give it a firm stroke from base to tip. The head was smeared with pre-cum and I groaned around the nipple I was sucking at how aroused he was for me. His cock felt like silk encased steel against my calloused palm. I stroked him until he was mewling and desperate for more. Only then did I release his nipple and cock.

I pressed my damp chest to his as I gazed down at his hooded eyes and flushed cheeks. "I love you so goddamn much. I want you so much, if I go too fast, tell me and I'll try to slow down."

His giggle was at odds with the blown pupils as he stared at me, his fingers still buried in the hair at my nape tightened. "You won't hurt me, and I want this. I want everything you have to give."

I didn't give him a chance to say more as my mouth claimed his in a demanding kiss. His whole body shuddered against mine and I struggled not to mount him like an animal. With care, I lowered my hand and cupped his balls, rolling them gently in my palm. He groaned into my mouth as I teased under his balls and slipped a finger down to his quivering hole. There was so much slick it was easy to spread it over the tight rim of muscle.

His head strained back into the pillow as he cursed and groaned after our lips parted. I teased him with gentle strokes, adding a little more pressure with each pass over his hole. When he bore down, I slipped my finger inside his hot channel. He cursed repeatedly as he encouraged me to fuck him with my finger.

"Fuck me. Fuck me with your finger, deeper, pleaseee!"

"I didn't know you had such a dirty mouth," I hissed when he clenched down on my finger and I considered how he would feel wrapped around my throbbing cock.

"It's your fault," he whined and thrust up, "Motherfucker!"

I clenched my eyes shut and buried my face in his neck, panting. His personal scent was stronger there and I inhaled deeply, hoping it would calm me. The heady smell did the exact opposite and my teeth gritted together when his hands fluttered over my back, heading towards my arse.

The shivery, light touches did crazy things to my heart as I sunk deeper inside him. The few minutes I took to make sure he was stretched properly were the hardest of my life as he drove me to distraction with his dirty demands.

Sweat coated my skin as I shifted and moved, putting most of my weight on my forearms as I lowered my mouth to his. "I might need to wash your mouth out with all those bad words tainting it," I rasped as my cock nudged his slick hole.

His hands moved back to my nape and he gripped tightly, his lust filled gaze holding mine. "As long as it's with your cum."

My own curse was swallowed in his mouth as he dragged my head down the couple of inches separating us. My cock bucked hard at his suggestion and I pushed against his hot flesh. He bore down and the head of my cock sunk past the tight ring of muscle.

I strained to hold still and let Sawyer adjust, while he chose that moment to suck my tongue deep into his mouth and his hips mimicked the motion, sinking me deeper inside him. Any thoughts of restraint disappeared as the heat penetrated the thin latex and desire spread through me. His hips rocked up and I thrust down. This time his moan filled my mouth before he sucked hungrily on my tongue.

Sawyer's need was like pouring petrol on a lit fire. It exploded through me, burning hotter than hell. His small hands seemed to be everywhere at once as he encouraged me to let go and take him the way I wanted to. The sounds of flesh hitting flesh filled the air as we both grunted and groaned our pleasure.

Teeth clacked against teeth as Sawyer took everything he wanted. We rolled across the mattress until he sat astride me, my cock still buried in his arse. His hands slid up my chest and rubbed at the hair before he gripped my pecs hard. His colourful hair was stuck up all over the place and his skin was flushed a deep pink. He looked wild and untamed and I'd never seen him look more beautiful.

As if to prove me wrong, he gave me a smile that would have stirred the blood of any male as he slowly rose off my cock before slipping back down in a sexy swivel. His arse muscles clenching in the most divine way. The stark need etched into his face left me breathless and achingly hard.

"Hold on," was the only warning I got as he braced his hands and started to ride my cock. He threw his head back and moaned at the ceiling, his whole body seemingly alive. His cock bobbed and dripped down onto my skin.

My own cock throbbed and swelled under the delicious assault it was receiving. I took hold of Sawyer's cock as my balls started to tingle, alerting me to my impending orgasm. I struggled to keep in time to his thrusts as he rocked faster, his pelvis slamming down on mine.

"Ohhhhhhh…youuuuuu…fuckerrrrrr!"   he bellowed as his arse clamped down painfully on my cock, causing my balls to tighten.

My neck arched and my head thrust back into the damp pillow under me. My body hung suspended in the throes of the most exquisite orgasm. Dimly aware of Sawyer's cum hitting my chest, my hips slammed up against him while his arse clenched around me. Spurt after spurt of hot cum filled the latex covering my cock and for a brief moment, I regretted it wasn't bare. Then my mind was flooded with sensations that made it impossible to think about anything other than the arse still clasping my cock in a tight embrace.

When my cock gave up trying to fire cum in Sawyer, I sank back against the mattress, exhausted.

Sawyer melted against my chest, causing my cock to slip free of his arse and I had a moment of regret at the lack of connection with him. Then it struck me that I'd have a lifetime of moments like this with him and a smile spread over my face.

Puffs of breath hit my neck as his breathing settled, and we lay for long minutes enjoying the afterglow as I gently stroked his sweaty back.

He lifted his head until I could see his face. His hooded eyes gleamed with pleasure. "What was that you said about washing out my mouth...Daddy?" He bit his lower lip and his demeanour changed.

My cock stirred and I silently cursed. *What was a Daddy to do?*

Chapter 20

Sawyer

Music floated up from the hidden speakers, but it wasn't loud enough to stop people having conversations. There was a heady scent of expensive perfumes and colognes, though it didn't quite mask the fragrant food that had been placed on large silver platters on tables throughout the room. The counters situated in the booths lining the walls around the room had been left free for people to put their glasses and plates on if they chose to.

My job for the evening was to make sure everyone always had a full glass and as I eyed the people filling the room, I grinned seeing no one without a glass.

Hours later, the satisfaction was a little diminished, my feet and back aching as I moved around the room with a tray laden with champagne. The only consolation was listening to people rave about the work that Boyd had done.

I'd actually planned to attend the party as Boyd's date and make it official to everyone we were dating, but Seb's request two days before to help out had put paid to that. I'd taken into account how supportive Seb had been with me and how I wanted to help Scott, who had been promoted to head waiter in this new venue.

Scott had discussed his misgivings about taking the promotion only last week, with the date to open imminent, when a few of us had gone to his home. If Luke worked in the evening and Scott was off, he tended to invite us round, not liking being left alone. It was on one such occasion that he'd mentioned how worried he was.

Earlier that afternoon, however, I'd felt nothing but pride at my friend's quiet confidence as he'd gone through the bar and restaurant to make sure everything was perfect before the invited guests arrived. In my books, it showed that Seb had made the right choice in picking him for the job. Now, as I caught sight of Scott through the crowd, laughing with the guests, I could see no sign of those nerves. In fact, he practically glowed, and I didn't need to look far to see who had given him that confidence.

His boyfriend Luke, also his Daddy, stood by the hand-carved bar Boyd had made of reclaimed wood, not that you'd know it at first glance. It was then I noticed Boyd stood next to him, his face showing none of the happiness anyone would have expected after completing a job.

It hurt my heart as my gaze lingered. Glenn had done so much more than try to delay the progress of the club. He'd struck at Boyd's sensitive heart in a way he had known would hurt the most. It didn't matter how many times he told me he was fine, it was clear he wasn't. The assumption that getting the police involved would allow Boyd to relax a bit more had been wrong. If anything, he'd gone into a state of hyper awareness that came out as overprotectiveness. His need to make sure I was okay had given his Daddy nature a serious workout.

I blew out a frustrated breath. I'd been going with it, hoping it would make him comfortable. After we'd made love for the first time, I thought we'd got past whatever had been holding him back. Only problem with that was he didn't appear to want to fuck me when I was little. As I always tended to be little when we were home together, I was starting to feel very frustrated. The freedom he'd given me to let go when we were together was hard to break when Boyd was so damn good at giving me what I craved. My cock, on the other hand, was starting to think I'd forgotten what to do with it and I wasn't sure how to go about changing it.

What about when you asked him to clean your mouth with his come? He didn't seem too inhibited when you were little then, did he?

"Sawyer, can you clear the few tables by the door? Then I'd suggest you've earned a break to spend some time with Boyd," said Seb, drawing me from my thoughts and the burgeoning arousal happening in my too tight trousers.

Shit, how long had I been stood staring at Boyd?

Seb lowered his mouth to my ear. "I'm pleased you've found someone to make you happy, he seems like a good man." He patted my arm before he walked off.

I chuckled, feeling a wave of heat spread up my neck as I wondered what Richie, his boyfriend and Adam's best friend, had told him about me. Our parties together seemed to be all about the sharing. The heat in my face increased at what I now knew about my friends' love lives.

On my way to do as Seb requested, I paused and counted how many of us that worked for Seb had a Daddy that I knew of—four!

I shook my head, trying not to think about what that said about us all as I cleared the tables, then went in search of Boyd.

"There you are, I've been looking for you." I grinned up at Boyd before offering a nod to Luke.

Boyd's caramel eyes lit up, but his expression gave little away, and I wasn't sure if it was because Luke was stood next to him or if it was something else.

Hoping to make Boyd relax, I turned my attention to both men. "The place looks fantastic. Boyd's done a wonderful job, isn't that right, Luke?"

Luke offered an apologetic smile. "I'm sorry, I was admiring the décor. What did you say?"

"I said, doesn't the place look fantastic? Boyd's handcrafted bar is so beautiful and the fact it's all reclaimed wood really speaks to his dedication to protecting the planet," I gushed, while Boyd's face turned a rather alarming shade of red. "And after all the cr—"

"Luke doesn't need to know about that, Sawyer," Boyd said, interrupting me. His caramel eyes spoke volumes, throwing out a clear "shush now" that left me flummoxed.

Then Boyd lowered his head and whispered, "I'm sorry, Angel boy, it's just with everything...listen, when you're finished, we'll go home and celebrate the bar completion in private."

"I'm just going to see if I can speak to Scott for a moment." Luke gave us a tight smile that made me realise how rude we were being. He didn't give us a chance to say anything in return as he spun on his heel and disappeared into the crowd.

When Seb came over just a little while later to tell me that I could finish for the night, I saw it as a sign for my plans to get Boyd on the same page as me. Not one to look a gift horse in the mouth, I went and grabbed my jacket then went in search of Boyd.

Boyd remained silent for the ride home and I chewed on my thumbnail, trying to think of the best way to approach what I wanted to happen when we got home. It took all my effort to keep seated in the truck when he pulled to a stop outside his home. As was his tendency, he unbuckled my belt and helped me out of the cab only this time, I didn't let him put me down.

The nerves danced in my belly as my little side came to the fore and I tucked my head into the crook of his neck. His breath gusted over my hair, making it move, but he remained quiet. He moved me to sit on his hip and I heard the rattle of keys as he must have dug them out of his suit pocket.

Once inside the house, I felt the tension leave his body as he focused on taking care of me. He carried me straight up to the bedroom and through to the bathroom.

He lowered me to the floor, patting my bottom, then turned on the taps to fill the bath, adding my favourite scents to the water. "Let's get you out of these clothes and give you a freshen up," Boyd said in a soft voice.

Carefully, each piece of clothing I wore was removed, his caramel eyes darkening with arousal. After he was done, he removed his suit jacket, but when he showed no signs of acting upon his desire, I swallowed my sigh of frustration.

By the time I was in the bath and he started to wash me, I was painfully aroused from his loving touches. "Daddy, aren't you gonna get in the bath with me?"

"It's late, and you must be tired—"

"I's not," I stated rudely, splashing him with water at the same time. The shirt he'd worn under his suit jacket plastered to his chest, turning it transparent so I could see the dark hair beneath. At thoughts of touching it with my lips, they tingled in anticipation.

He glanced down at the wet patch spreading down the front of him, then he returned his molten gaze on me. "You're being disobedient and that's because you're tired." His voice remained soft but still full of authority.

I shuddered and in answer, sent another wave of water careening over the side of the bath. His subsequent sigh sounded heartfelt as he shifted back and stood from his kneeling position.

He shook his head at the state of his sodden suit trousers. "You're playing up, so bath time is over." I hid my disappointment when he didn't strip, instead walking to grab a towel from the heated rail.

"No, I'm staying in the bath," I whined, taking hold of the bath rim to make my point.

Returning to the bath, he crouched down and looked me in the eye, offering a gentle smile that melted my heart. "No, Daddy's getting you out of the bath, right now, and there'll be no more nonsense." His firm tone did little to stop my cock from aching. The gentle way he lifted me out of the water and wrapped the towel around me added to my torment. He took a second to pull the plug from the bath before carrying me like a baby into the bedroom.

He laid me on the bed and used the huge bath sheet to dry me. "Let's get you dry, we don't want you getting any chapped skin." When he got to my groin, his eyes were drawn to my aroused cock. There was a noticeable tremor in his hands as he went to dry it.

A buzzing sound started in my ears as I held my breath and met his gaze, revealing what I wanted. His breathing became choppy, but he didn't stop the gentle strokes to my cock with the towel.

"Do I need to check if you're dry?" The rasped question was hardly audible.

"Yes, Daddy," I answered meekly. This time, when our gazes met, I could see that he understood what I was asking for.

Chapter 21

BOYD

My heart hammered against my ribs as I looked deep into Sawyer's eyes and saw what he really wanted. I sucked in a tremulous breath, hoping to ease the tight band constricting my chest.

Ever since we'd made love, I'd struggled to come to grips with what had happened afterwards. When he'd become little and asked me to clean his mouth out with my come, I'd found myself shocked at how powerful my second orgasm had been, following so swiftly after the first one. I'd become so painfully aroused so quickly, with the knowledge he enjoyed me taking care of him and giving him a punishment, it had me taking a step back trying to find my balance.

Did you find it, did you fuck? He is your balance, stop over thinking it and just go with it.

The words rang through my mind and were reminiscent of the conversation I'd had with Nathan earlier in the evening as I'd watched Sawyer work.

"Why the long face? You should be over the moon we completed, and on time." Nathan slapped at my shoulder. *"Look about, it's a fucking huge success."* He grinned when his gaze returned to me.

"I've got a lot on my mind." My eyes drifted to Sawyer as he stopped within a few feet of us.

"I thought things were good now that Glenn is fully out of the picture."

"Glenn is threatening to tell everyone all the sordid details of what I'm doing with Sawyer," I answered, looking back at Nathan when he released several curses.

"You're not going to dump Sawyer, are you?" Nathan growled, while he stood to his full height and gave me a steely stare that could have made a weaker man piss his pants.

I had to reel in my own temper at him jumping to that conclusion before I could answer. *"No! I love him and nothing Glenn can do will change that. I'm not worried for me, it's Sawyer I'm more concerned about. No one wants their private business splashed all over the papers, especially if it outs you to your parents."* I raked my fingers through my hair. *"I spoke to my father and my sister because I want them to accept that I'm in love with Sawyer."*

Nathan's face lost a little of its colour. *"How did that go down?"*

I chuckled at his obvious concern. "My father was a little shell shocked, but my fourteen year old sister was like 'that explains a lot about your domineering daddy side,' she then insisted I bring him on Sunday for lunch so she can meet him." I shrugged.

"Can you get Glenn to keep his mouth shut?" The deep grooves marring his forehead mimicked my own.

"Drop the charges against him." I held up my hand silently asking for Nathan to let me finish when his eyes darkened with anger. "I told him to go fuck himself. He didn't take it well. I think he's suffering financially and I was the solution. His claims of still being in love with me are utter bullshit, all he wants is access to my money," I ground out before taking a cleansing breath trying to rid myself of the anger. "Can we talk about something else instead?"

Nathan nodded, albeit reluctantly.

I glanced at the people within ear shot and lowered my voice. "I've a problem...letting go sexually...when Sawyer is little."

Nathan's eyes became shrewd, but with no condemnation. "You are new to the scene and have never been in that type of relationship before, so I'd expect that you might question what you feel. Can I ask, does it arouse you when he is little? Or do you separate it into compartments, like you love to take care of him, or make him happy by letting him be little?"

He'd kept his voice low but I'd heard him. I scratched at my beard, giving myself time to answer him. "Those things aren't separate because fundamentally, whether he's acting little or not, he's still the man I love."

Nathan beamed at me like I was a top pupil having just aced a test. "Then stop overthinking it and go with the flow."

A snort of frustration brought my attention back to the man wriggling in the bath sheet, his cock leaking onto his round belly. I edged back off the bed and stood up, feeling the weight of Sawyer's gaze on me as I slowly stripped off my clothes so he could see how he affected me. My cock stood proud and my balls felt heavy as I went to retrieve supplies from the drawer.

Back at the bedside, I made sure Sawyer was looking at me before I spoke. "I've been to the doctor and been tested."

Sawyer's eyes gleamed excitedly as he sat up clapping his hands together. "I have regular health check-ups, I's clear. I's not been with anyone for months and months before you."

I noticed the cute way he spoke, his little still in charge, but if I was truthful, I'd been stuck on the word clear and what that meant with my own negative test results tucked into my jacket pocket.

"Is that right?" At his eager nod, I threw the condom towards the bedside cabinet, not caring where it landed.

At the sight of him lying back down on the towel, his face softening and his eyes showing such trust, my heart expanded to fill my chest to capacity. The love was so overwhelming, I needed a moment to get a hold of it and be able to kneel on the bed clutching the lube.

The first time we'd made love it had been more frantic, our need firmly in the driving seat. This time it felt different, the need was there but somehow it felt gentler, but no less powerful.

I took my time softly stroking his body, exploring every curve, dip, and undulation, noting which ones made him sigh with pleasure and those that caused him to groan in need.

There was no need for words as he lay there, open and vulnerable to me. His eyelids hooded as his face became flushed. When I finally touched his cock, there was a pool of pre-cum gathering on his belly.

"Oh, Angel boy, you've made yourself all wet again. Daddy is going to need to dry you all over again." I tutted and ran my finger down the side of his slippery hard length that had the sticky residue of pre-cum coating it. "What should Daddy use? The towel? Or my hand? Maybe my mouth?"

His breathing became erratic at the last suggestion, his eyes pleading with me. "Not the towel, Daddy," he whined.

"Should you get to choose after you were misbehaving in the bath?" My brows arched as he gave me a beseeching look that forced me to stop myself pouncing on him. With more effort than I liked, I slowly lowered myself onto my stomach between his legs when he remained quiet, but the look on his face persisted.

His legs opened wider to accommodate my shoulders. "Good boy, Angel." Rewarding him, I took hold of his leaking cock and lapped at the head, tasting his salty essence with each sweep of my tongue over his slit. He mewled and pulled a corner of the towel to his mouth and sucked on the edge as he had a habit of doing with his blankie when he was happy.

My heart beat uncontrollably against my ribs as I pleasured him with my tongue. My saliva dripped down over his balls and slicked his skin. I continued to suck his cock, watching him as he sucked on the corner of the towel between his lips, a serene expression on his face. All the while, my fingers used the saliva to stretch him.

I used my free hand to feel over the cover for the bottle of lube I'd laid down earlier when he was ready for two fingers. He whined at me as I released his cock, then his brow formed into a scowl when my finger was removed from his body right after. "Shush, Daddy needs lube, I don't want to hurt you, Angel."

That placated him and the serene look returned. It centred me in a way I'd never expected and though I was painfully hard and leaking against the cover beneath me, I didn't feel the need to rush.

Patiently taking my time to make sure he was ready, sweat coated my skin when I finally deemed he was. His eyes looked like I'd drugged him, and his lips were parted, the towel forgotten. His whole body was flushed a rosy pink as I rose over him and slowly lowered my body over his. He moaned low in his throat as my weight pressed him into the mattress. My cock nudged his slick, hot skin and his eyelids dipped.

His mouth softened and I carefully pushed inside him, inch by inch, taking my time. The minute seemed to stretch like a long mile in front of me before my pelvis met his. The raw pleasure at being inside him without a condom was overwhelming and my heart skipped several beats.

There were no words to explain how I felt in that moment, with him tightly pressed against me. My hair stuck to my forehead and my breathing mimicked that of a runner. The heat and strength of his muscles clasping my cock worked to undermine my control. I gritted my teeth, my jaw bunching with the strain of keeping still.

Moving the towel out of the way, I gently kissed his lips, showing how much I revered him and this moment. One kiss led to another until it felt like we were almost in a dream like state. Inch by inch, I slowly pulled out of him, then sunk back in at the same slow speed.

Every time I sunk fully inside him, he'd whimper into my mouth. On and on for endless minutes I continued to move slowly, dragging my cock out of his body, giving him pleasure. His whimpers increased as his channel pulsed, but he continued to remain still, letting me remain fully in control of his pleasure.

Why hadn't I wanted to do this before?

Fuck knows!

The powerful feelings running through me felt like a flat battery that had been charged into new life. With each slow slide into Sawyer's pliant body, I felt the energy inside me increase. It was like he was recharging me in ways I'd never considered possible.

Breathless with love and need, I released his now puffy, slick lips and stared down in wonderment at the gift that I'd been lucky to find: Sawyer. "I love you," I gasped and pushed back into his body.

He came apart under me, his body didn't push up, but merely sunk deeper in the bed. I felt his cock pulse and throb against me as warm heat spread between us. "Oh, Daddy," he whispered in wonderment.

Those words were my undoing as my whole body strained and spurts of cum filled him until it leaked out of his body. The release felt brutal compared to anything I'd experienced before as I struggled to keep my full weight from crushing Sawyer. My limbs shook, and in the end, I gave up and rolled onto my back, pulling Sawyer on to my sticky chest.

He never complained, instead burying his head in my neck and nuzzling at the skin. A hand came up and he twirled his fingers in my beard and hummed to himself.

Overcome with how happy he sounded, my heart cinched in my chest. If this was wrong, then I never wanted to be right, because I'd fight tooth and nail to keep this, to keep Sawyer happy like this.

What if Glenn does what he's threatened?
Then I'll cross that bridge later.

I shut my eyes and blocked out everything but Sawyer and how he made me feel.

Chapter 22

Sawyer

The bright, hot sun soaked through my thin T-shirt, causing it to stick to my back as I peddled at a slower pace up the newly tarmacked drive towards my house. I slowed to a stop and placed my foot down to balance as a smile spread over my face.

Over the last few weeks, since Flamingo Bar had been completed, Boyd had focused all his attention on completing my house. Not that it was going to *be* my house, I'd decided. Since we'd had the discussion about living together on a more permanent basis, it had been agreed that we'd choose at a later date which house we'd live in. The thing was, as much as I loved what Boyd had done to the house, it didn't feel anything like a home to me. I'd thought I wanted it, but truth be told, I adored his home more.

So, after he'd left for work this morning, I'd made a call to my lawyer, Mr. Norris, to see if he could squeeze me in for an appointment. To my joy, he'd had a free slot this morning, although I'd not left his office feeling all that joyful.

I sighed at the talking to he'd given me when I informed him I was going to be putting my house and land on the market. It was hard not to tell him to get lost when he'd insisted on knowing the reason for my decision. As I'd never talked about Boyd to anyone other than the guys I worked with, I could see why it would seem a little out of the blue to want to sell what I'd been so desperate to have, and move in with someone.

There was, however, no way I was going to talk about what I needed with my lawyer and he'd seemed completely dissatisfied with my answers. I shrugged off the anxiety that still weighed heavy inside me at the conversation Boyd had with me about Glenn threatening to out us. We'd talked about it at length and we'd both agreed that we wouldn't give in to his demands.

That decision was swiftly followed by the acceptance I'd had in his childhood home from his father and sister. I'd considered if I should bite the bullet and talk to my parents. Boyd hadn't pushed me to make a decision, as much as my little wanted him to. I got this wasn't something my little should decide, but it would have made things a lot easier.

As I dismounted my bike, I worked to quell the continued fretfulness, and left my bike against the wall of the house. The front door was open, so

I stepped straight through into chaos. My smile returned at seeing beyond the chaos to how far the job had progressed.

I easily blocked out the shouts, thudding, and clattering noises as I waved to a couple of blokes I knew by sight, when I strolled through the large open plan room. Dodging several piles of reclaimed wood, I walked through to the dining area which opened up onto a large wooden deck.

Someone had opened the bi-folding glass doors, I assumed to let in a breeze when I felt it brush softly against my bare arms and legs. The last few days had been sweltering. The deep blue sky held not a cloud, the sun shining down as I stepped out onto the deck. My gaze swept the garden the landscape gardeners had started to work on.

I rubbed at the centre of my chest at the little twinge of regret that I'd never get to sit and enjoy an evening in the garden, like I'd planned.

You'll make new memories at Boyd's.

Reminiscences of last night followed the thought and the twinge disappeared with the image of Boyd and me dining alfresco. We'd watched the sunset as I curled in his lap on the porch swing he'd purchased after I'd said I wanted one. It had been perfect.

I swung around and headed back inside and shouted over the din, "Boyd, where are you?"

Stu's head appeared from the kitchen area. "He left to go and grab some sandwiches. He'll be back soon, but if you want one, you'll need to give him a call." With that, Stu disappeared and I shook my head.

At the angry growl my stomach made, I dug out my phone from my shorts. I'd only opened it when it started to ring. I eyed the number with a sinking heart. *Bloody hell, that was fast!*

I swallowed hard as I hit the accept button and put the phone to my ear. "Hello, Mum."

Not giving me the same courtesy of a greeting, she got straight to the point. "What's this nonsense, Sawyer? How am I hearing about you selling your land and house from our lawyer?"

"He's no right to breach my confidentiality like that," I whined, and slouched as I walked back outside, not wanting anyone to witness my humiliation.

"Don't give me that nonsense. I'm one of the executives of the estate that manages your inheritance. He has every right to consult me when he's worried my son is making rash decisions."

"Didn't you raise me to be independent and take control of my own life? Wasn't that the spiel you fed me when you left me with strangers to go and conquer the wrongs of the world?" The hurt I'd buried deep inside me came pouring out, my little side coming to the fore as she continued to berate my life choices.

Tears fell uselessly down my cheeks and dripped onto my T-shirt as I stared blindly out at the garden, no longer feeling the warmth of the sun.

"Independent, not stupid, there is a difference. Where are you right now?"

My heart beat erratically as the air got trapped in my chest. I couldn't get a word out past the misery.

"Sawyer, what are...oh my god, what happened, Angel boy? Did Glenn do something?" The second Boyd saw my face the bags he held were dropped to the floor and he swept me up in his arms, seemingly not noticing the phone at my ear as he continued to fire questions at me.

I buried my face in his neck and sobbed, my hand clutching at the phone as my mother continued to insist I answer her.

I was unsure if Boyd had noticed the phone in my hand or could hear my mother's strident voice, but the phone was taken from my trembling fingers.

"Hello, who is this? What have you said to upset Sawyer?" The angry demand rumbled up his chest as he continued to hold me tightly against him while talking.

I couldn't hear my mother's response, only Boyd's noncommittal noises. Then the world seemed to whirl by in fast forward mode when he replied.

"We're at the house now. Yes... Okay... We'll discuss this fully when you get here." His voice was firm and the one he used when he was Daddy.

With nowhere to look but up at Boyd, I peeked at him from under my eyelashes. His face showed strain around both his mouth and eyes as the lines deepened. "I'm sorry," I sobbed.

"I think we should sit down and you can tell Daddy what happened that led up to that call"—he brushed his hand through my hair—"do you think you can do that?"

He sounded resigned but not cross, so I met his gaze. While he still held me cradled in his arms with the warm sun heating my head, I regaled what had happened since he'd left to go to work.

"I thought we were going to discuss the house at a later date?" His question sounded full of frustration, but his hold remained gentle.

"I love your home. This place doesn't feel the same. I don't know how else to explain it. This is part of my old dream I had. I have a better reality and I don't want to swap it."

His expression went from pensive to exultant in the blink of an eye. He took my lips in a kiss that I felt singing through my veins until I remembered my mother was coming. I muttered against his lips, "You'll look after me when my Mother comes, won't you?"

He chuckled, his warm breath filling my mouth. "Am I not your Daddy?" I nodded. "Then stop worrying, I'll be right there to make sure she listens to you." Then he sighed and disappointment flooded through me when he moved his mouth away from mine. "This might be a good time to talk about...Glenn with your Mother."

Although he sounded hesitant, there was something that said this time it wasn't something I should think about, more something I should do. I reluctantly nodded, knowing it was always best to pull the plaster off a wound in one fell swoop.

With my agreement, Boyd suggested I have half his sandwich, but with my stomach jiving to some music I clearly couldn't hear, I declined. The time seemed to drag as I listened to the men chat as they sat on makeshift seats eating their food.

When they all headed back inside, I heard a car coming down the drive. I took hold of Boyd's hand, not looking at him, as I led him around to the front of the house.

Sensing no tension coming from Boyd, I tried to follow his relaxed stance as my mother got out of the car and eyed us both. Her gaze remained on our intertwined fingers before moving to my face.

Something flickered over her face and, for a moment, I thought it was regret before it was gone. When she started to speak, I shook off the thought.

"Now what have you got yourself mixed up in, Sawyer?" Her voice was as strident as it had been on the phone, only now there was an added extra, disappointment.

About to answer, Boyd took half a step forward still holding my hand. "Please do not speak to him like that. There is no need. He has not got himself into anything."

Boyd seemed to gather himself while I silently cheered him on.

"Shall we take a step back and start again? I'm Boyd, I'm your son's partner, we are living together in a house I've built and paid for with the business I own. Your son is not being taken for a ride. I'm in love with him and will do anything to make sure he *is happy*."

When he finished his speech, he held his hand out to my mother who, for once, seemed at a loss for words. Then the hand I held tugged me into his body and hugged me into his side protectively.

If ever there was a moment I'd want to frame it was this right now, right here, where he'd verbally, then silently declared to me that he was my Daddy and was going to take care of the little side of me no matter what.

I blinked back the tears and let him hug me into his side as I took solace from his confidence and faced my Mother knowing, for the first time in my life, that I could be me and that was enough.

Epilogue

BOYD

The feel of my heartbeat thrumming madly against my ribs distracted me as I walked with Sawyer into Flamingo Bar for the first time as members. The place was busy and most of the tables and booths were full. I was glad I'd had the foresight to book a booth for us as we planned to have a meal.

The tension riding through me eased, and my stomach unknotted, when I noticed several men were dressed in outfits similar to the one partially hiding under Sawyers coat. It appeared the setup of the bar and restaurant meant there was no need to hide, with the entrance to the second floor through the underground carpark maintaining complete privacy for all members.

I'd not appreciated that until Sawyer had come down the stairs this evening dressed in a beautiful, pale lilac adult sized baby grow that had sprigs of lilacs in deep purple all over it. He'd taken my breath away when he'd looked at me, his face soft, his expression open and vulnerable as he clutched his blankie. I'd watched him tuck his dummy into his pocket, and instantly known what a big deal this was for him if he required his dummy. It was only used when he was especially anxious or upset by something.

Clearly, he was worried tonight might be more than he could cope with and I'd been in half a mind to say we'd stay home. Then I'd recalled how long it had taken for him to consider if he wanted to go out in public with me as a little, even in a safe space. So I'd not mentioned the dummy and let myself be guided by him as he'd waited for me to put his coat on.

His anxiety had lessened the closer we'd got to the club and been replaced by excitement as he'd chatted about the possibility of making new friends like him.

The last six months had been a journey of discovery, and there were moments I still couldn't quite believe this was my life. After all I'd endured with Glenn, I'd acknowledged what I felt for him was a pale imitation of what I felt for Sawyer. The joy he brought into my life was precious, a gift to be treasured.

Glenn had based everything we had on what I could give him financially. That he'd been shocked when he'd come back with fresh threats and I'd not given into his blackmail, might be a slight understatement. My ears had rung for days from the names he'd called me before I could point out that if he outed me, then people would tar him with the same brush. His reputation, the one thing he appeared to think more of, had stopped him dead in his tracks, thankfully. He'd eventually admitted to what he'd done, and why, to avoid a long drawn out court hearing he didn't want or need. Money was the root of all evil, in Glenn's case, it was all he could see.

It was water under the bridge and after meeting Sawyer's parents, I'd understood that it needed to stay that way as they'd struggled to come to terms with Sawyer's lifestyle. They were not as accepting as my family were and, though I might have been a little hasty in outing myself to them, it meant Sawyer was never worried how they'd react if they called around and he was little. It seemed my sister had taken it upon herself to understand what being little meant and spent a lot more time at the house than she did before.

I shook off the thoughts, wanting to concentrate on Sawyer having a good time. He squeezed my hand and I looked at him. His sunny smile was there but it was tinged with apprehension.

"Do you think they'll like me?" he asked, his gaze moving back to where the play area had been set up for littles. There were four men knelt around the edge of the makeshift table.

The moveable stage I'd built had been pushed into the far corner of the room and now housed things a child might enjoy playing with. There were books, toys, paints, pens, playdoh and much more scattered across the surface of the wood.

"They'll love you. Why don't you give me your blankie, so it doesn't get lost? And do you want to take your coat off?" When he handed over his blankie but hesitated before letting me help him take his coat off, I had a moment to wonder if he was ready to share his little side with others. I kissed his upturned mouth. "If you don't want to stay then Daddy will take you home."

His brows knitted together as he sucked his lower lip between his teeth. "I wanna play."

"Then go and play. I'll be right here. Also, remember that when I call you for dinner, you have to come with no messing."

"Allllrighhttttt."

The exasperated response caused me to cough to stop from laughing at his antics. I patted his bottom. "Go on. I'll get you a juice. Do you want a glass or a sippy cup?"

"A sippy cup, a colourful one." With that he bounced off, only looking back once.

I stood watching him for long minutes as he sat down on the floor next to a man wearing a similar outfit in dark blue and Sawyer started to point at what the man held in his hands. At home, he tended to like to play on his own and only occasionally invited me to join him to build something with his Legos. Those moments were exquisite. So much so, I'd built a cabinet for the things we'd built together so they could be displayed. Sawyer had cried when he'd come home from work to see what I'd done.

A ball of emotion got caught in my throat, so I headed to the bar.

"Hey Boyd. It's good to see you," Scott enthused, his eyes dancing with laughter when he shifted his gaze to where Sawyer was and back to me. "He didn't waste any time, did he?"

I chuckled. "No, he didn't. Can you put Sawyer's coat in the cloakroom for me? I don't want him to lose sight of me."

Scott reached out and took it from me. "Cool, I'll take it. I've also situated you both in the booth closest to the play area as it's Sawyer's first time."

I was aware Sawyer had talked to Scott about tonight, and though Theo was his best friend, he'd grown close with Scott and even allowed him to come to the house when he was little, in preparation for tonight.

I glanced back at Sawyer and found him watching me with uncertainty, so I gave him an encouraging smile and pointed to the booth Scott had allocated for us. I mouthed, "I'll be right there."

His face brightened and he returned his attention to the table, ignoring the man he'd been talking to and grabbing one of the large colouring books. He stared at a box of crayons near another man. His face showed indecision and I struggled to stay where I was, fighting the need to go and get what he wanted for him. It had become such an ingrained habit to look out for his little I hardly noticed myself doing it.

When the man nudged the crayons towards Sawyer and offered him a shy smile, Sawyer gave him a meek look in return before picking up the box.

I rubbed at my chest, feeling the love blooming inside me. Each day it seemed to get bigger, bolder, to the point I wasn't sure I'd be able to contain it all.

How could an overheard conversation and a job, change a person's whole life?

Does it matter?

A smile spread over my face as Sawyer bit his lip and wiggled his bottom, once more casting a glance in my direction. At seeing me, he grinned and went back to colouring. The answer was obvious. *No.* There was nothing that mattered more than making Sawyer happy and I wouldn't change that for the world.

Coming December is the third book in this series...
Can you guess which boys will get their turn next?

Check out my website to find out!

BOOKS BY THE AUTHOR

Standalone
When Fake Changed Everything
Christmas beyond Christmas
The Elves and the Bondage Daddy (Grim and
Sinister Delights Book 5)

Series
The Potters Creek Series
A Christmas Wish (book one)

The App Series
The App: Daddy kink (book one)
The App: Littles (book two)
The App: Puppy play (book three) - January 2021

The Flamingo Bar Series
Always More (book one)
The Little Side of Me (book two)
3 is the magic number (book three) - February 2021

La Trattoria Di Amore Series
Puzzle Pieces (book one)
Dominated but not Subdued (book two)

The Playroom Series
Mine, Body and Soul: Part One
Mine, Body and Soul: Part Two

Audio Books

Mine, Body and Soul, Part One: The Playroom Series
Mine, Body and Soul, Part Two: The Playroom Series
Mine, Body and Soul, Part Three: The Playroom
Series
Daddy Kink: The App (book one)
Always More: The Flamingo Bar (book one)
When Fake Changed Everything
Ferron's Journey: Damaged Part One
Ferron's Journey: Hidden Part Two

ABOUT THE AUTHOR

Hi all,

My name is Jayne and I live in the Isle of Man. A tiny place in the Irish sea. It's an island steeped in folklore and history and just begs to have stories written about it, and one of my first inspirations. Over the last few years that has changed and now I find inspiration everywhere.

I'm an eclectic kinda girl so I've written contemporary and historical gay romance with a paranormal twist, daddy kink, fake boyfriends, out for you and enemies to lovers. My head is so full of ideas. I never know where it will take me next. I had a twelve book plan for 2020 and I smashed it and will release fourteen books and already I've a few new ones bubbling inside me waiting to be written 😊

I hope you have enjoyed this book, and if you are in need of more, then you can find all my other books, on Amazon and in KU.

If you would like to give me any feedback or just have any questions, go ahead and friend me on Facebook, and I would be happy to answer anything. Well, almost anything. I hope you enjoyed this book as it was a little different for me. If you would also like to leave a review, then I would love to read your thoughts.

Thank you for taking the time to be part of my dream.

JP SAYLE

www.ingramcontent.com/pod-product-compliance
Lightning Source LLC
Chambersburg PA
CBHW020821180626
46814CB00001B/61